Executive Lunch

Mismanagement Meets Its Match

Maria E. Schneider

Bear Mountain Books

A Bear Mountain Books Production
www.BearMountainBooks.com

Maria E. Schneider

Printing History:
POD printing April 2011
Second POD printing August 2011
Third POD printing June 2012
E-format November 2009

Cover Art:
Elements of the cover were used with permission from:
http://www.openclipart.org/
Special thanks to Johnny_automatic and pianoBrad

ISBN-10: 0615448747
ISBN-13: 978-0615448749

Acknowledgments

A special thanks to the ladies on the Amazon Cozy Forums; you've been a huge support to me. Danna at http://www.cozy-mystery.com/blog/ --thanks for a great blog and for welcoming me. Yvonne, not only do you have a wonderful blog at Socrates' Book Reviews, your Goodread's EReaders Unite group is a happy place for readers and writers. A big shout-out to Kerrie at http://paradise-mysteries.blogspot.com/ halfway across the world.

Throughout the series, I have been privileged to receive valuable encouragement and feedback from LeAnn, Joan, Cinderspark and April. And to my earliest supporters, a special thanks: Holly, Paula, Renee, Cathey, Marty, Kevin and David. For all the fans who read one of my books and came back for more, Thank You. To Old Granny, Dreams and Elisabeth: your support came at a key time. Your enthusiasm is priceless. To Libraries and Librarians everywhere, thanks for being keepers of the magic.

Mom and Dad, you probably deserve the biggest thanks of all. How did you put up with me all these years?

And to my husband: walking through life with you is exactly where I want to be.

Executive Lunch

Chapter 1

The hallway at Strandfrost wound along the windows on three sides of the floor. This design ensured that everyone was equally deprived of a window office with the exception of the managers, who all sat along the north side in windowed offices. Since I was just a computer lab rat, I felt lucky to have any kind of office, even one without a window. In order to have a metallic nameplate with "Sedona O'Hala" gracing the door, I had to rip apart an old manager's nameplate and rig it with card stock.

I was on my way to the lab when Sally Bunker, our adorable, very scatterbrained secretary screamed. If I hadn't had an armful of papers, I might have covered my ears. Sally was frequently what one might refer to as unprofessional, but she was so well liked that no one ever actually mentioned it.

More worrisome, the next sound from down the hallway was remarkably whimper-like. Sighing, I headed around the corner. I expected to find Sally frantically plaguing anyone that wasn't already at lunch to help her speed-dial restaurants--she had probably forgotten to get Allen Perry, our overweight director, lunch reservations.

I was not expecting a six-inch switchblade.

I stopped short and stared. The papers I was carrying fell on the floor with a loud thump. "Ohboy." I should have minded my own business. It certainly would have been better if I hadn't heard Sally scream.

At the end of the hallway, past the guy with the switchblade, there was a guy with a bull neck holding Sally against the corner window. He trailed a knife down her neck. A chunk of her long auburn hair, usually sprayed neatly into place, severed and fell to the floor.

"Wha..?" While there might be some petty cash in the drawer, Strandfrost was a very ordinary computer company located in a fourteen-story office building outside the downtown area of quiet Denton, Colorado-- an unlikely spot for a mugging.

"You can't do that," I squeaked. The guy swore and looked over his shoulder at me. He screamed, "Beee...itch!" loud enough to wake Sally from the dead had he pushed her out the window.

"Well, you can't," I defended meekly, looking at Allen. He was stuck against the wall next to his office, held quietly in place by a tattooed arm that reached out from the office doorway. The tattoo was a harmless sword. The gun in the hand attached to the arm didn't look so benign. Allen's beefy face dripped sweat from his receding hairline down his neck and cheeks.

"Sedona--" Sally cried.

For the first time in my life, I wished for a boring meeting to discuss options. Sally looked like she would be more than happy to go get the donuts.

With great reluctance, I pushed my foot forward. The guy with the switchblade just looked at me and then at bull neck. He didn't stop me.

The next step wasn't any easier, but I didn't think about it until I had scooted up behind bull-man. Weakly, I tugged on the hand holding Sally's breast. "Let her go."

Incredulous, he swung my way, beady black eyes flickering hate.

"Seriously." The plea came out in a squeak, not very persuasive. I stepped back and let go of the tree trunk that served as his arm. I scurried backwards, my knees knocking together hard enough to bruise.

Whoever was behind Allen yanked Allen backwards into the office. Continuing to backpedal seemed like a good idea. I didn't need to wait around until the thug was finished with Allen and free to come after me.

"You crazy bitch!" A look that shouted, "charge" came across bull-man's face.

Sally slumped against the window, clutching protectively at her neck.

Bull-man spread his feet and rolled forward, evil anticipation floating across his face.

Sally's hazel eyes came alive for a moment, and she mouthed my name. "Sedona!"

"Uh-oh." There was a very sinking feeling in what was left of my stomach. The first guy with the switchblade was still behind me. Drawing the only conclusion possible, I leaned down and kicked my left leg straight up backwards.

My foot snagged a gun rather than a knife and knocked it into a high arc. It was just like in my old karate class, only then the weapons were plastic.

I caught the gun. It was heavy. "Well." I blinked at the barrel pointing at my chest. Gingerly I turned it around and made it aim at something else. Backed against the windowed part of the hallway, there wasn't enough room to point it at both the bull and the guy that had been holding the gun.

In class, the exercise was over. We bowed politely and went home. No one here looked ready to leave.

"You want to play?" Bull-man smiled like it was Easter Sunday, and he had the prized golden egg, only instead of a harmless egg, he balanced a knife between two fingers.

He was definitely the better target to point the gun at, but even with me waving it around, he threw the knife. It was like the games my brothers used to play, except they threw darts and they weren't all that lethal. Oh sure, if they had struck my eye I would be dead by now, but that didn't concern them much at ages eight and twelve. It obviously wasn't the number one worry of the guy throwing the knife either.

I swallowed bile, dropped the gun and grabbed. Thinking of the game made me reach out for the knife. Human vision was just slow enough that by the time the knife was visible, the sharp blade was by, and the handle rested in my hand.

I didn't expect to catch it.

No one else expected it either. The guy that used to have the gun was mid-flight, arms wide, headed for my tiny, unprotected body.

I kicked as hard as I could. He fell with a grunt, holding his private parts.

"Help!" I screeched. I should shoot him, but I had dropped the gun. *Where was it?*

Bull-man came straight at me. His hair looked like it belonged on a suit of armor, sticking straight up in some kind of plastered Mohawk. His dark eyes were devoid of anything but mean.

I stabbed with the knife praying I'd miss, and at the same time praying I'd get lucky and get him the first try.

I missed. He kept coming, running through the imaginary red blanket and right into me, the untrained matador. "Help!"

The knife hit the bone in his shoulder. "Uuuungh."

Mashed by his weight, my bones ground into sand, ready to become part of the glass behind me.

The injury on his shoulder finally registered somewhere inside his bovine brain. He shrieked and stumbled backwards. "Aaaaaaaaagh!!!!"

With the weight lifted, I melted to the floor. The gun was by my right hand. I couldn't shoot right-handed. I wasn't certain I was all that good left-handed either.

Sally screamed, "Oh my God, oh my God!"

No one ventured around the corner of the hallway. Allen yelled 911, but something told me he wasn't dialing. I finally had a use for the marketing people with their ubiquitous cell phones, but their lunch hour was more like two and the fast-talking types were nowhere to be found.

The sounds of sirens registered. "Plug her!" Bull-man screamed. He jerked a step or two down the hall, but stepped on his fallen buddy. Bones crunched. Bull's arms windmilled, and he went over backwards, landing on his bad shoulder.

Since his buddy didn't have the gun, and his hand was now broken, it didn't take a genius to surmise Bull-man wasn't talking to the guy on the floor. I scrambled to my feet, using the wall to prop me up. "Uh..." It was the guy with the tattooed arm that had been behind Allen.

He stalked me.

"Eeee!" I tried to jump away, but the only place to run was after the thugs hobbling backwards towards the intersection and the fire exit. "Nnnn... nnn…"

"Plug'er and let's beat it!" Bull-man grunted in pain but leaned against the wall, sadistically waiting to see my brains scattered across the window.

I tried to swallow and couldn't. This guy wasn't stupid, but for half a second…I honestly don't know if I had a sudden brain tumor or an epiphany, but something was wrong here. Where Bull-man had an absence of presence, this guy looked different. His dark brown eyes were hard, but they looked regretful. Despite the evil sword tattooed down his arm, he didn't look much like he wanted to hurt me.

"You--" My mouth dropped open in surprise, silencing the mewing sound in the back of my throat.

He snarled, "Time's up," and threw himself at me, launching us both four feet down the hall. His arm behind me kept my head from cracking open, but he wasn't finished. He growled, pulled back his fist and took aim.

Damned if he didn't give me time to defend myself. I was so stupefied, I didn't move.

He pulled back, yanked me up and stuffed me at the window like a rag doll. "St..op," I stuttered. For a nice guy, he was playing rough. He put the gun in my chin. For longer than it takes an elevator to get up to the fourth floor I thought I was dead.

His buddy yelled encouragement, "Nothin' but smear!"

I hung there, already a body bag.

He reached higher with the gun to smack my head. My arm, feeling like someone else's, blocked. He struck again. His arm was solid muscle and his blow had to have broken something. There was nowhere to back up to, but sliding sideways out from under his arm worked.

Had he let me?

He threw punches faster. I backed away, dancing over my own feet, blocking another punch that nearly shattered my jaw even with my defensive maneuver.

I whimpered again, and he snarled, "Fight."

I don't think his buddy heard. *Did he want me to beat him? Was he crazy?* He was six feet tall to my five-seven if I stretched in the morning. He must have gotten a false impression from my earlier luck.

With a frustrated grunt, he reached for me again and struck pay dirt.

"Ahhhh!" I screamed in rage. "You bastard!" I ripped his offending digits off my breast and plowed him over backwards. He hit the wall opposite the window and bounced, my head in his stomach. The gun dropped from his hand. I was pretty sure I hadn't hit him that hard, but I was going to. I put my hands together and took a magnificent swing.

Crack!

His head snapped backwards, denting the cheap plasterboard. His buddy stopped yelling and headed for the stairs. I fell to my knees. There wasn't enough air in my lungs to keep a gnat alive.

The guy stumbled away from the plasterboard and ran for the exit. On the way, he knocked over Ross Canton, the head of marketing, just coming back from lunch. A doggie-bag full of leftovers flew through the air and splattered on impact.

It mixed well with the blood and disaster.

Chapter 2

I was so sore, I missed work the next two days. That was fine by me. I was too embarrassed to show my bruised face anyway. Instead of being calmly led away to give a statement, I dissolved into a teary, hysterical mess.

Because there were conflicting stories, someone insisted I be taken to a hospital. No one seemed to know if I was injured. Of course I was injured. I had bruises the length of my arm. One palm was cut, but I couldn't decide if that was from catching the knife or wielding it later. Someone had scored a hit on my eye, and my lip was split wide open. I was pretty sure that was from biting it in fear. I didn't remember getting hit in the mouth.

When my eldest brother, Sean O'Hala, picked me up from the hospital, he figured it was my mouth that started it. "Did you insult somebody? Just because I'm a lawyer doesn't mean I can get you out of every trouble spot you create."

"I am not discussing it," I grumbled out the good side of my mouth. "I told you on the phone that muggers broke into work. You're not the police so don't start with the twenty questions."

"I'm calling Mom and Dad."

"No you aren't!" I tried to glare at him, but it was impossible to do from the wheelchair that the hospital insisted he use to cart me out to the car.

"Of course I'm calling them," he snapped, stopping the chair just short of his old maroon Accord. "You can't expect me to pick you up here and just neglect to tell them." He flapped his arms against his body. "You look like hell." He peered closely at my face and then carefully patted me on the head. My long brown hair matched his except for my highlights and the fact that his was military short while mine desperately needed to be collected into a ponytail.

He jerked opened the passenger side door. "Get in."

"They'll worry if you tell them." I heaved myself into the car. "They might even fly here."

He gave the wheelchair to a nurse, and then walked to the driver's side.

I stared out my window. My parents were great people. So were my brothers. They, and only they, were allowed to torture, tease and malign me. My father would have shot all three of the cowards, unlike his daughter. I still didn't know why I hadn't shot them. I knew how to use the gun. My father was a perfect shot. Sean, the only family member who lived in Denton near me, was also a good shot. I was lucky Sean didn't know all the details. He'd be getting his gun if the guys he knew on the police force had had time to give him the lowdown.

Sean meandered through my sub-division as if he had never seen it before. He took extra turns and looked out both windows as though searching for the right address. When we finally pulled up to my house, he studied it before asking, "So. Got any food?"

I rolled my eyes. "I've been working and just got released from the hospital, dummy." I got out, expecting him to drive away. He followed me to the front door.

"We should go get your car from Strandfrost." Normally he squeezed my shoulders as a goodbye, but because of my current bruised condition he refrained.

"I mentioned my car at the hospital."

"I wasn't sure you were alert enough."

"Uh-huh." He took my keys, opened the front door and came in behind me. My brown-tweed second-hand couch looked lonely across from the silent television. I didn't remember whether the place was picked up or not, but it was clean even by my relaxed, dusty standards. It was good to be home.

"I have to use the bathroom," he decided.

I folded my arms. "Just search the place."

He disappeared into the main bedroom, his lanky form tracking quickly through my small, but treasured patio home. He took less time in the spare bedroom because it contained only a bed and was barely bigger than the hall closet. The closet took him longer because he actually checked the top shelf. He also opened the refrigerator, but then turned away in disgust.

"You must be dating too much."

I rolled my eyes again and sat before I could fall.

As brothers do, he noticed. "You want to get your car?"

"Sure." I didn't mean it.

He shrugged and went out to the Accord. He came back. He had his gun case. My eyes flew to his. The worry lines were there, across his forehead. He had been so nonchalant...I was tired.

"You remember how to load it?" Without waiting for an answer, he loaded it, unloaded it, checked the safety and showed me each move. "I won't come to the back door without making sure you know it's me." His eyes locked with mine, dark blue-gray to my greenish-gray, serious and needing some reassurance.

"Yeah."

He paused for a beat, and then put the gun back. "Why didn't...I heard you had one of the guns."

I shrugged.

Sean sat back against my black pillow cushions. "You know how."

"I could have, but there wasn't time." Not to shoot, but to decide. I hadn't had time to make certain I could live with it. And the tattooed guy could have killed me several times over, but he hadn't.

Sean handed me the case. "Brenda and I will bring your car by tomorrow."

I should have known when he didn't bring his wife along that he was going to give me the gun. "Okay." I held the gun case like a lifeline. It gave me something to look at besides him. He patted my shoulder awkwardly. He squeezed hard. I hoped he wouldn't hug me. If he did, I'd burst into tears, and then he'd really be worried.

When he left, I wandered into my bedroom, still carrying the gun. The bed wasn't made, but I rarely did more than pull up the covers. Sean must have actually checked under it because the side I didn't sleep on had one corner of the ivory cotton bedspread stuck up on top.

The gun was a heavy presence, the best protection a brother could buy. I sat on the edge of the bed and rolled over to put the gun underneath. I was only going to rest there a few minutes and then change for the night, but contrary to my expectations, it didn't take me long to fall asleep. Firefighters could have run drills in my living room, and I wouldn't have woken.

* * *

Morning arrived a little later than usual. There wasn't much point in doing more than call and reassure my parents. The weekend was another day away, but I didn't plan on going in on Friday anyway. Suzy Daniels, my best buddy, stopped by to get the scoop, and although she invited me over for dinner, I had to decline. "It's not that I don't want to go, but your five-year old might find my appearance rather frightening."

"No really," Suzy reassured me, "Jimmy loves you so much, he won't care!"

"So what do I tell him? That I fell out of my bunk bed?"

She studied me carefully for a few seconds before saying, "He's been a little wild on his bike lately, trying to ride in the street. How about we tell him you were in the street and a car ran over you? Maybe then he will be more careful." She eyed me critically. "We could even mess your hair up a little more. You're going to have to get it cut anyway. It looks like some of it got torn out."

What are friends for? "Thanks. Speaking of Jimmy, why isn't he with you today?"

"I left him with Robert. They are having a man's day--bring your kid to work thing." She helped herself to another cookie. "It gave me a chance to go and get the rest of the things I need for the baby." She patted her stomach. "God should have made pregnancies six months instead of nine. The last three are hell."

"If he made it too short, you wouldn't be so anxious to get to the delivery part. Even knowing the pain that you're going to be in, after these last three months of carrying her, you want it over with so bad you'll gladly endure the pain of delivery."

She eyed me dolefully. "I will not "gladly" endure that pain. Do you know that Dr. Stanley had the nerve to call and warn Dr. Evans about me?"

My head bobbed up and down enthusiastically. "I don't blame Dr. Stanley one bit. You ripped part of his beard out, Suzy. Do you know he has to shave now because that spot never grew back? What did you expect him to do, forget the incident?"

She sniffed and fluffed her frizzy ginger curls. "He fired me as a patient and refused to be my doctor for Emily. When he recommended Dr. Evans, I think he could have just left the beard incident out of the history. Besides, I told Dr. Stanley I was ready for the epidural. He should have given it to me."

Pointing out that the dear doctor didn't think it was the proper medical time to dispense the medication had not helped Dr. Stanley's cause at the time, nor since. I wisely said nothing, but she wasn't through.

"Furthermore, Dr. Evans is female. I can't rip her beard off no matter how much pain Emily causes me."

"I'm sure he was attempting to protect Dr. Evans in general, Suzy." Knowing she was quite temperamental at this stage, I decided not to push the point. "Sounds like you've picked the name Emily for the baby?"

"She seems to respond to it. She didn't like Emerald." Suzy drank some milk and then munched the last of her cookie. "Do you have more of these?"

Even though she was supposed to watch her sweets, I obliged and grabbed the cookie dough from the fridge. I pressed out a couple more cookies for the toaster oven. "The baby hasn't kicked you too hard yet?"

"I'm pretty sure the name will start with an "E." It's going better than the "A" through "D" names." She grinned and grabbed some of the raw cookie dough out of the bowl. "I better skip the cookie and just eat this. If I don't get going, I'll be late, and I promised Robert I'd be home by three. He seems to think if he limits my time out, he can limit my spending." Her eyes twinkled. "Wait until he sees what I ordered for Emily!"

"I don't think he meant the time limit as a challenge."

She shrugged and smiled happily. "Maybe not. You better get some more rest. You look like you were in a room full of pregnant women that didn't get their epidural!"

Chapter 3

Even after my extended weekend, work was awful. Instead of a bright, up-and-coming genius in her twenties, I looked like a bruised and beaten homeless person. No one would meet my eyes, but every person that had ever met me for ten seconds had to stop in and see how I was doing. I was a bad traffic accident that everyone cursed because it slowed down traffic, but they all stopped to stare just the same.

My boss, Turbo, kind person that he was, didn't stop in until very late in the day. Nicknamed after his coding style, he spent most of his time behind a closed door, usually without showers or food, until a final product was shoved into testers' hands. His hair was on the longish side, except for the round bald spot in the back. He was closing in on forty, but he dressed like a teenager. Today's t-shirt was an old company one that had the faded letters spelling, "Strandfrost," across it. His shirts were never tucked into his ubiquitous jeans.

"Hi." He pretended not to notice my bruises, but only a blind man could miss them.

"I sent the performance figures in on Friday since I couldn't be here in person," I offered in greeting.

He helped himself to the chair on the other side of my desk. "Got them. Glad you could send them. From home." It was an oblique reference, his idea of offering to talk about what had happened if I wanted to unload.

I didn't.

After what he considered an appropriately polite pause, one in which I could have left, gone to the ladies room and returned, he decided I wasn't in the mood to talk. "Don't forget the patent dinner is Friday."

"Uh...huh. Yeah."

He looked at me a little sharper than usual, but his anti-social behavior resulted in him having little insight into other people's heads. In this case, it was a good thing because I had completely forgotten the dinner. "I'm going to rerun a couple more tests," I said to change the subject.

"You look like you could use an easy week. Right?"

There it was again, another offer to spill the beans. He was more curious than usual, or he had something he wanted to tell me. "I'm fine. Is everything okay here? Did I miss anything?"

"Well, security has been improved."

My eyes narrowed at this understatement. "I noticed the hired security people running around on the floor. Does someone think the thugs will come back?"

Turbo actually smiled. The only time he smiled was at one of his own jokes, and no one but he understood those. Okay, there were two other guys in the company and maybe six other people worldwide, but other than that, he was on his own. "There's this little problem. No one seems to know what they were after."

"Sex?" I hazarded. "Money?"

Turbo looked very serious again. "Well, it could have been random, but the chances of that, according to statistics, are less than one percent. Especially since there has been no other sign of gang violence at any other business in the area."

"Seems to me they were a little old to be in a gang."

He nodded, pleased with my observation. "Of course." He rubbed his hands together. "They knew exactly where Allen sat. It's likely they were after him specifically."

"Really?" I couldn't fathom it. "The man is incompetent. He spends more time golfing than in the office. What would they want with him?"

Turbo waggled his eyebrows, causing them to disappear and reappear from under his long choppy bangs. "Personally I think he may have been gambling."

"Gambling? Whatever for? He's paid enough. All he does is sit around, drive a nice car and wear brand new polo shirts that the company orders for him."

Turbo sat back, disappointed that I didn't agree. "It's the latest thing. People get in over their heads."

"Mmhmm." I wasn't convinced. "Maybe he lost a golf bet."

He shook his head vigorously. "It has to be something bigger than that. They were going to make him suffer."

"By attacking him?"

"He and Sally."

"Why Sally?"

He looked at me as though it should be obvious. It wasn't. He could see the deficiency on my face so he began explaining. "Before you got there, they were threatening Allen. They wanted the money or else."

"Or else they were going to hurt Sally?"

He nodded.

"But--"

"The guys that broke in didn't know that Sally isn't important to Allen." He waggled his eyebrows again.

I finally caught on. "Meaning all low-life scum sleep with their secretaries? Come'on. She's twenty-five, and he's an ugly old fart." I shook my head. "Why not just go after Allen's wife?"

He sat back and looked at his shoes. His face got very red.

I swallowed. He still wasn't looking at me. "Turbo."

He tapped on the side of his chair. He mumbled something I couldn't hear.

"Turbo!"

Without looking up, he said, "They threatened his wife. A couple of days earlier. They...they broke two of her fingers, one on each hand. They promised to come back if Allen didn't pay up."

My stomach dropped and churned. I had almost convinced myself that I was right not to have shot them. Now I was pretty sure I should have.

Turbo departed abruptly, leaving me with a queasy stomach and the feeling that I had missed my best chance at protecting myself. I just hoped it wasn't the only chance; better yet, I hoped I never needed another one.

Chapter 4

Tuesday morning, first thing, I had no choice but to call and wheedle until Angela agreed to squeeze me in for a hair appointment after work. If I had remembered the patent dinner, I could have gotten my hair set on Friday before the dinner, but this late, I was lucky to get an appointment period.

As I hung up, Sally stopped by my office. Her hair was newly styled. Instead of a shoulder length cut, she now had a neat bob, stopping at her chin. I tried not to stare or think about why it was shorter.

"I would have come yesterday..." She inspected her manicure as though the answers to the universe were hidden between her fingers and her nails. "I'm awfully glad you did...what you did." She gulped air quickly. Either she had just swallowed her gum or she was having a hard time keeping her stomach down.

"I wish it hadn't happened." My own fingernails were suddenly interesting.

Sally sat and dusted the desk between us, removing invisible crumbs. "They promised they would come back if Allen didn't pay."

"Pay what?"

Sally swallowed again. "I don't know." Her voice was mousy, a small child with a secret.

"But you think you know."

Frightened eyes danced around the room. She was up from the chair and bolting for the door before I could say anything else.

"I have no idea," she squeaked around a deep breath. "Why would anyone think I know anything?"

I shrugged. "I'm sure no one thinks that. You're his secretary, but it's not like you handle his personal affairs."

Sally nodded emphatically. "No way. Not very many of them anyway." She slowly edged back inside my office. "Really, the only thing I can think of is the equipment deal that didn't happen. He put in an order by accident and everything was messed up."

"What equipment?"

"Last quarter he turned in equipment expenses for over a hundred and fifty thousand dollars." She leaned forward. "But no one in the group needed the equipment, and I was told to cancel the order." She waved her hand. "It wasn't that big of a deal because the equipment never showed up at Strandfrost or anything, but there was a check cut for it, and then there was a big tangled mess while I tried to figure out what happened."

"Sally, those guys didn't look like the type of people that got promised a business order that fell through. I'm pretty sure none of them would be selling computers to Strandfrost."

"I didn't think so either. I mean, I had forgotten all about the expense report until those guys started demanding money from Allen, saying he owed them business."

"They said that?"

She nodded. "What other kind of business could they have meant?"

"I don't know. And neither do you. So if anyone asks, just keep telling them you don't know anything."

She didn't look reassured. Wiping her hands along her navy pantsuit, she backed towards the door again. Before scurrying down the hall, she looked both ways.

* * *

I almost missed my hair appointment because people interrupted me all day, and I couldn't get my work done. Unfortunately, things didn't get any better at the beauty salon. I should have waited until the gossip about the break-in died down. Of course, by then my hair would have been long enough to wrap around my waist where I could cut it myself.

"Was it terribly frightening?" Angela demanded, waving a brush wildly as if it were a dangerous weapon.

"Not much scarier than having a woman dressed in a pink leotard with pink tennis shoes do your hair." I dodged the swinging brush.

"Hey, my older clients like pink!" She put her hands on her pink-dressed tights and tapped her foot at me. Her hair was mostly a highlighted brown, but she had dyed one pink stripe across part of her bangs.

"Uh-huh."

She snapped her brush at me again and demanded, "So what happened? Tell us, girl! Details!"

While she started on my hair, I filled her in with the minimum of details.

She oohed. "What about the samurai?"

"The what?"

"I heard there was a guy with a sword as long as his arm."

"Uh…" It took me a minute. "There was a guy with a tattoo of a sword on one arm."

"No real sword?" Her scissors froze in the act of making a precise cut.

"I saw a small knife," I told her apologetically.

"How big was it?"

I put my hands out the approximate length.

"Oh honey, do you want to get your nails done today too?" she asked, spying the broken ends.

I curled my fingers under my hands. "No thanks. I'll just file them." The bruises on my arms weren't gone. I had purposely worn a cotton-knit long-sleeved sweater to keep the greenish-blue spots hidden. Today wasn't going to be the day I rolled my sleeves up and gave her even more of an excuse to hover.

She worked on my hair, but didn't stop talking. I ignored the rumor about one of the guys having a peg leg. Maybe it came about because by the time the thugs ran off, one of them was limping. I was half asleep when she said, "I heard they didn't catch any of them. Emma was telling me she heard from her nephew that they plan on coming back and getting even."

"What?" I sat up, bumping the hand that held the scissors.

"Sit still! You know that nephew of hers has been in and out of jail. I guess he must know some of them."

My heart beat faster. "He knows who did it?"

"That kid has been in a lot of trouble. Wouldn't surprise me if he was in the getaway car."

"Emma told you this? Emma who?" I demanded.

Her scissors stopped cutting for a heartbeat or two. She glanced quickly at the other stylists. "I don't know as I should tell you that. I mean, gossip like that could get someone in trouble."

I had to bite my tongue to keep from screeching. Now was hardly the time for her to get high and mighty about gossiping; it was the reason half her clients came in! "I don't need Emma's name. Just tell me her nephew's name."

"James." She eyed me carefully and then stole another quick glance in the mirror at the others in the shop. "And I don't know his last name. It's not the same as Emma's." She sniffed, focusing back in on me. "You really could do with an updated hair style. Next time you come in, let's look at some books."

"Okay, but if Emma's name isn't the same as James, couldn't you tell me her name?"

Snip, snip went the scissors. I started to fear for my hair.

"No. She'd know I said something."

I didn't nod, for fear of the scissors, but it was hard to sit still. I pleaded with my eyes, but Angela refused to look at me. "It was so scary," I said. "I have a lot of trouble sleeping at night." Which was mostly true, except for the first night. "I sure hope the police find out who did it."

Angela said, "me too," but then pushed a couple of magazines my way. "Pick out a new style. You really need one next time. You're too young to let yourself go."

I thought that description was a bit harsh, but she was the one with scissors. I dutifully flipped pages, trying to think of a way to convince her to give me the name.

Angela kept up a constant patter, but suddenly none of it was about the break-in. Maybe I could call her later. Maybe she'd tell me on the phone when no one else was around.

When I paid my bill, out of habit, I automatically pulled up the sleeve of my sweater to sign the credit card slip. A dark line of golden-green bruises showed. I hurriedly slid it back down, but Angela stared even after the sleeve covered them.

I signed quickly. Angela looked over at the other two ladies cutting hair. She didn't say anything. When she took the slip back, she separated them, and then wrote, "Jackson," on my part of credit card slip. She pushed it over to me.

I clutched it. "Thanks," I said, all inclusively.

The minute I got home, I called Sean and told him about Emma and the nephew. "Do you think you could get one of your policemen buddies to look into it?"

He grunted. "You don't have a last name for James? Address? Age? Anything?"

"No," I admitted. "But he's been in jail, and you have the aunt's name, Emma Jackson."

"That only helps if she happens to be his guardian. I'll just have Derrick check out every James that was ever arrested. No problem. The police always appreciate huge tips that make the job easy."

I ignored his sarcasm and cautioned, "This James kid might have just been bragging, shooting his mouth off."

"Let's hope so," Sean snapped back. He hung up, but I knew he'd try to find out more about James just in case. That's what brothers were for.

Chapter 5

The week didn't improve much, but no more thugs visited Strandfrost, so I counted that as a huge improvement.

By the time Friday rolled around, most of the bruises had faded enough that I could cover them with makeup. The grand ball for the company patents was held in the Whispering Pines Resort. Technically I shouldn't have been invited, but Turbo had two patent awards. His wife was beside herself at the opportunity to attend such a huge event, which is probably where he got the idea that I would like to go. He wangled an extra invite and gave it to me.

The pickings in my closet were lean. The blue silk top was one I usually wore with business suits; the black skirt had been on sale. I almost hadn't gotten it because I couldn't remember the last time I needed to wear anything with a slit. Make-up brightened the gray of my eyes, but blush just made my cheeks look like those of a chipmunk. I took it off. I was more an unfinished canvas than a masterpiece; the reality was "okay" but I kept hoping for the day I would wake up stunningly beautiful.

Getting dressed was depressing because I wasn't nervous over a date. It was a little hard to get excited over impressing the valet parking guy. My mother kept telling me to get into the nineties and ask someone out, but she didn't work with the men I did.

I drove myself, although Turbo had offered to stop by and get me. I didn't want to spoil Irene's night out on the town.

My Civic was the least fancy car in the lot. "Geeks." Obviously Strandfrost engineers were making up for their nerdiness by driving cars that no one else could afford. At least that's what I told myself since I couldn't afford a Corvette or a BMW.

The valet looked like he would park the Civic. "Thanks," I mumbled, stepping out. I assume he took all car keys by two fingers as if he were removing a soiled napkin. I wasn't so certain of it that I felt obligated to tip him, however.

Inside, bright lights danced across tablecloths dressed with flowers and fine china. Even with the crowd milling about, Turbo managed to get me seated next to Irene. Paul, one of the guys that worked in the lab with us, was on my other side. He was single, early-thirties and just starting to lose his straight brown hair. He made up for it by sporting a bushy mustache.

"Hey, Paul."

He aimed his knife at me with a grin. I looked at him soberly.

"Sorry." He put the knife down, sheepishly. "Some of us write code, some of us are Karate Kid."

Turbo looked confused as though he didn't get the joke. Irene pressed a white-laced hand against her heart. "We aren't going to talk about that, are we?" She blinked rapidly, smoothing a hand down her lilac dress. "I mean, not at dinner anyway."

Paul smiled, kind of like a kid caught kicking under the table. "No way. I just wanted to tease Sedona."

I turned my attention to the waiter, who rushed over and filled one of the glasses with water.

"Would the madam like wine or champagne?"

"Water is all."

Whisk, away went the extra glass. "Are they serving dinner yet?" I asked.

"Just rolls so far." Carefully, Turbo handed round the basket. There were little silver dishes with butter, but the rolls weren't hot, so I passed them along. If I were going to get fat, it wouldn't be over a cold roll with cold butter.

Generally speaking, the night started out fine. I only embarrassed myself after dinner when I asked for hot tea instead of coffee. The waiter didn't look ready to accommodate the special request and by the time it arrived, the speakers had already started.

I was lucky the order took so long because the tea had time to cool. That didn't stop me from choking on it when I realized that the speaker on the podium was none other than the guy that had grabbed my chest last week at Strandfrost.

Chapter 6

Paul pounded my back, trying to be discreet while I struggled not to gag dinner back up. Irene waved one of her gloves in my face, either to provide an inadequate supply of air or stuff it down my throat because I was embarrassing her so badly.

Turbo handed me a glass of water. I managed to get some down without swallowing my tongue. Obviously, I was hallucinating. Thank God the speaker couldn't see down into the dim room.

I looked again. His hair was about right, but his skin was lighter than I remembered. He...had the same eyes, bold, steady and honest. He spoke slowly; he didn't hiss. His arm was covered by a suit so it was impossible to tell if he had a tattoo. Of course I was imagining the whole thing.

"Who is that?" It came out more like a sneeze and everyone was already studiously ignoring me. I looked at the program. There was a glowing description of some guy that served on several impressive company boards. He was currently CEO of I.C. Inc, and had been vice president of some other company in his past. "Steve Huntington." Who was he? And why had he been threatening Allen?

I gulped some of my tea. It was bitter and barely lukewarm. I didn't care. Had the food been poisoned? I hadn't taken champagne or wine. I hadn't even eaten much of the wine sauce that had been on the fish!

I dared one last glance to test my sanity. He was looking right at me! I nearly shriveled and died on the spot, but his eyes moved on. Bolting was out of the question. I would be calm. "I have to go."

Irene looked aghast. "I don't mean to the bathroom," I explained. She looked worse, like she had swallowed her own glove.

If I got up and left, he might notice. What did I care? I had to be mistaken.

Mercifully, his speech was short. The two that followed were like sitting through a church sermon on a particular sin right after I'd committed it.

At the end, the music came back on and Paul tugged at my shoulder. "Don't you want to get dessert?"

Instead of serving dessert at the table, someone had decided that milling around would give the inventors time to show off their awards. Maybe now was a good time to escape. I stood. Paul reached out a hand. "Are you okay? You look kind of pale."

"I don't think dinner agreed with me." The speakers certainly hadn't. I edged around the table.

Irene fluttered politely at someone, and Turbo had his back to me. It would be rude to leave without saying goodbye.

I touched Turbo's sleeve to get his attention at the same time I heard the person he was talking to say, "It's a pleasure to meet you."

It was him. I stood stock-still.

I was nearly out of air when I realized that Turbo hadn't turned to acknowledge me. I sucked in a deep breath. "Good-bye," I muttered and stepped back. Paul grunted when I came down hard on his left foot.

I would have sailed right around him, but Paul grabbed my arm to keep me from plowing him over. Turbo turned around. "Oh, Sedona."

Mr. Huntington was bending over Irene's hand, responding to her ridiculous Victorian gesture.

I sidled along like a crab, moving around behind Huntington to make good on my escape.

"Your husband is a talented inventor," Huntington said to Irene. He stepped backwards and pivoted to include Turbo. Pain shot through my foot.

"Uhmph." I didn't mean to push him, but it hurt, and I was trying to escape. He stumbled forward into Irene, who gasped for the millionth time. He caught himself and Irene, steadying her.

He turned quickly then, brilliant blue eyes lighting on me.

I froze. His eyes were blue, not dark brown.

There was no sign of recognition. He apologized. "The room is a little crowded."

"Oh." *His eyes were blue.*

Paul, bless his heart, stuck out his hand. "I'm Paul Carter. I've been wanting to meet you."

"I didn't." I said it low enough that no one noticed. The creep had brown eyes, not blue. He had slammed against me, holding me to the window. He had tried to kill me, but his eyes were brown.

Paul began discussing his patent. Huntington's eyes turned to me.

I looked at the floor. There I was, ready to accuse the man of horrible crimes just because he happened to resemble some nightmare.

Before Huntington could ask about my contributions, Paul volunteered information. "This is my date, Sedona."

Paul may as well have knocked me down. I gaped at him, wondering what part of the conversation I had missed.

Huntington stretched his hand towards mine. I stared at it before managing to get mine into proper form. "Um. Nice to meet you."

"How is your foot?"

"No problem. I was on my way out anyway."

He stared at me in silence for a moment. "It's great of you to show your support." He included Irene in the comment, and out of the corner of my eye, I swear I saw her simper. I settled for staring at the floor and tried to concentrate on dying. If I held my breath long enough maybe I could just expire and the whole nightmare would end.

While Paul blathered on about his patent, I made a polite noise and edged away. I made my smile as vague as Irene's. Let him think I was an idiot. I had covered any sign of intelligence with an astounding display even my own family wouldn't have recognized.

Paul reached out and snagged my sleeve. "Did you want to sit down? Let me just finish telling Mr. Huntington about the new design."

By the time Paul turned back, Huntington had turned away. Within seconds, he was lost in the crowd, smiling at other attendees, playing host. Paul looked annoyed.

"Who is he?" I gulped out.

Paul pulled out a chair and sat heavily. "He's the new board member. Don't you read the annual report? He was just elected to the board this year."

Sure I read it, and I always checked to see how much the executives were making. I just never paid any attention to the board member's names. I couldn't imagine why a board member would attack Allen.

I closed my eyes. I was under too much stress.

Even closed, I could see blue. The attacker did not have blue eyes. Maybe Huntington had a brother.

Paul didn't apologize for telling Huntington that I was his date. I hadn't realized until that moment that Paul pitied me because I didn't have a shiny patent of my own. I attended to show support for my colleagues and boss. How was I to know they considered me an outsider?

Feeling no more need to hang around, I made polite good-byes, this time without stepping on or pushing anyone. The whole night was an absolute bust.

* * *

For weekends like this, I needed my best friend, a good book and a poolside chat. Unfortunately, Suzy was busy with her five-year old. After calling her in the morning and lying about what a great time I had, I settled for the book at the pool by myself.

By Monday, when I had to face people again, I was almost prepared. I stuck to the lab doing my job. In the middle of the afternoon, Turbo called me into his office. I figured he was going to lecture me on my bad behavior.

"I'll be right there," I said on a sigh, hanging up the phone.

I dawdled, but there was only so much time I could waste. I peeked around his office door, hoping something had called him away in the last five minutes.

Sadly, he was still there, waiting. His office was crowded with computers, ongoing inventions, and an oscilloscope. Four stuffed heroes--Dilbert, Taz, Bugs Bunny and Marvin the Martian--had a place of honor on top of his monitor. Turbo sat in the middle of this mess with his hands folded across his stomach and his feet propped on the support under the desk. He stared intently at his email with an expression that could only be described as smug.

Turbo was often deep in thought, sarcastic, lost in code, or even tired, but smug, well that was a new one. "Come in," he waved me to a chair.

I sat.

He grinned.

Uh-oh.

"New assignment for you," he said heartily.

"Since when do new assignments make you laugh?"

He looked a little sheepish, but still pleased. "This one is right up your alley."

"Me? Not us?"

"Well, you work for the customer and so do I. Technically that would be us." He wagged a finger at me and sat up. "Remember when I told you that Allen was up to his neck in gambling debts?"

"You mean when you were speculating?"

He leaned back and gave me one of his long, disapproving pauses before saying, "The board of directors wants our help." He cocked his head sideways. "Well, specifically yours."

My eyebrows left my face. "Mine? They don't even know I exist!"

"I suggested you to them and the Federal Agents working the case."

I had already lost my eyebrows in surprise; now my eyeballs popped out of my head. I wasn't sure I liked the idea of being "suggested" to Federal Agents-- for any reason. "Uh…"

"After the patent dinner, the Feds, several of the board members, Paul and I all got together. Turns out that the board is looking for a candidate to help infiltrate a problem that has cropped up at Strandfrost."

"What problem? Allen's gambling problems?"

"No," he said dismissively. "Money disappearing." Before I could say anything, he continued. "There are certain funds missing. Basically it looks as though Allen has been skimming money from the budget that should have gone to charities."

Sally's comments came to mind. She hadn't mentioned charities, but had said something about money for stuff that hadn't been needed. She never said how the mess was cleared up. "If Allen is skimming from charities, why not just arrest him and make him go away? What do they need me for?"

"Well," Turbo sat back and folded his hands again, "that's where it gets interesting. The checks to the charities were signed by Allen, but the charities never received the monies. No one knows exactly who cashed the checks, but they were cashed. The Feds are pretty sure Allen had help from someone getting them cashed. Of course, he kept at least part of the money himself."

I thought of bull face and his friends. "You think the guys that broke in here were due some money from the scheme?"

"It's quite likely. They seemed to think Allen owed them for something. All we know for certain is that the board doesn't know where the money is, and the Federal Agents aren't leaving until we find it. That's where you come in. You're about to be an up-and-coming executive, and you're going to horn into Allen's territory."

I was a lab rat, happy to play with equipment for hours on end. I took things apart, I put them back together, I ran analysis. My favorite uniform was blue jeans and a casual shirt or sweater, but on Fridays and bad hair days, I had been known to show up in t-shirts. I almost always tucked them in. "Uh, I don't think that will fly. I haven't exactly acted interested."

"It really doesn't matter what Allen thinks. It's his associates that matter-- we're hoping that whoever is behind the check-cashing scheme will push Allen aside now that he has made mistakes. They will be looking for a new, malleable person with signature power willing to sign off on company contributions to charities. Management has noticed you and your potential because of your bravery, of course, so it's only natural that you'd be promoted."

My eyes narrowed. "My bravery?" Foolishness was more like it. "Who is telling management that they noticed me?"

"Well…" he hedged. "Not everyone thinks this is a good plan, but the board wants to talk to you. If they agree you are the right person, you'll get promoted a few levels and be able to work on this problem."

"Um…I don't think this is a very good idea."

Turbo sat forward again. "Sure it is! You can take care of yourself! You're smart, you've been asking about being promoted, and here's the perfect chance!" He pounded a fist into his open palm. "We can stop those bastards!"

"We? Are you going to be promoted too?"

He shrugged and sat back. "Of course not. I'll just be the technical representation."

"Oh boy."

"The meeting is tomorrow at nine."

"The meeting?"

"The meeting to talk to the Feds and the board."

"Oh boy."

"Do you think," he frowned with intense concentration. "Do you suppose you could wear something that made you look like you wanted the job?"

I glared at him. "No. Not until someone gives me a better reason."

He knew me well enough not to argue. He thought hard for a few moments, but let it go. "The group should be able to answer any questions you have, if they know the answers. I guess they need you because that is what they lack the most. Answers."

I was less than pleased and not nearly as excited as Turbo. Apparently Turbo and Paul not only thought I was lacking in patents, they must have thought I needed fear in my life also.

Chapter 7

I shoved Turbo and the promotion out of my mind. The day was over and Monday night was shooting night. So my brother Sean had decided, anyway. I met him at the range. He hadn't said anything about bringing Brenda, so I was surprised to see her. "Hey, guys." I glanced quizzically at my eldest brother. He looked like a man who had lost a fight with his beloved wife.

"You decided to learn to shoot?" I asked Brenda.

She glared at Sean. She was a very pretty woman, smaller and more petite than I. Her hair was dark enough to be called black and cut short in a little pixie haircut that made her resemble a very cute elf. "Yes. If you need to learn to protect yourself, I guess I do too."

"Well now." I squirmed.

Sean took over. "It isn't as though you get into trouble all the time like my sister does."

"Hey!"

He silenced me with a look. "She," he pointed an accusing finger in my direction, "has been like this all her life. She gets chased by horses, falls down stairs, jumps out of moving vehicles, runs after purse thieves and gets mugged."

"I was only three! How was I supposed to know the horse would charge?"

"She needed a gun even then." His lips tight with anger, he slapped his credit card on the table. "We need three targets." He put another gun case on the counter. I added the case he had given me that contained the twenty-two. It wasn't exactly a killer weapon, but Sean knew it was the one I shot the best. It had very little kick and was accurate.

He pointed to his thirty-eight. "You use this one," he snapped at me. "Brenda can learn with the twenty-two."

It was an indoor range, which was a lot more claustrophobic than outdoor shooting. Sean led the way to the edge of the pop-up targets. Immediately, my stomach rebelled. I didn't view shooting as a sport and shooting at police training targets was not amusing.

Sean set Brenda up with ear protection in a nice quiet booth. He pushed the button, put the target on the platform and sent it out. Since I was standing there looking like one of the targets, he turned and pointed at me. "You know how to use it."

And I hadn't, and he was angry. Sean was a lawyer and a good one. The problem was that he represented victims; rape victims, robbery victims, and little old ladies that had been mugged. He only hated two things about his job: the fear and the grief that resulted from the weak being too weak or too unwilling to protect themselves.

Like a good little soldier, I loaded the gun. I preferred semi-automatics to revolvers, but I also preferred rifles with nice safe scopes and targets that were very far away and didn't resemble people.

The codes for controlling the targets were more complicated than just point and shoot. Fully focused on the instructions, I nearly jumped out of my shoes when Brenda screamed. Heads turned in our direction. Screaming in a place where there were guns and high adrenaline was probably not a good idea.

I peeked around the cube. "What happened?"

Sean's face had absolutely no color. For a second I thought Brenda had shot him and that he was about to tumble to the ground like a felled tree.

Brenda gulped and backed away from her husband. Sean had never raised a hand to her, but he looked like he might want to start.

"Next time," he took a deep, living breath, "wait until my arm is away from the gun before pulling the trigger."

I swallowed bile and stepped back into my booth. There were three targets. While I shot at the first, the other two moved forward and back before popping up again. I set the thing to the slowest speed and braced my arms.

Brenda didn't scream again so she was either dead or she had killed my brother and fainted. I hit the first three targets before they ran full up to me. If they got up to the end of their tethers without getting shot, a bell would ring, and I guess that meant I was technically dead. Since I hadn't set the reload number, I got killed after the first round, plus I missed a target entirely. Dad had taught us to shoot with both of our eyes opened, but in the last couple of years, my sight had diverged, and I was having a hard time of it.

Five rounds in, I gave up. I could hit the targets. I could even hit them where it counted most of the time. What I didn't know was whether or not I'd do it.

Sean probably intended to practice also, but he changed his mind. It wasn't good to practice when you're tense, and it looked like it would be a few days before he calmed down enough to speak without yelling.

On the way out, his shoulder twitched. I decided it would be a good idea for me to get back into karate. Sean would feel better, and his wife might not shoot him accidentally.

He left the thirty-eight and a large box of extra bullets with me. I was thrilled, of course.

Chapter 8

Tuesday morning it was raining. Thinking about Turbo and his Fed friends made me nervous so I ate leftover cookies from my fridge, and then stopped at McDonald's for a breakfast burrito and orange juice.

Once inside my office, I booted my machine to check my email. There was a reminder about the nine o'clock meeting. Too bad it hadn't been a dream. Turbo had sent me a couple of reports to look at, and I still had some tests that needed to be run.

I went to the lab to get one of the tests started. Paul and Turbo were both there. "Hi guys."

Paul looked up. He tugged on his mustache and frowned. "I thought you were going to wear something nice."

"What's wrong with sneakers and jeans? They're clean."

Paul looked a little like my dad the first time I wore pants to church instead of a dress. That isn't the point," he huffed.

Clean pants at church hadn't impressed my father either. "I haven't decided if I want the job, Paul."

"Why not? You don't want to be stuck testing the rest of your life, do you?"

I shrugged. "Maybe I'll have a great idea one day and get a patent or two. Then I can be like you."

Paul stroked his mustache again. He opened his mouth, shut it and looked unhappy. I imagine he was trying to find a nice way to tell me that if I hadn't made it already, it wasn't ever going to happen. Funny, until the patent dinner I didn't know he secretly felt sorry for me.

Nine rolled around before I even got the correct software loaded. With little choice, I followed Paul and Turbo downstairs to the meeting rooms. We rarely had visitors upstairs because our hallways were filled with old equipment or new equipment that hadn't been unboxed yet. No need for anyone important to see our mess.

My heart, though I had prepared it, beat a nervous tune when the three of us entered the narrow meeting room. Huntington, the guy from the awards dinner that looked so much like the attacker, and four other men in suits were waiting. A coffee urn sat on the low counter attached to one wall. From the cups on the table, these guys had been here long enough to get settled.

Two of the suits looked like they had guns; forced relaxation, hands on the table, their jackets roomy enough to accommodate shoulder holsters. They sat funny, looking a lot like my brother's cop friends when they were carrying.

Huntington sat between two other board members that I recognized from the awards dinner, Christopher something and Vic Towers. Vic was either nervous or impatient. He tapped his fingers against the table in a choppy rhythm.

Huntington didn't make it any easier for me to separate him from the attacker when he started off with a snide remark. "I thought you said she was capable of playing the part of up-and-coming executive?"

Hadn't I had this argument already this morning? "I haven't decided I want the job, Mr. Huntington. No point in getting dressed up if I'm not going to the party."

Unlike Paul, Huntington's blue eyes didn't waver. "Was the dinner the other night the best you could do?"

Turbo sat down and rolled his chair sideways. He was either trying to get out of my way or get within kicking distance of Huntington.

I kept from snarling, but my voice was strained. "I wasn't trying to dress like an executive, then or now."

"Let's just hope you weren't trying all that hard to impress your date."

For a minute I was confused. Then my face colored. I had forgotten about Paul's escort claim. I sat down, off-balance.

Vic, the board member closest to me, hurriedly started introductions and explanations. He had a slight accent and a nice tan that indicated that at least some of his managing was done in the great outdoors. "We really need an inside person on the team, someone that the embezzlers can approach now that Allen has made enemies in his own camp," he said. "I think you'll be very intrigued by our plan."

Huntington continued to glower, obviously not a big believer. I noticed that his shoulders were wide. He could be carrying a gun, like the other two. He had huge hands. I remembered those hands; grabbing, shaking, threatening.

Turbo leaned over and touched my hand. "Did you understand the question?"

I hadn't even heard it. "What? Uh, no, I wasn't paying attention, sorry."

Huntington rolled his eyes heavenward. "She hasn't got the brains to pull this off."

I frowned, trying to shake the image that kept intruding, but other than blue eyes, this guy was the attacker. That thought prompted my first question. "Do I get to carry a gun?"

Fed number one, a black guy named Bruce, looked startled and shook his head sharply. "No way. Executives don't go around packing." He was a broad-shouldered man, but unlike Huntington, he held himself inside as though he didn't want to appear threatening. His hair was short; his clothes neatly pressed. He looked to be in his mid-thirties, probably a few years younger than Turbo.

"Executives aren't supposed to go around stealing either," I said. "I think I deserve some sort of protection. Those guys already attacked once." I very carefully didn't look at Huntington when I said it.

Bruce shook his head again. "You aren't going to be Rambo, you're going to be a civilized executive. You're going to act a part. You'll have signature power. Hopefully someone will approach you and offer you the same deal they made with Allen."

"Don't you think it would be a little strange for someone to approach me? I'm pretty unknown. Maybe they don't want to run anymore deals since this one didn't work out so well for them."

Bruce didn't smile, but his brown eyes were friendly, helpful. "Yes, but they are missing a lot of cash. We don't know where it went and neither do they. Allen isn't talking, but if we can catch one of them offering you a hand in, we can get the goods on all of them. Once we have something, Allen will spill everything he knows."

"Why don't one of you just step into the director's spot and take over?" I dared a glance at Huntington. "You're new, and you're already an executive. Maybe they will approach you now that Allen has been caught."

Huntington's blue eyes narrowed. "I have too much of a reputation. They wouldn't approach me or any other board member. I can run the operation and provide direction, but I can't play stoolie."

I ignored the possible insult. "But why me?"

"We need someone they aren't afraid to approach," Bruce said. He shifted in his seat and looked down at the table. So did Vic.

Huntington cut to the chase. "What he means is, you're a woman trying hard to get ahead. You're approachable--and probably easy to manipulate."

My face froze.

He held up his hands in an innocent pantomime. "So the thinking might go."

Bruce cleared his throat and started talking before I could think of an appropriate reply. "Let's go over the details. Your part of the job won't be that difficult. All you have to do is wait for someone to approach you like they did Allen."

I forced myself to concentrate. "And then I report to you?"

Bruce nodded.

At this point, the job sounded a little like someone saying "test this, I know it works." Engineers never wanted to give details. They wanted the least amount of work possible to get testers to sign on the dotted line. Just like with my lab job, I didn't think this was going to be as easy as everyone hoped. "Tell me about this scheme of theirs. How did it work? What am I supposed to watch for?"

Bruce looked at Vic for permission. When he nodded, Bruce said, "We know Allen was skimming. He approved checks written from Strandfrost to various charities, but cashed them himself. He had help filtering them through false accounts, and he got a small percentage."

I interrupted. "He took money from Strandfrost and only got a small percentage? Why not keep it all?"

"Because he didn't dream up this scheme on his own," Bruce explained. "Someone helped him set up a bank account that could accept deposits in the charity name. Then, at least two names were listed on the temporary charity accounts as executors, but the names were always tied to false IDs."

"Fake names? Not Allen?"

Bruce nodded. "If Allen's name were on the accounts it would be too obvious. All charity accounts have someone listed who manages the money. Two or three people usually have the authority to deposit checks, move money around or withdraw money for expenses. In this case, several local banks allowed temporary accounts to be opened for deposits from a local charity drive. The IDs used to open the accounts were accepted as legit until the money was taken out in a large cash withdrawal. In the second case, the money was transferred to a different account that was then cashed out immediately."

"And you think Allen was working this scheme with a few people, but once he learned the process, he found a place to deposit a couple of checks and didn't give a share to his buddies?"

Bruce nodded.

"Why not just arrest Allen and be done with it?"

Huntington took over explaining. "We could arrest him, but we'd miss the people he has been working with--remember they used false identities to open the accounts. While Allen would probably finger one or two under enough pressure, he may not know enough about the organization for us to get them all. We'd like to catch them in action--follow them, photograph them, and catch them red-handed. We can't use Allen, because he's a liability. Not only was he skimming from Strandfrost, he was skimming from his cohorts. No one is going to deal Allen in anymore."

Generally I preferred pacing when I was thinking, but since the room wasn't big enough, I settled for rolling the chair forward, then pushing it back. "What if the amount his buddies is missing is more than the charity checks? What if Allen was taking money out of the budget for say, equipment that he didn't really order?"

I managed to surprise them. Huntington hid it better than the others; his eyes only widened for a fraction of a second. I didn't tell them that Sally had given me a hint about a funny expense report. Let them think I was brilliant. My reputation needed a little enhancing anyway.

Turbo smiled like a proud parent.

"What makes you ask that?" Bruce asked cautiously.

"I order equipment all the time. The records are such a mess, in some cases it would be hard to tell if the equipment is missing or if it had ever been ordered in the first place. We get things in all the time that we didn't order. Then there's the stuff we order that never shows up, so we order it again. On items over ten thousand dollars, the signature authority would go up to Allen's level. He could claim things in his budget that were never ordered." I shrugged. "How he got his hands on the payments…I don't know."

Bruce exchanged glances with the men. "It's possible."

I looked around the room. Turbo was the only one that didn't look smug and secretive. This wasn't going to work unless I had more details. These guys knew more than they were sharing. "Gentlemen," I said, "if you're going to ask me to help with the laundry, I need to know what kind of dirt is on the clothes. And I want to know about all of it, not just the easy stains, because if I'm going to help, I don't want to be the next person they come after."

Huntington said, "We are attempting to protect you. The more you know the more dangerous it will be for you."

I shook my head. From my line of work, I knew it was necessary to know what made a machine tick before I could make sure it ticked the way it was supposed to. "If you tell me what it is you are really trying to find out, maybe I can help you. I'm guessing Allen must have taken more money than just a few thousand charity dollars to cause all this trouble."

I waited, but instead of telling me that my guess was correct, Huntington sat back and folded his arms. "Before we get into too much detail, we need to know if you can do the job."

"You tell me what really needs to be done, and I'll tell you whether or not I can do the job." I gave him my stubborn stare, the one that I used when engineers didn't want to give me the information I needed. Unless he pulled a gun or slammed me against the wall, I could afford to wait him out.

The room was silent for a few heartbeats. Huntington didn't look happy, but eventually he reached into his briefcase and pulled out a list. It was in Powerpoint and many, many pages long.

Chapter 9

Exact details of my new job could have been jotted down on the back of a grocery list, but executives couldn't keep things that simple. Boiled down, the basics entailed a few thousand dollars to advance my wardrobe and a bunch of nonsense ideas on how to invent a whole new persona: a desperate-to-impress manager one.

I listened to about half of Huntington's ideas, but when it came to dressing for success, I would look to my mother. Huntington might serve on the company board and have lots of money, but my mother could wear clean clothes from the Salvation Army and make them look good. Through many reluctant lessons, I knew about tasteful elegance, even if I couldn't carry it off with anything close to her grace.

I could have bought off the rack, but most clothes would require altering for a perfect fit. My mother would have been happy to make a classic outfit or two, but that would have meant a lot of explanations. I called my hairdresser, Angela, instead, hoping she could recommend a seamstress.

"Angela, I need someone that can make me a really nice outfit or two. Do you know anyone that can sew?"

"You need a seamstress? You pregnant or something?"

I nearly choked. "You just saw me!" Maybe my fashion instincts were worse than I thought. Of course, she had known me a while and I had never shown interest in needing special outfits. "I'm just, um, it would be easier to, you know, get promoted and stuff if I dressed better."

"Well, well, well." I heard her put something down against a hard counter top. "I have been telling you that you need a new hairdo for how long? Don't you worry. I have the perfect style--"

"Angie!" I broke in desperately. "Clothes! I'm starting with a new wardrobe."

She didn't stopped prattling. "And your nails could use buffing too."

"Angie, do you know anyone or not?"

She laughed. "Calm down, girl. You sound desperate. Must be one hot date, is all I can say." I heard her tell someone she'd be with them in a minute, and then she typed on the shop computer. "I got a friend that can help you out. But once you get this outfit made, you come straight in here, and we'll fix the rest of you up."

"Okay, okay." I jotted down the number.

"Get yourself something in a deep purple or dark blue," she advised. "It'll bring subtle attention to your gray eyes. You're a winter, girl. You need dark colors to enhanced that olive skin of yours."

"Whatever you say." Although O'Hala sounded Scottish, my grandfather was at least half American Indian. I had his angular face and skin tone, but my mother's Irish temper.

"You want to make your hair appointment now?"

"No, no, later. Not until I have the outfits ready."

She didn't believe my excuse, but she hung up, and I called her friend.

We met at Barbette's Bobbins just past the mall. She knew a guy in Hong Kong and, if I was willing to pay, she could get certain raw and silk twills. I was a big fan of cotton also, so she promised me some comfy kick-around pants.

On Friday, Turbo stopped by my office and closed the door. He sat down and dropped a huge stack of papers on my desk.

"Tests to run?"

"Tests?" He shook his head and looked stern. "You're being promoted, remember? This is your new house."

It took me a few seconds. "My--" I blinked rapidly. "My what?"

He pushed the papers over. I looked down and read the address. Denton wasn't a very big city. There was still a touch of country, a quiet air that outsiders liked. We had the Whispering Pines Resort for skiing, golfing and mistress boffing, and next to it was a section of town that was known as the place to live.

"I'm moving to Alpine Hills?"

Turbo nodded. "Don't get too excited. It's not one of the estate homes," he said apologetically.

I looked at the address again before typing it into my computer. The Hills had mostly estate homes, but on the very edge--gasp, there was set of condominiums for those that wanted to be in the place of money, but couldn't actually afford one of the mansions on the winding hillside.

"I'm moving to a condo in Alpine Hills?" I was impressed. "Wow."

Turbo handed me a pen.

With my eyes half popped out of my head, I signed.

He shuffled the papers around, handing me another bundle. "Just one more thing."

This time, I saw my own address, the real one. "What's this?"

He looked unhappy. "Huntington insists that you sign over your place to him until this is over."

"Oh, no." I pushed the paper back at him. "Not in this lifetime."

Turbo rolled his chair away, refusing to take the paper. "He just turned his condo over to you."

"I don't care."

Turbo sighed. He turned my monitor around to face him. "May I?"

I pushed the keyboard his way.

When he was finished, he turned the monitor back to me. County records. I scanned them. My mouth dropped. "You've got to be kidding me."

He shook his head. "The condo is worth more than double your little patio home."

"That's only because my house isn't in Alpine Hills, and I don't have a golf membership or live two blocks from the course."

"Huntington doesn't want any problems getting the condo back when this is over."

"Hmph." I twiddled the pen. "There has got to be a better way! Can't he just trust me?"

Turbo shook his head.

I fiddled with the pen and moved the papers around, but he didn't leave. It took me a long time to sign the second set of papers. With each letter of my name, I thought about backing out. I had a feeling that Huntington had done this before. What bothered me was that I didn't know which Huntington was real, the attacker or the board member. Every time I saw the man, I was certain he was both.

Chapter 10

I drove to Alpine Hills Saturday afternoon to see my new condo. Even from the outside, it appeared to be as fabulous as advertised. Pulling into the parking lot, I decided I'd better pester Huntington about a new car. I was thinking black, maybe a Mercedes. I was not a Corvette person. I needed to be able to see above the dash, and no one in high heels looked good hauling themselves out of a car that cruised a foot above the ground. Hopping down from a high leather SUV seat or inching one's skirt up delicately to get in... whole different thing.

There was valet parking and a doorman. "Hello," I said in my brightest, happiest voice.

Neither smiled, but the valet looked ready to park the car, and the doorman opened the door and gave a half bow. He looked like he was still in high school, scrubbed clean and stuffed into a band uniform.

The inside of the building was more to my taste than the outside, because it was discreet and quiet. Don't get me wrong; I wasn't giving up my little house in suburbia just so I could live in the neighborhood, but as a temporary thing, I thought I could stand it.

My number was 324 and it took up one quarter of the floor. The place was decorated with white walls and a barrage of new and old. The living room was all plush leather and sink-in carpet. The bedroom contained a gorgeous antique dresser and a matching carved vanity. The bed looked brand-new except for the bedspread, which may have been purchased at a garage sale. Either that or it had been attacked by a guard dog and chewed on for a while. Even if I didn't have an image to uphold, the giant, faded flowers were ugly.

Next, I inspected the kitchen. Culinary tools were minimal. The Lenox china was nice, but without pans to cook in, having delicate white china with gold borders wasn't going to be too useful. The place was spotless. I wondered if the condo had its own cleaning team. That wouldn't do at all. I could keep up an image for a while, but there came a time when my sweat pants needed to come out of hiding.

I grabbed my backpack from the couch, grimacing at having to replace it with a briefcase, and rummaged through it for Huntington's phone number.

It took me a couple of minutes to find the phone. I hadn't been in the study yet, but it came complete with a computer, two phone jacks and an astounding desk that likely had been dragged in from a junkyard. It tilted rather dangerously and bowed in the middle under the weight of the computer.

I dialed Huntington's number and realized it was a pager. He probably didn't trust me with his cell phone number.

While I waited for him to return my call, I checked the refrigerator. Empty. That would have to be fixed immediately. I found another phone in the kitchen, but no phone in the bedroom. That must be where all the rich people kept their cell phones. Go figure.

The phone jingled, kind of a puny sound. I went to the study. "Hello?"

"Ms. O'Hala?"

"This is Sedona."

"You paged?" Huntington made it sound like I was a solicitor.

I already knew he didn't like me. He didn't have to send a postcard. "I need to know if I can hire my own maid to clean the place." I was nervous about asking him for anything and found myself babbling. "I also need a Mercedes or BMW, black, preferably an SUV. The place needs a new bedspread and someone should spend some time at Williams and Sonoma getting a full set of cooking utensils. Maybe a set in copper or Calphalon that can be hung in the kitchen."

There was a silence on the other end and some static. "Will you be at home for a while?"

I didn't know why he was asking. "Here? Uh, I wasn't planning on staying all that long."

"I'll swing by with dinner." He didn't give me a chance to refuse; he just hung up.

I stared at the handset. "I might have to go somewhere," I told the empty phone. I looked at my watch. It was almost five. I would have preferred running to the grocery to at least stock some basics rather than sit around. Maybe I had time. Maybe I didn't. He hadn't said when he would be by. I guess he expected me to cool my heels.

The phone rang again. I snatched it up with the intent of telling him where to put his dinner. "Listen, Huntington, I don't have time to wait around here and be your lackey--"

"Good afternoon, Ms. O'Hala. We have some deliveries. Would you like them sent up?" The cultured tone hit my brain just after my mouth started spewing.

There was an uncomfortable moment while I corked my mouth and re-established communication with my brain. "Uh, hello?"

"This is the front reception," the voice repeated in my ear. "If now is not a good time for deliveries, we can hold them here."

I sighed. "I'm sorry, I thought you were someone else. Now is fine."

"Of course."

How did the doorman manage to sound so icy and civil at the same time? I put the receiver back down, much gentler this time, although I wasn't feeling all that nice.

It wasn't long before a polite knock sounded. I assumed from the lack of demand, it must be the guy from downstairs. I opened it. A young blond kid held three large packages for me. Two were overnight packages from Fed-Ex. One looked like the Georgiou order I had spent Friday agonizing over. Excellent.

The guy handed me a clipboard to sign. He had on the same regulation black pants and white shirt as the valet parking guy. This guy looked slightly older, maybe even twenty. His hair was short, but it stuck straight up on top like a bristle-brush. "Do you always bring packages up? I'm new here."

He nodded stiffly, not meeting my eyes.

"Sorry about the phone. I know I get regular mail downstairs in my box, but I see these are too big to fit."

He nodded again. Breaking the ice was going to be hard. Asking if he lived around here was way too stupid a question even for me, so I shuffled my packages onto the couch and let him leave. I would have tipped him, but I had a feeling he would have gotten even more insulted, so I just let it go.

Georgiou had come through with a silk twill dress that was sleek and professional. They weren't normally in my price range. Victoria's Secret had delivered the silk underwear that I thought it only fair to purchase. Not that I expected anyone to see my underwear, but I had a part to play and one doesn't dress well on the outside without taking care of the inside, right?

The doorbell rang again. Before I could move to open the door, the deadbolt clicked and it swung open. There I was standing with my brand new camisole in front of me like a kid playing dress up. I swallowed the part of my heart that hadn't leapt all the way out of my chest. "I knew I needed a gun," I muttered.

"Nice." Huntington had the nerve to give me a cheeky grin. "I see your taste is improving."

I shrugged and lied even as my face flamed. "Same old, same old."

"I bet your date never even guessed."

"He wasn't my date!" I grabbed the boxes from the couch.

Huntington paused on his way to the kitchen and looked up at the light fixtures, hopefully contemplating my idea of hanging some decent pans. He then peered sideways out the balcony. "Maybe I should take a look at the rest. Make sure all your ideas are on target," he suggested from across the kitchen bar.

I stopped on my way to the bedroom and looked back, confused. "You haven't seen the place? I thought you picked it out." He raised a suggestive eyebrow at the boxes in my hands. My face flushed again. "No!" I flounced into the bedroom to hide my goods.

By the time I came back out, he had dished Chinese onto two plates. Not even my mother would serve takeout on such fine china.

"So, you want a maid and a new car."

I nodded and took a plate from him. "Did you bring anything to drink?"

He moved around me and opened the sliding door under the bar. "Voila."

It was fully stocked. Not a leftover hunk of bread in the refrigerator, but the bar was stuffed. Remarkable. "No thanks, I'll have water."

He helped himself to some kind of bubbling beverage.

Nervous, I sat at the glass table. Marring it with fingerprints seemed like a crime so I stood and started searching for napkins.

"In the drawer by the stove."

I found some linen napkins and sat down. "So did you live here or did you just purchase the condo for the Strandfrost investigation?"

"It's actually mine. I spent some time here after I first bought it."

I chewed on that and the Chinese for a while. Nothing in the condo fit any of Huntington's various personalities. "So the napkins are yours?"

"Previous owner."

"Guess you haven't had it long. I read in the pamphlet at the patent award dinner that you're fairly new to Strandfrost's board."

A happy cat smile, one that was smug and quite ready to pounce, passed across his face. "They hired me onto the board specifically to solve this problem. I have a history of solving corporate problems. Usually companies prefer I do so without groups like the Feds being involved, but in this case, it will save me the trouble of turning over evidence."

"It must pay well," I mused, thinking about the cost of the condo.

His smugness went into hiding. "Sitting on corporate boards pays well even without the inside assignments. Running my own investigation company doesn't hurt either."

"So you'll keep the condo after this project?"

"Thinking your new position will provide the extra cash to buy it?"

"Not my style," I said. "But as long as we're on the topic of style, it needs a new bedspread and a new desk."

"You don't seem to be having any trouble fitting into this new lifestyle," he observed. "You hoping to live it up big and keep some of it?"

I blinked. "I'm playing the part you hired me to play!"

He didn't look convinced. "You certainly seem to be enjoying yourself. Why ask for an SUV? Why not ask for a Lexus? Or a convertible?"

I had no trouble with that question. "A Lexus is too...bitchy. It's a, "I got my money from my husband" car. A convertible is too carefree. Doesn't go with the climbing the ladder image."

He stopped chewing and set his fork down. "And the SUV represents mountains? Where does the black color fit in?"

"Black is discreet, powerful. Red shouts for attention."

"What about blue?"

"Too ordinary. Not enough statement. Blends."

He thought about that a while. His eyebrows frowned as if he couldn't decide if I were trying to take advantage of the situation or just make fun of it. "Anything else?"

I wasn't certain if he was annoyed or not, but since he asked for suggestions, I obliged. "The place doesn't look lived in. Could use some plants, some personality."

"Personality?" He grunted. "I didn't know they sold those."

It took all my self-control not to suggest that he buy one for himself to go with the condo.

We finished dinner in silence. When he was done, he got up to rinse the plate.

I was impressed. At least he didn't think I was going to do the dishes for him, even if he did bring over dinner. I followed him into the kitchen, but not too close. Getting to near him reminded me of the attack. I couldn't get over feeling that he was the same guy.

Huntington took my plate and rinsed it, adding it to the dishwasher next to his. That left me with nothing to do so I backed off feeling like I was in his house, rather than one that was supposed to be mine.

I wandered into the living room.

"So what about the maid?" he called out from the kitchen. "You can't handle cleaning the place?"

I pulled on my last bit of patience. "Yes, but I don't imagine anyone else in the building does their own place. And if we hire the same person that cleans the neighbor's places, that person might gossip with the other owners."

He watched me over the bar without saying anything for about a minute and a half. We shared no trust. As far as I was concerned he could be a thug or a boardroom executive. I wasn't certain there was enough difference between the two. He found me an extra burden the rest of the board members thought was a good idea.

Never good at playing cat and mouse, I broke the staring match by escaping to the balcony.

It was the right choice. "Wow." A view of the mountains and a sparkling pool waited beneath my feet. Suzy was gonna love this.

I hadn't realized I was smiling until Huntington crept up behind me. "Gloating again?"

I thought about banging my head against the rail. "I am not gloating."

He was closer than I would have liked. I could smell his cologne. He could pick me up and throw me into the pool. Maybe I'd land in the water. Maybe I wouldn't.

"Don't get too used to this lifestyle," he advised sharply.

Through gritted teeth I said, "All business. Nothing more."

He looked down at the pool and then back inside. "Right. That's why you need a new desk, of course."

"Have you seen the desk that's in there?" I nearly bellowed. "It's not my fault the place looks abandoned."

"Abandoned?" he snorted.

I pointed sideways. "See those other balconies? They all have plants. It makes it look like someone lives there on occasion."

He never took his deep blue eyes from mine. "Plants." Then, the cat smile was back for just a half-second. "Fine, I'll buy some plants."

I wasn't sure if it was a challenge or if he thought it was funny that of all the things I asked for, he offered to get the plants.

He sauntered back inside. I stayed on the balcony while he took his leave. Even though it appeared he had his own key, I locked up behind him.

After he left, I called Angela. She was thrilled when I made an appointment for the new hairstyle.

I didn't sleep at the condo. No matter what the paperwork said, it wasn't mine.

Chapter 11

Sunday morning rolled around, and I had to put in an appearance at church. Don't get me wrong, I probably needed the word of God more than most. I just had this thing about sitting still long enough. Sadly, if I didn't show up now and again, brother Sean got worried and started nagging incessantly. If it went on too long, he dragged my parents into it, and they all started worrying about me.

I sat in the pew behind Sean and Brenda so that he wouldn't have to watch me fidget. Derrick Sawyer, one of the policemen Sean worked with quite often, sat next to Brenda. Derrick looked more like the kid next door than a policeman. His red hair was always on end, and he had a face full of freckles. Yes, freckles. From the attentive look on his face, he was getting more out of the sermon than I was. I sighed and tried to pay attention.

Sean heard the noise I was making. He twitched.

I scooted to the edge of the pew. Maybe I should just go to the cry room. Suzy was probably in there, and I couldn't wait to tell her about the condo with the pool. I had already decided on a half-baked story about watching it for someone.

Sean turned slightly, catching my eye. I smiled weakly and settled back. It probably wasn't a good idea to go to the cry room without a baby anyway.

After the service, I hopped up and looked over the sea of heads, trying to spot Suzy. Sean caught my arm. He had to shake it twice to get my attention. "What?" I asked in exasperation.

He rolled his eyes. "I said I need a favor."

I narrowed my eyes warily. Sean had stopped asking me for favors after the incident at the homeless shelter. He couldn't believe that someone as skilled as I in the kitchen had started the place on fire. It wasn't my fault, but he didn't believe me. "What kind of favor?"

Must not have been the right question. Sean's mouth formed a tiny little line. I finally noticed Derrick standing just behind him, looking at his toes and shuffling.

"Well, what is it?" I repeated.

"Can you come outside?" Sean was a gentle man, even though he was my brother. He only half dragged me into the parking lot, which was rapidly emptying.

"Slow down, I have dress shoes on." I noticed that Derrick followed meekly, rather unlike him.

When we got to his car, Sean planted his foot on the fender of the Accord. "Okay," he said. "Here's the deal. Derrick has made arrangements to meet with a battered wife." My eyebrows shot up. Sean raised a hand before I could interrupt. "Mrs. Harrison has some evidence, not on the beating, but on her husband's drug distribution habits." He glared at his friend. "He was going to meet with her without any backup."

"Why?" I asked.

"So that she will talk freely," Derrick said.

"Probably to get setup," Sean growled.

I knew what Sean meant. Beaten wives tended to turn on their husbands for brief periods of time before running back and living under the same conditions. If Derrick had a battered wife lined up, she may have intended good things when she called him, but that didn't mean she would keep her word. "This doesn't sound good."

Sean agreed grimly, "She has one prior complaint against an officer for sexual harassment. As Derrick's lawyer I've advised against the whole thing, but he insists on going through with it."

"It's important," Derrick put in earnestly. "We've been trying to find out when the drugs are coming in. This guy is a likely suspect, but we don't have enough evidence. We're pretty certain that the drugs come to him in specific cars through Larry's Body Shop where he works. We figure he's the middle point right before street distribution, but we need some hard evidence or a witness that will testify about where the extra money is coming from." Derrick was obviously at ease with his decision, but not with Sean's assessment.

"So where do I come in? Why not another officer?"

"Marilyn--Mrs. Harrison insisted that I come alone," Derrick said. "But I think I've convinced her that I need to have someone--not a cop--there to talk to her about the battering. She hasn't exactly agreed to it so she may not show."

Sean nodded. "But she will if she is setting him up. If Derrick takes another cop it'll be two cops protecting each other. If he takes a caring civilian, it will hold up better in court if it comes to that."

I was skeptical. "What makes you think anyone will believe I can help a battered woman?"

Sean smiled. It was his courtroom smile, an evil one that didn't reach his eyes. "You're an outsider. You've got self-confidence, and you aren't a counselor. Real counselors wait for victims to come to them. You're not real."

I was pretty sure he didn't mean that as a compliment. "So...when?"

Sean spared another glare for Derrick. "I just found out about this before Mass when I asked Derrick about your mess and the unknown James."

"Did you find James?" I asked eagerly.

Derrick shook his head. "Not yet. Not enough info. We need a last name or at least his last arrest date or why he was booked. Can you get that?"

I sighed. "I'll try, but…most of what I get is just second-hand gossip."

He nodded. "I know how that is."

Sean said, "To get back to Derrick's project, the meeting with the possible informant is Tuesday at eight o'clock in front of Sedmons."

"Sedmons? Where is that?"

"In Edgewood," Derrick replied glumly. "Which is why it would be far safer if I went alone."

I shot him a glance. "Riiight. No one is safe in Edgewood, not even in daylight." I couldn't believe my own brother would send me there, not even to protect Derrick.

"There will be two undercover cops in the area. I'll be perfectly safe without an escort," Derrick said.

"Unless Mizz Harrison rips her shirt off and starts yelling rape. Unless the other cops see what happens, you're in a mess with no witnesses."

"Well," the shuffle again, "there is that."

I sighed mentally, only keeping it quiet to avoid reminding my brother of my behavior in church. "Okay. But I'm wearing black. And I'm taking a knife." And a gun. Only Derrick didn't need to know that because I wasn't licensed to carry concealed. He would never go for that.

"No weapons."

I gave him my haughtiest glare. "You're leaving yours?"

He nodded.

I blinked. I stared at my brother in disbelief. Sean looked like he might kill Derrick rather than wait for it to happen naturally. I suggested, "You could at least insist that she meet you somewhere reputable like Denny's or something!"

Derrick just shrugged.

I could have refused. It probably would have been better for everyone if I had.

Chapter 12

Monday wasn't a bad day. Gary Marcus, Allen's boss, came by my office, and we chatted a bit. I was now officially a peer of Allen and reporting directly to Gary, the vice president of the division. Gary was in his fifties and an avid golfer. Any signs of athleticism had faded, as had all but a ring of gray hair forming a semi-halo just above his ears.

Gary assigned Turbo, Bruce, and to my great humor, Paul, as direct reports to me. He also assigned Tam Wong and Jerry Zercroft to my group. They were both excellent technicians with expertise in equipment, soldering, and testing.

"You'll be heading the special technical team. I expect some great new products that we can qualify into our library of recommendations. I know you'll need to order some new equipment; Allen had been about to do that before you took over."

"Of course," I demurred to his expertise.

"I'll need you to project the equipment requirements, the overhead, salary, and any other expenses. Get back to me on a burn rate. We've already done similar hardware designs so you can ask Dan Thorton for his past numbers and get a good idea of what you'll be spending."

"No problem." I had only an inkling of what he was talking about. "I assume I'll be doing the performance reviews for my people?"

"Absolutely. I'll have their paperwork transferred over to you immediately. Turbo will switch from reporting directly to Allen to reporting to you. It might make the transition easier if you let Turbo handle things like performance reviews until you decide if you want to make any changes."

That was definitely a good idea. Once this whole thing was over, and I got demoted again, the guys might not like me knowing all their salary information. Turbo could have that job as far as I was concerned. Since he had also been handling the equipment budget, I sent him an email to get a copy of that information. I sent another email to Dan, the department finance guru, to see if he could get me last year's expense numbers.

Tuesday night rolled around way too quickly for me. Despite the meeting with Derrick, I went and got my new hair style right after work because I had already made the appointment. I was pretty sure getting a new cut was a bad idea, but I couldn't put it off since I was supposed to be making all kinds of changes to prove to an invisible enemy that I was dying to get ahead.

Angela had already picked out my new hairdo, a kind of layered at the bottom, long look. I let her have at it, while I concentrated on more important things. "Did Emma ever tell you why James was arrested?" I asked. "You know, was he a burglar or into car theft?"

She wasn't fooled by my casual attitude. "No idea. According to Emma he was arrested because he was hanging out with the wrong crowd. You know, he didn't do anything wrong himself."

"Could be true," I allowed generously. "What did the crowd do?"

"No idea."

"When was the last time he was sent up?"

Angela glanced at the other ladies in the shop. "It's not really the kind of thing you ask about, you know?"

When I checked out, my hair looked great, but my credit card slip had no names, dates or other good information.

Derrick swung by my house around seven. His green Dodge was clean inside; no empty soda cans or take-out bags littering the floor. If he used the vehicle for stakeouts, he didn't park his trash in it.

"Hey," I said.

"Hello," he replied, holding the door for me. "You ready?"

I shrugged and pulled my baseball cap down lower. It was a shame to have to cover the new hairdo, but I wanted the hat. "I suppose I'm ready. All I have to do is sit quietly, unless you give me a signal to start talking, right?"

He nodded.

I added, "And under no circumstances am I to leave you alone with the lady."

He grunted. "Sean's been filling you in."

My turn to nod.

"Harrison could be important. Even if she takes it back later. I'm going to try and get permission to record it, but I don't expect her to agree. I can't do it without her permission unless I get a judge's order and since she isn't the guilty party, that won't happen."

I was big on the right to privacy, but since my Tuesday night was being eaten up by driving into a very avoidable area, I was thinking maybe the law was too strict. Downtown Denton in the daytime wasn't that nice. The south side was horrible, especially after hours, with bums and discarded trash billowing down the streets and alleys. The closer we got, the higher the ratio of boarded up buildings.

Apparently, one of the restaurants was still open and had been converted to a bar. That didn't mean it wasn't boarded up. The place only had three windows intact; the other two were crisscrossed with two-by-fours and some plywood. The door didn't need to swing open, because it was propped and rotting. It was probably easier to stay open twenty-four hours than get the door shut.

Derrick held back and let me go in first, although he couldn't seem to make up his mind if it was polite on this side of town. Taking the lead could mean getting the first bullet.

Personally, I think he should have let me hide behind him, but I'm against letting men be too protective, or so I told myself.

No shots rang out when I stepped through the door. Of course, it would have been hard to see me because of the smoke. Most of it seemed to be coming from the kitchen, but I was willing to bet no one was going to come and ask us if we had a smoking preference.

"Booth in the back," Derrick whispered in my ear. He took my arm to guide me.

I only tripped twice. The second time, I moved the bill of my cap up a bit, but it didn't help. The floor seemed to be made of brick or uneven cobblestone. Apparently that served as an excuse to let debris gather.

"Shit, the health department ought to shut this place down," I grumbled. Derrick tightened his grip, warning me to be quiet.

The back booth was by one of the windows that wasn't covered by boards. I did not want to sit down. It wasn't the presence of the diminutive lady crouched against the window that turned my stomach. It was the roaches under the table.

Granted, I couldn't see under the table, but there were roaches waiting to crawl up my leg. Women can feel roaches from blocks away, and I knew they were there.

Derrick shoveled me towards the booth. I had pretty good purchase with my sneakers. In fact, I may have stepped in some gum, and I think it helped glue into place. He grunted and pushed harder.

My foot caught against one of the uneven ridges in the floor and I catapulted, face first into the vinyl-torn seat. "Ack!"

My half scream made the lady jump. "Who is she? I told you not to bring anyone!" The window probably wouldn't hold long if she pressed any harder against it.

"It's okay, Marilyn. She's not a cop. She's here to help. In case you decide you want it." Derrick was a tall man, bigger in the dim light. His boyish red-haired charm looked freakish in the smoke. He sat beside me and put his hands in plain sight on the scarred table. I knew Derrick, and even I wasn't reassured, but that was mostly because I was trapped in a roach infested building with him between me and the door.

"I want to record this conversation if you will agree," Derrick suggested gently.

Marilyn shook her head mutely, pursing her thin lips closed. Her hair was frizzy, maybe a little gray or maybe just a light brown; it was impossible to tell in the dim light. She wore no make-up and her eyes looked tired. "Her...you gotta make her go!"

"She is here to help," Derrick said patiently.

I did my best to look helpful. I didn't want to chance smiling, because I was pretty sure if I moved my lips at all, something fowl might fly in.

I almost jumped out the window when a harsh voice demanded our order. "What'll it be?"

"Ah!" I swallowed the rest of my scream. Marilyn must have seen the waitress coming through the haze because she didn't jump.

Derrick turned slightly, but he was tense and not much happier than I. "Three cokes."

"Cokes?" She snapped her gum. "Rum and coke?" She started scribbling on her pad.

"No," Derrick corrected. "Just coke. No rum."

He may as well have shouted, "I'm a cop." I closed my eyes.

The woman taking our order faded backwards quickly. She must have worked here a long time, because even walking backwards, she never touched another table.

Derrick turned to Marilyn. "I won't record the conversation. I just need you to tell me how your husband works his deals."

Her eyes slid away to the window. "There ain't no deals. Where's the recorder?"

Derrick sighed and pulled it out of his jacket pocket. He took the tape out to prove the recorder wasn't turned on. About that time, the waitress showed up with our sodas. I rolled my eyes and pulled the cap lower. I did not need to be seen with a cop that had to keep looking like an idiot cop. He had just marked Mizz Harrison as an informant. Good God, we were all going to be killed.

The funny thing was that Marilyn didn't seem to know or care. She looked out the window again, moving her head sideways to see around the grime that coated the pane. She mumbled unintelligibly, "--to do."

"What?" Derrick leaned over the table a bit. "We know he is dealing drugs, Marilyn. I need you to tell me what you know. Do you know what days the cars come in? What kind of cars? Does he bring the drugs home?"

I looked out the window hoping to discern what she was trying to see. It was difficult to distinguish the actual outside from the dirt on the window. There were lumps in the alleyway that might have been trashcans.

"I ain't talking. You brought someone," Marilyn whined.

Derrick sucked in a deep, frustrated breath. "I want you to feel safe. I want you to know that there are other women that have gotten away from men that abused them. That you could start a new life too."

Marilyn glanced at me. I gave her a sickening smile. I couldn't imagine being abused, and one woman to another, she knew it. I was more like the enemy than an empathetic friend.

"Come sit next to me," she suggested to Derrick halfheartedly. "I don't want her to hear."

That wasn't according to plan. Sean had specifically told me to make sure that Derrick didn't get too close and that he in no way blocked her exit. If he sat next to her, she could claim she felt threatened, unable to escape.

"Uh," I started.

Derrick stood up. I grabbed his sleeve. "Derrick!"

"It will be fine." He tried to keep moving.

"I won't tell anything I hear," I promised madly. I glanced outside the window, looking for an excuse, a message from God or a train to run over us both.

What I got was Huntington. He was handing something to a shorter individual that looked a lot like...Huntington? I blinked, the dual images in the dirty glass impossible to sort out. My mouth dropped opened, and I swung my arm around to point. Instead, I knocked over both my soda and Derrick's. Bubbles spilled across the table right into Marilyn's lap. She screamed.

I nearly jumped out of my skin. It was time to leave. Without delay, I scrambled out of the booth and nearly knocked Derrick over in my hurry. He grabbed me to keep us both from falling over.

"Git yer hands off my wife!"

Derrick was holding me up, so he couldn't go for his gun. Oh yeah; he wasn't carrying a gun.

A guy the size of a small truck moved in, swinging a baseball bat and yelling about his precious wife.

"Eeek!" I tried to backpedal, but the table was behind me. Bat guy finally got a glimpse of me and stopped with the bat raised over Derrick's head.

"You--?" He decided to swing anyway, but by now Derrick had turned and was able to duck away.

I rolled off the table. "I'm not your wife! Don't hit him!"

The bat hesitated on the second swing. The guy's eyes darted around, searching. He finally saw Marilyn back in the corner. "Stupid bitch."

All of a sudden, I understood the look of hopelessness on her face that had appeared when Derrick mentioned abused wives.

I had been right. There was no way she would mistake me for an abuse case. I lacked the fear. Fear that I suspected would never leave her. She cowered against the window, tears rolling down her face. She didn't try to run. She didn't even look like running really occurred to her.

I would have broken out the window to get away from that bat.

"Hey!" The barmaid decided to intervene. "You take yer filthy fight outside!" Now that the bat wasn't actively swinging, she hefted her bulk over and grabbed at the weapon. "I don't need no trouble, Ted." Her beady eyes were aimed at Derrick.

I was willing to bet that normally the barmaid had a gun, but she knew Derrick was a cop.

Ted gave one last scathing look towards his wife and then shouted, "Gimme a damn beer! I want a beer!"

He didn't relinquish the bat, but he sat down. He stared at Derrick defiantly.

I remembered to breathe and nearly choked on the smoke.

Derrick leaned across Ted's table and got in his face. "Don't use that bat on your wife."

Ted didn't answer. He smiled a crooked kind of missing-teeth smile. "Nah."

I looked back at Marilyn. She was studiously looking out the window. "Come with us?" I whispered.

She shook her head, just slightly. Fingernails bitten to the quick clutched at her shirt, holding it tight across her chest.

I had a picture of her ripping her shirt and screaming, giving the signal for Ted to come running. But I had knocked the soda on her lap and startled her into a scream too early.

"Just for tonight," I whispered.

Another mute shaking.

"Do you need a job?" For some insane reason, I thought that might help.

This time, out of surprise, she turned her head and almost looked at me. Confusion crossed her face, probably because it was a stupid question. She shook her head again, this time more noticeably.

I sighed and checked on Derrick. He was watching Ted, making quiet, earnest suggestions about cherishing women.

"Go somewhere else tonight," I said. "I know you think it'll be worse later, but hell, you'll live to see another day."

She did turn enough to look at me then, but it was with a hollow emptiness that beheld the promise of a bad beating. For a moment, she almost looked as if she relished it, and I could only imagine it must be because maybe she would die, and then she wouldn't have to be hurt again.

"I'm sorry." I didn't know what else to say. I couldn't make her come away. And what did I have to offer her? I didn't really have a job to give her. I couldn't start her life over for her either.

Derrick was suddenly looming over me again. "Let's go."

He watched Marilyn for a moment, but he had dealt with her before. He already knew she wouldn't come with us. He must have figured out that she had been trying to set him up. He was more saddened than angry.

Once freedom was in sight, I didn't move slowly. I still felt prickling on my legs as we left the building. As soon as we got in Derrick's car, I rubbed my legs up and down, praying nothing went squish. The rubbing didn't help. A million bugs were crawling up and down my body. My stomach had knots big enough to moor a boat.

"You okay?" Derrick finally asked.

"Yeah," I lied. I felt for my cap and realized it was missing. It must have come off when I fell over. "You?"

He didn't say anything for a while. When he did, it was punctuated with his fist hitting the steering wheel. "Your brother was right."

"About the setup?"

"About a lot of things."

I didn't know what to say, so I watched the dark buildings turn into homes with friendly lights on. "I don't guess Ted will be complaining about you mauling his wife though."

He glanced over at me. "Hardly. After you jumped me, there wasn't room for her." A small grin threatened his features.

"I didn't jump you!"

"Man, it's no wonder those guys that attacked Strandfrost didn't get anywhere. You start moving, you're hard to slow down." This time he really smiled.

I thought of the guys at Strandfrost and shivered. The window had been very dirty. What was Huntington doing in that neighborhood?

Then again, all I had really seen was two figures by a dumpster. It couldn't have been him.

Derrick reached over and touched my shoulder. "Hey, thanks for coming along, even if it didn't work out. I guess I should have listened to your brother and just tried to get her to talk to a counselor."

I shrugged sheepishly. "No big deal. Sorry, I, uh…" I wasn't sure what I had done. She hadn't really intended to talk to him. As it was, we both ended up sticky and reeking of smoke and grime, but no one had gotten arrested or killed.

Derrick pulled into my driveway. The motion detector light came on. He got out and walked me up the sidewalk.

"Really," he said. "Thanks. And I'm sorry about your hat."

"I'm sorry about the soda." Some of it had splashed onto his pants and shoes.

He looked down and grinned. "You're something. Your brother told me to keep an eye on you or you'd do something crazy. Why in the world did you throw the coke on her?"

That made me mad. Sean shouldn't have asked me if he didn't think I could do it right. Never mind that I hadn't exactly kept to the script.

Derrick saw the scowl and grinned harder. "Don't worry. I won't tell."

He was lying. He was going to fill Sean in because he was an honest cop, and he was Sean's friend. When Sean asked questions, Derrick would tell Sean I had panicked and made a fool of myself.

"I thought I saw someone…" There was nothing I could say that was going to make sense.

"Don't worry about it." He clucked me under the chin. "I guess it's a good thing you moved when you did. The lady looked to be out to cause trouble."

Marilyn's plight was horrible. "Is there something we can do? Tonight, I mean, to keep her from getting hurt? If she isn't already dead or bleeding somewhere?"

"I'll call in an extra watch on her house. If we get a domestic call someone will get there faster." He shook his head and deep sympathy showed in his hazel eyes. "There isn't a lot we can do unless she asks for help, you know?"

"Yeah, I guess not."

He gave me a crooked grin and backed away. "I'll call it in. You lock up."

I got myself locked in and took a long shower. It didn't completely erase the bugs. They were still crawling about. At least I didn't have anyone waiting to beat the shit out of me.

Snug in my favorite pajamas, I was halfway to bed when the doorbell rang.

I sighed. "Derrick, I'm going to kill you."

I grabbed a robe and marched out to let him in. "What now?" I demanded, opening the door.

Had Derrick not just left, I never would have opened the door without checking to see who it was. It didn't occur to me that anyone besides him would be standing there.

"Aaah," I screamed, backing away.

"What is wrong with you?" Huntington advanced into my living room, forcing me further backwards.

Derrick was long gone and…my gun was under the bed where it wouldn't do me any good at all. Huntington must have seen me at the bar and now he was here ready to…my brain stopped there. "Eeek," I screamed again and made a dash towards the bedroom.

Huntington grabbed me from behind. "This isn't a game," he hissed. "Just because I hired you for a job doesn't mean you get to play detective and follow me around."

"Help!"

I couldn't tell if he was trying to shake me or I was quaking so badly he was just trying to hold on.

"What kind of idiot goes into that part of town late at night and sits in that bar of all places? Why did you follow me?"

I struggled, but couldn't break away.

He finally released his hold.

Faster than any rat that lived downtown, I backed against the nearest wall, wondering what he was going to do to me.

"Sedona, you can't go following me into dangerous situations. Or any other situation," he boomed out.

I shook my head, inching towards the bedroom again. "Fo…followed?" I'd feel much better after I shot Huntington, Ted and any other boogey-men that might happen along.

His shadow moved. I jumped a foot in the air. We stared at each other in the half-light for several seconds. "Oh for…I knew you were a mistake," he said softly.

He disappeared out the way he had come, slamming the door behind him.

It took me a long time to peel myself off the wall and re-lock the front door. Afraid I was having a heart attack, I emptied the medicine cabinet, but there was nothing in there stronger than aspirin.

It had been Huntington I had seen through the window. For some insane reason, he was up to something, and he thought I cared enough to track him into the worst part of town and sit at a roach infested table to watch him through a filthy window.

"Not likely, damn it." I shivered and clenched my fists. I wish I'd had the presence of mind to tell him so, but I hadn't been thinking of anything except fight and flight.

I took the gun from under the bed before I got up the nerve to go back into the living room and check the doors. They were both locked. The windows, painstakingly checked, one by one, were all intact.

I took two aspirin since that was all I had and started pacing. It was two hours before I managed to think about crawling under the covers.

I didn't sleep. Every creak and shift of the house was an enemy come to get me.

Chapter 13

Getting out from under the blankets when it was time to go to work wasn't easy. I wasn't talking just a bad hair day either. Modern makeup couldn't make a dent in the puffy black circles around my eyes. Extra mascara merely made it look like I added false eyelashes to the mess.

I turned up at work looking like I had lived through a fire, but only by sacrificing my hair, my sanity and mashing my face repeatedly against a window.

Turbo, ever polite, only stared for a fraction of a second before ignoring me. I checked my tests in the lab and then, equally polite, locked myself in my office. I called Abba, my karate teacher. He taught Shodokan, a Japanese form of karate. Shodokan didn't involve high leaps or dancing flips. It relied a tad more on strength than was good for me, but I was less likely to break any of my own bones if I kept both feet on the ground.

Abba was pleased to hear from me. "Seedona!"

"Hi, Abba. Do you have an opening in a Saturday morning class?"

"Of course, of course! Saturday, you Americans like to sleep in. My students, they like the after work so they already awake!" He had a bit of an accent, but it wasn't hard to follow. I signed up for a couple of months worth of classes, and he willingly put it on my credit card.

While I was making phone calls, I called a locksmith and made arrangements for him to double the locks on my doors and add some sort of window security. With the people I was hanging out with, I couldn't be too careful.

Even in my current state, someone had the nerve to knock on my office door. I sighed and let Turbo in. He was trailed closely by Bruce, the Fed guy that had been in the first meeting to discuss my up-and-coming job. Bruce didn't appear to be wearing his shoulder holster.

"Hi," I mumbled. My official promotion was supposed to happen Friday. I wished this meeting could wait until then. Despite my new power suit, a set of summer silk navy pants and matching jacket, my second impression with Bruce was going to be worse than the first. I looked like a drunk returning from a long binge.

"Bruce Heldon is going to take over your testing so I wanted to get your status." Turbo studiously inspected his pencil and notebook.

Bruce took one look at me and tried to swallow his tongue.

I began the stats in my best monotone. Bruce took a while to start paying attention. He was going to look like a fool when he had to ask Turbo for help. Turbo would probably talk to him in his extremely patient voice, the one that made me feel like an idiot.

"So, uh..." Bruce trailed off into silence. He ran his hand across the top of his black nubby hair. "Uh..."

"You do know how to run performance tests, right? You have to run direct attach tests, which is Alpha, and then pound the disks with network activity. That you start Beta testing from the clients."

"You look kind of tired," he blurted out, completely ignoring my question. He was obviously wondering how I was going to pull off my new position.

"I got a makeover." I smiled because he was beginning to be funny. "I guess the make-up didn't agree with my skin."

Bruce nodded before looking suspicious. "So you scrubbed it off?"

I shrugged. "Well, you know how it is. You can't get it off before your face swells. Hasn't your wife ever gotten her face done?"

He struggled mightily with that one. I wondered how he intended to let me know that his wife had never returned looking like a monster. Turbo, damn him, took pity on the man.

"I'm sure the swelling will be gone tomorrow," he said. "Nice suit by the way."

Bruce took a second, but then nodded emphatically. "Yeah, nice."

I smiled again and fought against laughing. "I'm thinking of trying a new makeup line at Macy's since this one didn't work out. Botanical. Maybe it won't bother my skin. What do you think?"

Turbo rolled his eyes. "Could you just email the test results you have so far? And put together, in writing, the tests you would run if you were going to complete the sequence?" He knew as well as I that if I didn't write it all out, Bruce was going to be in his office asking for details because poor Bruce hadn't been paying the least bit of attention to my directions.

Sally popped her head around the door before I could agree to send the stuff. Women are better than men when it comes to concealing surprise. We can look you right in the eye and think, "you fat cow," but it doesn't show on our faces. She smiled at the men, barely spared me a second glance, and said, "Oh, I can come back!"

I shook my head. "Not necessary. Have you met Bruce? He's our newest performance engineer."

Bruce stood and shook the hand that Sally offered. "I heard," she looked shyly at him, "that you were new. You must be taking Sedona's job. How nice!" She turned to me. "I just found out in the staff meeting that you are getting promoted. I stopped by to say congratulations!" She was dying to know how I had pulled it off. Instead she got a bonus, because not only had she confirmed that I knew about the promotion, she got to meet my replacement.

I nodded. "Thanks. I'm still a little stunned."

Her eyes narrowed while she considered whether that was a good opening for mentioning my battered appearance, but decided against it. Women didn't talk about that sort of thing in front of men unless they intended to be insulting. "I think it is just fabulous!" she said instead. "Allen told me you'll be moving to the other side of the hall, in the corner office. You'll just love it. It's bigger than your office and has a window!"

She then turned to Bruce apologetically. "Will you be moving in here?"

He nodded, his brown eyes darting back and forth between Sally and myself. She looked fabulous and professional. I looked...like a homeless person dressed to play a part.

"Stop by when you get a chance," Sally suggested cheerfully. "We can plan the move." She waved and as she turned to go, she mentioned the suit. "That color looks great on you. You'll have to tell me where you got it."

By the time I faced the gentlemen, Bruce had decided to go back into his stoic Federal character. He carefully blanked his face and let his training take over. I guess he figured if Sally could ignore my looks, he could. He stopped stuttering and asked a couple of intelligent questions. "What operating systems do I test under?"

"You'll need to do all the Windows operating system stuff. Don't worry though. There are plenty of people that can help you if you need it."

He nodded. "Send the test plan, and I'll stop by if I have questions."

Turbo smiled politely and ushered him out of my office. At least we all parted on friendly terms. I hoped Bruce called Huntington and complained about my appearance. That bastard deserved to worry about his precious plan for saving the company. God only knew what he had been up to in the dead of night. Whatever it was, I wanted nothing to do with it, or him.

I just had to figure out how to get myself out of this assignment. There had to be a way.

Most of the day went by in a tired, hazy blur. Several people stopped by to congratulate me. Each time, I felt more the fraud.

That evening, I returned to the condo, planning on packing my stuff and hightailing it home. Maybe Strandfrost management would be forced to let me keep the promotion even if I told them to hell with the side job. The only problem was that I wasn't certain quitting would make me safe. Huntington knew I had seen him.

I was so tired, I laid down on the bed for just a few minutes. The sheets looked clean and the bed wasn't lumpy.

I slept like a dead person.

Sometime during the night, I must have crawled under the covers, but I didn't remember doing so. When dawn finally woke me, I couldn't figure out where I was.

The antiques in the room came into focus. I remembered.

"Is it Friday yet?" I whined. I thought about calling in sick. No one would doubt it after seeing me yesterday. But I had to keep some job, promotion or not. "What have I gotten myself into?" With very little energy, I dragged myself into the shower. My eyes were hardly swollen at all anymore, and I was starved. Everything I had mail-ordered had been delivered to the condo. I didn't have an iron, but I shook out another power suit, this one a charcoal gray. At least today my iris was visible.

Grabbing the jacket that went with the pants, I was on my way to the door when the doorbell sounded. Warily, I stopped. Wrong address? More packages?

I thought the doorman was supposed to announce guests. Or maybe I was supposed to ask him to do so. I couldn't remember.

I opened it. The chain wasn't on because anyone, including someone my size, could break right through it. For some reason, Huntington had decided to knock politely this morning.

"Hi."

My eyebrows shot up. "What?"

He ignored my surprise. "Breakfast?" He held up two bags. They were unmarked.

"I don't think so." My stomach didn't agree with my answer, but I didn't care.

"I came to apologize."

I still didn't care. "I don't want to be late."

"Executives are allowed to be late."

He didn't push into the condo as I expected. I wish he would have. It would give me an excuse to shoot him. Not that I was feeling all that brave, and I didn't have my gun. "I'd like to go now." I addressed his shoes.

He proffered one of the bags and reached into his jacket pocket. He pulled out some keys. "Your new vehicle."

I looked at the keys. I shook my head. "Keep them for a while, would you?"

He sighed. "Look Sedona, I was angry because I thought you had done something incredibly stupid by following me. When I came by to talk to you, you wouldn't answer the door. It wasn't until you finally answered that I realized you must have been in the shower. Then you started to scream and--"

I pushed past him out into the freedom of the hallway. He reached out and touched my arm lightly as I passed. "Take the breakfast. I'll stop by tonight and explain."

"Explain?" I looked over my shoulder and then down at his hand as he pushed the breakfast bag into the crook of my arm. "Explain." As if he could explain why he had been at Strandfrost and downtown in the scurviest part of town possible. Was he crazy?

I couldn't walk away fast enough.

Chapter 14

My first meeting of the day was with Gary and his staff, including Allen. Whether I decided to continue with the undercover assignment or not, I still had to do the company job to which I was currently assigned--at least until I figured out what would happen if I quit the undercover part.

I took the breakfast burrito that Huntington had given me into the meeting and sat down. There was orange juice and coffee in the bag too.

"Coffee, anyone?" I offered. "I don't like coffee."

Allen looked at me like I had sneezed in it. "Why did you buy it?"

"It must have been an error," I lied. "I didn't order it."

Gary looked up. "I'll take it."

I pushed it across to him, and he smiled, the perfect avuncular businessman. "Hey, that reminds me. There's a conference in Tamarron this coming week. We need someone with a strong technical background."

"Oh--," I choked out, wishing I could shoot myself.

Dan Thorton, the finance guru, smirked. He always wore business slacks and a button down, just in case he was asked to present to clients unexpectedly. He patted his brown ubiquitous businessman cut with his well-manicured hand and gave me an up-down condescending look. "I was planning on going to that conference if it's all the same to you. I think that's what Gary meant." He winked to make it all friendly, the kind of wink that told me I was dismissed.

Gary looked up from whatever he was reading, peering over his reading glasses. "No, I was talking to her. You can both go, but I'd like her to present to the clients. You're planning on talking to the financial analysts right?"

Dan managed to get his mouth closed and act like he was in agreement. "Of course, of course. But I can certainly handle the technical sales."

Gary nodded, but Dan knew him well enough to know it wasn't a nod of acquiescence. "Sure. But Sedona needs the exposure and experience. I'm glad you'll be there to lend a hand though."

Now the guy found himself volunteered as babysitter. Oh goody. I was just making friends all over.

Allen shifted his gaze between Gary and the rest of us in the room. He adjusted the collar on his yellow golf shirt. A tiny bead of sweat might have been forming just at the edge of his dark hair. His eyes finally settled on Gary, waiting for him to invite him to the conference. Of course, Gary hadn't said Allen wasn't going, he just hadn't mentioned Allen at all.

Gary finally put down the papers he was reading and began talking to us.
The meeting was a lot of numbers and nonsense, most of which didn't make
sense to me. I used Allen's technique; nodded a lot and kept my mouth shut. I
scribbled notes that weren't much more than doodles. Maybe they would
matter someday, but I doubted it.

By the end of the day, I still didn't know what to do about the job. I went
home to my own house. It was dark, but comforting with its shiny new locks.
Even better, unlike the condo, there was pasta in the cupboard.

I tossed some in boiling water and mixed up a casserole. Normally, I'd
have grilled the chicken, but I sautéed it in butter so that I didn't have to go out
on the back porch with the shadows.

I was done eating when the doorbell rang. I stared at it a while before
opening the door.

Huntington dangled keys again. "Gary called and said you were going to
the meeting in Tamarron." He smiled. "I'm glad."

I grunted. "I haven't decided to go, not exactly. Besides, I thought hiring
me was a big mistake?"

"Can I come in?"

I didn't answer.

He leaned against the door frame, his blue shirt and light khakis making
him look like he was just another handsome guy out for a casual, enjoyable
evening. "Bruce happened to be checking in with one of the local police
detectives and your name came up. There's a story going around about you and
a mercy call downtown."

That was one description.

"I guess you weren't following me after all," he said softly.

He was too big for my doorway. I stepped away from him without
knowing it. He took it as encouragement and came in, shutting the door behind
him.

I backed up another step. His black hair was just a tad long, curling
slightly at the ends near his neck. His button down shirt was short-sleeved. He
didn't have a tattoo. His eyes reflected an even deeper blue than usual, picking
up the color from his shirt. They were not brown.

"I came by to apologize again." He put his hands on my shoulders,
keeping me in place.

He must have noticed that I was considering running. The two of us stood
like that, almost dancing, until I remembered that I needed air. I decided that I
also needed more exercise. Breathing hard on short notice was going to kill me.

He said quietly, "I'm not going to hurt you. I wasn't going to hurt you the
other night either. I just want you to stay safe and following me isn't a great
way to achieve that."

"Women die of heart-attacks too, you know."

He laughed. "I suppose." He rocked back on his heels a bit, relaxing his
grip but not letting go. "I'm sorry I made you afraid in your own home. I

thought you were playing detective."

"Just because you aren't who you pretend to be doesn't mean everyone else is up to something," I blurted out.

He dropped his hands. "What is that supposed to mean?"

I took a deep breath. "What were you doing at Strandfrost with the bad guys?"

His shoulders tensed. "What?"

I didn't back down. "It was you. At Strandfrost. What were you doing there if you're so busy helping with this problem?"

He eyed me carefully, those same eyes I kept seeing. "So that is where this started."

"Surely you recognized me!"

He shrugged. "Of course. But you never--" His head tilted. "Mm."

I waited another heartbeat. He didn't look as though he had decided to kill me so I moved back into the living room and sat down.

He followed, but not too closely. Without making eye contact he said, "I've been hired onto Strandfrost's board to help them clean up their financial scandal. The board voted to solve this internal mess as quickly and quietly as possible, and I am an expert in financial problems. Ideally, the police would never have been involved, but the IRS happened to notice that Strandfrost's deductions for charity funds weren't being delivered to the charities."

That didn't tell me why he had been at Strandfrost with the bad guys. "And?"

"And I'm solving the problem any way I can," he said. "I don't want to see you or anyone else get hurt. I'm the one that will take the risks, do the real infiltrating where necessary. How I get the job done...is my business."

He dangled the keys. "All you have to do is play executive. Stay out of dark alleys. Leave everything to me."

The keys were alien chains that would tie me to the project. I did not reach out and take them. "It doesn't seem to me that playing executive is danger-free. Why don't I just go back to doing my old job and not be in any danger at all?"

His blue eyes darkened. "I think that is a great idea, but the board thinks otherwise. They want someone on the inside. If it isn't you, they are just going to pick someone else." He reached out and took my hand, turned it upwards and dropped the keys into it. "All you have to do is drive around and let the board think you're doing your part. I'll take care of the real problem. You'll get paid, have your promotion and walk away clean."

He stood up and walked to the front door before turning back. "Nice new locks." He grinned.

I rolled my eyes. New locks weren't going to do me any good if I kept letting the bad guys in.

After I was sure Huntington was gone, I peeked into my driveway. A shiny, new, black Mercedes SUV filled the space. My mouth dropped open.

I looked up and down the street before racing outside to get the thing inside the garage. The leather seats were...plush. The whole package was beautiful. Sleek. And noticeable.

If Sean saw me in the thing, he would think I had robbed a bank. Being Sean, he'd started doing background checks on anyone that had talked to me in the past decade.

I didn't have to drive it, I just needed to get it to the condo. Well, unless I was going to keep playing this silly game.

Chapter 15

Gary was in the break room swearing at the coffee machine when I arrived Friday morning. As appropriate to his stature, his curses were mild. His bald head stared down into his cup at though trying to read the coffee grounds.

"Morning," I said.

He glanced up at me with a grimace. "How tough can it be to make coffee?"

"That stuff will rot your guts, I've heard." I helped myself to one of the pints of chocolate milk I had stored in the refrigerator. Before I could peel the plastic lid off, Dan walked into the area. True to form, he immediately staked out the territory between Gary and myself and began talking about himself, his latest project and his progress.

"Hey, Dan." Gary greeted the younger man without paying any attention to the patter. "You going to get in any golfing this weekend?"

Dan nodded enthusiastically, taking a golfer's stance even though he wore penny loafers and slacks. "Sure, sure." He swung an imaginary club. "I'm playing out at Meadow Hills. Last time I played there I hit a drive off the first tee so straight you could have followed it with a laser!"

Gary grinned and leaned around Dan to include me in the conversation. "Do you golf?"

"Uh..."

Dan moved in front of me before I could answer. "We should get the group together and go play a round. I'm sure that Sedona would love to join us." He never turned around. I could have choked on my milk and died, and he wouldn't have noticed.

"Maybe our next company outing," Gary reflected. "Hey, they have golf up in Tamarron. You get your tickets?" Gary leaned over and directed the question my way.

Not only hadn't I gotten tickets, I didn't golf. But golfing was asking a bit much for playing the part in my opinion. "Sally said something about taking care of it," I said.

Dan had no choice but to move sideways and include me in the conversation. By now a couple of other people were milling around. I nodded towards Bruce and Paul. Gary stepped over and slapped me across the shoulders. "If you don't play, I think you should learn. You'd love it. Very competitive sport."

And the place where all business deals were done. It would just be my luck that Allen's thieving buddies were golfers, and Huntington would deliver clubs to my door tonight. Why couldn't I have a job where I got to make deals in dark alleys like everyone else?

I was thinking bleak thoughts and forgot to keep an eye on Dan. From right behind me, he said, "Let me know if you need lessons. I can recommend someone."

I jumped because he was speaking directly in my ear. Before I could move away, the oaf actually dared, in front of all those people, to goose me in the ass. I saw a color between red and hazy purple.

With every ounce I had, I shoved my elbow through his stomach hoping like hell it didn't stop until it reached his spine.

"Ooof…"

I turned around to tell him what I thought of him. The look on Gary's face gave me pause. Executives did not engage in street fights. They used drawn out ladder-climbing wars to get even.

Too bad there wasn't a ladder around. I'd hit Dan over the head with it.

No, no. I could be professional about this. I could play polite executive and still call him on it.

My voice squeaked, but I forced the words out, hoping for shocked innocence rather than rage. "You scared the daylights out of me, patting me on the behind like that!" Dan was not yet able to get air. "Here, quick," I rushed over to the water cooler and filled a paper cup. "Have some water."

I tripped. Really. I mean, I don't know what I had planned with the water. I had a half-baked idea that I could force it down his throat while he wasn't able to breathe, but he was bent over, gasping for air. When I tripped, the water sailed out, soaking his head.

He sputtered, and his face got redder.

"Uh…" I backed up. I grabbed some paper towels from above the sink. "Let me get that."

Okay, I should have stopped there, but I was still angry. I took a half-hearted swipe at mashing his nose, knowing it would look like I was dabbing his face, but he moved. I ended up slapping the top of his head. The towels caught in his now wet hair gel.

He backed up a step. One of the paper towels was still gummed to his head. I reached to retrieve it, but succeeded only in knocking it sideways. It slid down the side of his face, taking his hair with it. What looked like brown, perfectly combed hair was a toupee that slid right off the top of his head and then dangled over the back of one ear.

No one said anything. The room was deathly quiet except for Dan's gasping, and in that moment, even he stopped trying to breathe. Out of the corner of one eye I saw Turbo walk up.

He snapped his mouth shut and moved back down the hallway without looking back. I don't know if his pants were on fire or if he was trying not to cry in public. His prize pupil, undercover agent, executive extraordinaire had just participated in a petty hair-pulling contest.

I cleared my throat. "I, uh, do believe, perhaps I will just...not help any further." I stared at the torn paper towel in my hand, not sure what to do with it. I was still mad, but it was nothing compared to the beast in front of me. Thankfully he was more concerned about righting his missing hair than attacking. I used the time prudently and followed Turbo's tracks, moving at least as fast as he had, maybe faster.

Huntington was going to fire me now for certain. I wasn't so sure that it was a bad thing. He was crazy if he thought I was going to put up with getting grabbed just to catch one lousy thief. "No way, no how, mister."

Of course, at this rate, even the criminals looking to find a new contact weren't going to want anything to do with me. Huntington may as well fire me. I just hoped that Gary would at least let me go back to being a lab rat.

I sat in my office stewing and waited for the phone to ring.

It wasn't ten minutes before Sally knocked. Maybe they sent her to tell me the bad news. Cowards.

She came into my office and shut the door. She leaned against it, her short auburn hair catching static from the door and dancing wildly. "Tellme, tellme!" She bit her lip and held her hands prayerfully towards the ceiling. "Tell me that you actually did cut Dan Thorn-in-my-ass' balls off?"

My eyebrows shot up at the venom in her voice. "Well, uh..."

She spun around gleefully. "A toupee?" Her voice was nearly a shriek. "There is a God!"

I was afraid she was going to have a stroke from sheer happiness. "Uh..."

"That little prick grabs my ass every time he has an excuse to visit Allen! I've complained several times and all I get is the, "are you sure?" from the morons in human resources and from Allen."

"He does?" While the good old boy network didn't like a scene, surely they wouldn't look the other way if it were that serious. "Why haven't they done anything?"

She took two steps forward and sat down in the visitor chair. "Allen promised to talk to him, and he did. Since then, Thorn-in-the-ass has taken to accidentally running into me. He gets close and gets his hands on me, but I can't say he actually grabs anymore."

That didn't cut it with me. "I'd have--" I blinked and stopped. "I guess I already did that."

She chortled happily. "I know! I want details! Details!" She leaned forward, her brown eyes full of fire. "Did he actually *cry*? I heard there were tears running down his face!!!"

Her enthusiasm was rather catching. A grin worked its way across my face. "It is not funny! It was an accident."

"Yeah, just like his little accidents. In some ways, he's worse than those thugs that came in and attacked." She shivered. "I mean, I expected it from them, or at least..." She faded off. "But every day I see Dan, and every day he acts like he's one of the boys, and I'm just here for his entertainment. You know what I mean?"

I kind of did, but I wasn't sure I had ever felt as bad as the look she was giving me. "He's a real loser."

She shook her head. "But he's not. He has everything. He's got a great job. He's paid tons of money, and he gets to travel all over. For a loser, he gets it all. I guess it's always that way."

I bristled. "He'll get what's coming to him."

She touched her pink lipstick on the corners and grinned at me slyly. "He just did, now didn't he?" Then she giggled. "They'll never fire him for something as trivial as grabbing an ass now and then. Not when he's the big finance marketing guru. But a toupee! I can't believe we never guessed!"

"It appeared to a be a rather small one. Woven into his hair, you know?"

Sally grinned. "A toupee! This is just great! I'm going to collect hair jokes off the web and put them up on my door. This is going to be soooo good!"

The guy probably would have been less embarrassed had I cut his suspenders off and his pants had fallen on the floor.

"There's this other guy," Sally gushed. "His name is Chris Ladwell. He sits down on six. Next time he comes to my office, can I call you?"

I rolled my eyes. "No! I'm trying to get ahead here, remember?"

"At least you have hair!"

We busted out laughing until a knock on the door interrupted.

Bruce had a question, and Sally used the opportunity to breeze down the hall to make sure everyone else had heard about the incident. Dan was going to have a hard time facing his co-workers for the next several weeks. Too bad. He should have kept his hands to himself.

After Bruce left, Tam came by to help me move my things to my new office. He poked his head around the open door and said, "Jerry was going to help, but I offered instead." He smiled shyly. "Gotta suck up to the new boss."

"Come on in." I wasn't sure I should bother to move things. They were bound to fire me later this afternoon. I looked at Tam, not wanting to tell him that I was a failure and the move was off. Then again, what harm was there in moving? They could fire me here or there, it didn't really matter. "Glad...you're here to help." Tam was one of the best guys on the team, a short Asian with typical straight black hair. He was incredibly intelligent, but he had one or two nasty habits. Namely, he misplaced things. He could spend two straight hours doing a magnificent soldering job under microscopic conditions and then lose the board on the way to installing it.

Turbo regularly did a check in the men's bathroom on three different floors to retrieve forgotten soldering tools, miscellaneous capacitors, hard drives and other paraphernalia.

"I'll help you pack the boxes," I said, eyeing my desk trying to decide what to save.

Tam was too quick. He dragged in two boxes and started piling pens and papers into the first box. "Nah, you don't have much stuff."

I grabbed my laptop and winced when he put my little steeple clock on top of the other stuff in the box.

"It won't get broken, don't worry," he reassured me. "I'm going to move one box at a time." He traipsed out into the hallway.

I called Turbo and told him the move was underway and asked him to check the bathroom in the next couple of hours.

He grunted. "More likely it'll end up in the lab. He tends to stop there to check on his tests. As long as he doesn't start unpacking the boxes in there, we should be able to recover most of it. Are you going to be in your new office or your old one?"

Tam popped back in. Getting work done in either office would be impossible, and I really didn't want to talk to Turbo right now. He was bound to bring up the incident with the toupee. "I'll stop by if you need something. Otherwise I'm going to go home and start packing for the trip to Tamarron. Is there anything I need to know before I leave?"

There was a rather lengthy pause before he said, "No, it can wait. Have a safe trip."

Tam absently stuck one of my favorite pens behind his ear. He draped a power cord over his arm and a mouse around his neck, all while continuing to put some stuff in a box. He mumbled something about needing a cart for carrying the computer monitor and off he went to the lab.

I snagged a notebook that I liked and snacks from a drawer before heading out for the shortened weekend.

Chapter 16

Saturday I managed to miss my karate class. Since I was out of shape anyway, it was probably a good thing. I used the day to buy some decent luggage and travel stuff. The entire time, especially as I picked out a few necessities for the condo, I ignored the fact that I hadn't quit the undercover work, even though I was pretty sure that I should.

When Sunday rolled around, I wasn't in the mood to deal with Sean and church. I knew Sean would hassle me about the fouled up favor, so I slept in and ignored the phone until it was time to leave for Tamarron.

I flew into Durango on Sunday afternoon. The resort was a half-hour drive up the mountains. In the summer, a lot of people took the train ride in Durango and maybe played a round of golf before they moved on. In the winter there was excellent skiing at Purgatory or Wolf Creek over by Pagosa Springs.

The resort catered to these types of tourists, and it was fabulous. When I walked in, I couldn't contain a whispered, "Wow." As far as I was concerned, if Strandfrost wanted to foot the bill, they could forget all about me and leave me here. It was possible that I had just found the first real hint of appeal to being an executive.

My biggest challenge was to keep my teeth from falling out of my open mouth while checking in. The front lobby came complete with a grand piano, a bar off to the side and a discreet front desk. I almost missed the desk because I was agog at the grandeur.

"Hi, I'm here for the conference," I managed.

The woman checking me in was more than polite. Refusing the bellboy's service was out of the question. He did not accept a tip.

There were two king beds in my room and a view of the mountains that was close enough to reach out and touch. The kitchen was better stocked than Huntington's condo back in Denton. Below the sparkling clean windows, a pool and hot tub waited. "Oh my!" I stared down, salivating. "That hour-long flight was exhausting. And how can anyone approach me with dirty deals if I am holed up in my room? It is my duty to go to the hot tub."

I sighed with regret over my horrible job, jumped into my bathing suit and grabbed the big fluffy hotel robe. I made a mental note to order a flowing beach wrap. In fact, deciding the robe just didn't cut my new image, I grabbed a luxuriously fluffy towel instead. On my way to the pool, I stopped in the resort shop on the lower floor. It was hard, but I purchased only two beautiful print cover-ups before heading outside.

It wasn't even Monday, and I was already having to shop and wait around in a hot tub for business. "Tsk, tsk. Will I never get any rest?" I giggled and stepped into the pool area.

I had dawdled long enough that someone had beat me to the hot tub. Two someones actually. I stopped dead in my tracks and barely stifled a groan.

Allen and Turbo were sitting awash with bubbles. Allen had a drink in a plastic cup. His thinning black hair was damp and sticking to the sides of his portly neck. Turbo looked better, but only because he was thinner.

"Hi," I mumbled unhappily. I glared at Turbo. Why had it slipped my mind to ask if he was coming?

Because he had no reason to be here, that was why. Warily, I untied my new wrap. It was hard not to screech with frustration. I had planned on slipping into an empty hot tub to wait for a Romeo. Allen and Turbo were more like a cross between The Simpsons and Dilbert.

Turbo lifted his drink in my direction. "Welcome."

Allen smiled rather blearily. "'lo."

I stepped carefully into the tub and addressed Turbo stiffly. "I didn't know you would be attending."

Turbo shrugged. "Allen and Dan needed some equipment setup for a demo."

I started to say that I thought I was going to be setting up the equipment, but Turbo gave me his bulging eye look. I clamped my mouth shut.

"Didn't see why Sedona couldn't do it, but I forgot...about the promotion," Allen said. "Con...grashulations."

"Thanks." The tub had been empty when I started down here. Allen must have started on the drinks way before the hot tub.

We chit-chatted for a bit, but it was a difficult mix. Allen wasn't comfortable using buzzwords with someone as technical as Turbo and myself, and Turbo and I were too smart to want to waste off-time discussing the pros and cons of a particular operating system.

When it got too warm, I tucked myself into the outdoor pool for a lap or two. It was heated with a window that didn't quite touch down to the water. Ducking under the panel, I was actually back inside.

Cooled off, I headed back to the hot tub to warm up.

To my complete dismay, Dan sauntered through the hotel door as I walked over. A gorgeous blond babe held onto his arm. I tried to remember if he was married or not. With his hard-to-resist ass-grabbing openers, marriage wasn't likely.

Allen jumped up enthusiastically. "Dan! Autumn! Houz are you guys? Come on out!"

Apparently blond-babe, Autumn, knew Allen. She waved and blew him a kiss.

Allen put one foot out of the tub and leaned to slap Dan across the shoulders. His other foot was still in the tub.

"Be careful!" I yelled.

The warning was too late. Allen's drink went flying. There was a magnificent splash as he slid back into the tub, rinsing off the drink he had just thrown all over himself and the tiles.

Autumn gasped. Dan reached a half-hearted hand towards the tub, but unless Allen's arms suddenly tripled in length, Dan wasn't leaning close enough to actually be of any help. Of course, with his girlfriend in tow, he couldn't really afford to get his toupee wet, now could he?

Turbo squeezed himself over to one side, trying to avoid getting smacked by flailing limbs.

Like a bad apple, Allen's head bopped back up after only seconds. "Fi..ne, Fine," he sputtered.

I closed my eyes. This was too embarrassing for words. Without wasting any, I turned to go, not even waiting to see if Allen could still walk.

Turbo caught up with me before I made it to the elevator.

"I hope you don't mind that I showed up." Turbo was ever polite.

I didn't answer. Looking at his knobby knees and unshaven legs poking from the bottom of the robe, I was ecstatic with my purchase of the swimsuit cover-up. I made an additional note to never be seen in the room slippers even if the hotel was on fire.

With my hand hovering, I waited for him to specify a floor. He was one floor up from me.

"You're showing up late tomorrow, right?" he hinted.

"Is there a particular time you want me to make an entrance?"

He tilted his head a bit. "I don't want you thinking you need to help with the demo equipment."

"Is that why you decided to come along?"

He nodded. "Dan was in the hallway the other day talking to Allen. Dan suggested to Allen that he was happy to have you along to do the grunt work." He smiled. "I thought it might tarnish your image."

My new image maybe. My old one, hardly. But Dan had already made it clear he was going to do everything possible to keep me in my place. "Gary just let you sign up? They never send techs unless they're desperately afraid the equipment won't work."

"Gary set it up, said it was a good idea."

"I think he knows about the Feds and the investigation," I said. "He seems to anyway."

Turbo swept a warning glance around the entire four-foot space, but unless the elevator had been bugged, our secret was safe.

I waved good night and got off on my floor, feeling depressed. Only a moron would approach this new team of people. Then again, the old team wasn't that impressive. Dan was a womanizer, Allen a lush, and between the two of them, they almost had enough brains to kill a mosquito.

At least the bed was comfortable.   I had a bad feeling that tomorrow wasn't going to be.

Chapter 17

The conference was a fairly large draw, partly because of its peaceful location tucked in the mountains of Colorado. Strandfrost had pulled out all the stops, providing enough demonstrations to fill a large ballroom. Partitions went all the way around the outside walls of the room, each blocking off a demo and providing a semblance of a private consultation. I found Turbo hard at work inside the partition where I would be giving my demo. Bruce was helping him. My fingers itched to dig in and get the setup running, but Turbo gave me one of his looks. He may as well have worn a sign that said, "Go Away."

"Hi."

"Good morning," Turbo replied in his most deferential tone.

I rolled my eyes. "You guys want some coffee?" This earned another dirty look, but hey, they were helping me get my show ready. I figured that some of the executives had to be human.

Bruce wasn't as wary as Turbo, so he nodded. "That would be really decent."

There was a table with donuts and goodies on the way in, so I made my way back there and got a tray with some food and coffee.

When I returned to the booth, Turbo reluctantly helped himself from the tray. "You might want to check things. You know, give us some orders on how you want this set up."

Turbo could do a more perfect job than God's angels when it came to setting up equipment. "Uh…yeah, right."

"Is this where you want this?" he prodded helpfully. It was a ridiculous question. The booth was ten by ten facing the center of the room where people could crowd at will. I didn't care how high a person was in the chain of command, there was only so much anyone could do with the space. "Yeah, that's great. Just perfect."

Bruce tried not to laugh and ended up snorting coffee.

"His stuff could be closer together," I said, just to goad him. "We don't want people to try and get between those racks and trip on the power cords." I batted my eyes at a now scowling Bruce. The only person small enough to fit through the space might have been me before breakfast, turned sideways and with no air in my lungs.

Turbo looked pleased enough to have kissed me except for the fact that it would have ruined everything. He helped himself to another donut. Now that he was certain I wouldn't screw things up too badly, he went back to plugging things in. Bruce gave me a snarl, but his heart wasn't in it.

I wandered off to check out the other demonstrations. On my way back around the square, I saw the woman that had been with Dan the night before approach Turbo and Bruce. What was her name? Alice? Autumn? Something like that. Bruce didn't bother to take his eyes off her cleavage, but Turbo stared politely at her face and answered a question. She must not be used to meeting men's eyes because she sashayed away pretty quickly.

It was almost time for the customers to start asking questions. Bald suits, tall suits, fat suits and skinny suits were lining up in front of the donuts. Dan had a couple of banker-types hanging on his arm, and Allen went by with an entourage.

The parade had started, and I was one of the caged. I scurried to find the fliers. The computer screens were big and bold and the lights on the storage drives flashed busily as the server commanded that data be moved back and forth. There were lights for failures and lights for idle and a pretty flow of numbers for the monitor.

The first two hours weren't bad; the only problem was that I was the only one doing the demo. My feet started to hurt, and I was hungry, but I kept on going. "Yes," I answered for what felt like the millionth time. "Let me show you." I turned to draw on my white board, but it was already full of scritches and scratches.

Turning to apologize, I noticed one of the hard drives had failed. Good. It gave me something different to brag about. "Don't worry folks. The data is still protected!" A few people stepped closer; the steady red light was like a beacon for trouble.

By the time I was done explaining the protection, it was lunch and the crowds started to thin. I had to replace the failed hard drive, so I set out a stack of fliers on the table and stepped behind the partition walls. The small hallway space stretched over to the booths next to me. "Mm." I sorted through boxes of packing material, but didn't see what I needed. Turbo had to have left some extra equipment somewhere.

Trying to hurry, I stepped over cables that were plugged into electrical outlets and made my way towards Allen and Dan's demos. Turbo probably figured I could handle my stuff and left the extra for the guys.

Given my grace and the dim lighting, it was inevitable that I tripped over a cord. Like a large sack of potatoes, I fell hard, landing on my knees. "Oomph!" I sucked in a breath of air and held perfectly still while the pain radiated through me. It took me a minute of whining before I could untangle myself from the cable. I then had to make sure it was still plugged in so that none of the other demos would be ruined.

With the thinner lunchtime crowd, I could hear Dan easily on the other side of the partition. "We can make a special deal. You don't have to go through

Strandfrost. I know someone that can help you. Come on back here where we can talk."

I froze. Back here? No one ever took the customers behind the partitions. The place was a mess and dangerous, not to mention kind of dark.

I looked around, trying to figure out if I was behind Dan's booth or Allen's. Either way, I didn't want to be caught back here, especially sitting on the floor checking cables. I scrambled to my feet.

"You tell me what you need," he said.

I paused in my panic. His voice wasn't getting closer. Was it?

"How...spending?"

He sounded further away. The only problem was that his conversation seemed to be something I should hear. Spending on what? What kind of deals was he making?

I jammed my way behind a stack of boxes. Maybe I'd be able to hear and not be seen. My foot hit something soft, twisting my ankle sideways. I nearly fell and took the boxes with me.

Holding my breath and the box in front of me, I tried to step over whatever cable had nearly killed me. I couldn't see it, but it...groaned.

My feet jumped a foot in the air. They came down, along with the empty box on the top of the stack. I stifled a scream.

The darkness whimpered back.

I spun around, smacking my shoulder against another tall box. In the dim light I could see an arm...a leg...it took me several heartbeats to figure out where the head was. At first there seemed to be a bunch of body parts completely unrelated to anything else.

"Hello?" My voice sounded like a badly oiled door.

The arm moved, but not in a threatening manner. "Ow." The head raised off the floor and the arm reached towards it.

"Are you okay?" My brain finally accepted that the prone person wasn't a threat. I scooted closer. "Ann?"

"No...it's...I'm Kathy."

"Kathy! Are you okay?" I barely knew her well enough to identify her in broad daylight. She worked in marketing under Ross, but I had never said more than "hi" in a Strandfrost hallway before.

"I think my head is falling off." She moved to sit up. I helped her.

"What happened?"

"We were out of give-aways upfront." She sat, dazed. "I ran into something." She pulled her legs in, crossing them and leaned her head down. "Oh my God, it hurts."

I reached out and felt along where her hands were touching. The bump was all the way in the back, towards the left side of her head. It was sticky, but she used a lot more hairspray than I did. I couldn't tell if she was mortally wounded or not. "We need to get you into the light. Can you stand?"

She sniffled. "Gimme a minute. It hurts. Damn. I must have fallen over these boxes. I've got another lump on my arm."

"I'm going to go get--"

"No, no. Just give me a minute." She leaned her head back.

I hovered nervously until she moved her legs to stand. When she was ready, I helped her up.

She was shaky, but she didn't sit right back down. "I need to go to my room. My God, I am a mess."

I wasn't sure how she could tell in the dim light, but it was probably true. "We can go back over this way. My booth is closer to the ballroom doors."

We walked carefully. She leaned on me at first, but got stronger as we went. Thankfully we were both in pants and low shoes. I peeked inside my booth before waving her out. "Come on."

She stepped into the display area, looked down and winced. Her pants looked like she had slid through a dust-bunny derby. I was slightly cleaner, but only because my pants were blue, rather than black.

I checked her head, but other than her hair sticking sideways, it looked intact. "Let's get you upstairs."

I took the outside, letting her walk along the partitions as much as possible. Most people were at lunch, so no one paid us much attention. Sadly, we both limped a bit. We kept our heads together as though conversing quietly, hoping no one would notice us. Kathy was shorter than me by a head even with her light brown hair sticking up. Her lipstick was chewed partially off, and she must have shed a tear or two because black mascara streaked underneath her eyes. Her skin was pale; tiny freckles stood out against smeared makeup.

Once we got to her room, I headed for the phone to order an ice pack. She leaned against the bathroom sink and waved me off. "I'll call room service. You go on, change."

"Do you want a doctor? I would guess the hotel has one or can get one."

"No." Her hands were shaking, but she peered at herself in the bathroom mirror. "Two lumps. One in front and one in back." The one on her forehead wasn't really a bump, but it was red. "No blood. I'm good."

I wasn't too keen on leaving her, but I wasn't sure what else to do. I made a note of her room number before going to mine to change. Once cleaned up, I called her room, checked on her again and then went downstairs. Lunchtime was fast fading. I hadn't eaten, and I hadn't gotten my hard drive yet either.

Boldly, I went straight to Dan's booth. He was gone, of course, still at lunch. I stared around at the posters and fliers. It was Dan's job to make deals. Just because he said something about not going through Strandfrost...shoot, he'd probably tell customers that he would build the stuff by hand if he thought it would make them buy it.

I tapped my foot. I hadn't even seen who he was talking to. Could have been one person, could have been a group of six. Before I could decide what to do next, a voice hailed me. "Excuse me, miss?"

"Huh?" I turned to find a customer waving at me from the other side of the table.

"Do you have any more free t-shirts?" he asked.

"I, uh--" Looking around, I didn't see any shirts. No one had given me free t-shirts to give away. Why did Dan get the best goodies? Remembering what Kathy had said about looking for give-aways, I said, "Let me look in back."

I scooted back around the partition. Looking through the junk, I spied a hard drive. There was an entire box of them, maybe two or three. I grabbed what I needed. Turbo could have left me at least one instead of giving Dan enough to triple his setup. Stepping back out front I said, "No, sorry, no shirts."

The guy, dressed in a suit that probably cost him several hundred dollars, looked very disappointed. "You gotta be kidding me! I told my kid I'd bring him one."

"Have you tried the resort shop? I'm pretty sure they have shirts in there."

"Those aren't free!" He blinked. "Are they?"

I rolled my eyes, but managed to direct the look at the floor. "Uh, no. I just thought your kid might like them better."

He snorted.

A loud clatter behind me got my attention. I turned, but couldn't see behind the partition. "Turbo?"

I started to peer around the corner, but then thought better of it. I didn't want to try and explain to Turbo that I had been back there working on replacing my own hard drive. I didn't have time to tell him the story about poor Kathy either--and doing so would only make the case for him that I shouldn't be back there doing my own work.

Whoever was back there grunted as they lifted something. I scrabbled out the front way to get back to my booth before he came out.

From a safe distance, I looked back. A few suits were wandering around, coming back from lunch. None were behind the table that was meant to separate the crowds from the demonstrators. I didn't see anyone that looked like Turbo or Bruce. In fact, I didn't see anyone come out from the partitioned area.

I frowned. Of course, it didn't matter. If Turbo had been back there for some reason, he wasn't likely to show his face to the public. It wasn't part of his job. Whoever was back there was probably like me, just grabbing something they needed for their own station.

Back at my demo, I got busy replacing the drive. Bending down, the first thing I noticed was my knees. "Oh, no!" The fresh, off-white pants I had just put on had a smear of dust across one side.

"How's it going, Sedona?" Gary's voice interrupted my dismay.

I turned to find Gary with two customers. "Oh...fine." I tried for a smile, but probably failed.

He grabbed some fliers. Leaning closer he confided in a loud whisper, "Don't worry. By three the place will be cleared out."

I waved, keeping my knees turned away from him.

When they were gone, I discovered that brushing at my pants only ground the dirt smudges in. Would anyone notice if I gave the presentation from behind the machines? Probably, because I'd look like an idiot.

By two o'clock, I was so hungry I almost started chewing on my sleeve. With the crowds thinning, I wanted nothing more than food and a hike into the blissful silence of the mountains. Unfortunately, I doubted those with devious purposes would find me if I was out wandering the hills. I kept working until three-thirty when the crowds were down to casual wanderers that looked more lost than interested.

Letting the machines continue to run their silent demo, I went upstairs and changed out of the ruined pantsuit into a new pair of dress shorts and a polo top. I looked professional enough in case my invisible audience cared.

I checked on Kathy again, but she wasn't in her room.

Intent on finding her, being available, and getting food, I went to the hotel restaurant.

It solved two problems, probably all three. Kathy was there looking a lot perkier than I felt. "Hey Kathy, how are you feeling?"

She chewed a big mouthful of sandwich and waved me over. A waiter followed me and took my order.

"I'm good," she said. "Got an ice pack. Had room service take care of my suit. You get them to clean yours?"

I hadn't thought about having room service do my laundry, but I was going to be short at least one pair of pants if I didn't. "I'm fine, no worries. How is your head?"

"Couple of aspirin. I laid down for an hour. Got a little queasy and decided I better eat. On the way through Ross stopped me, and I had to help with some clients."

"Oh no!"

She nodded and swallowed another bite. "That's the way it goes. I'm okay though. I don't know what I ran into. I'm just glad you were there when I fell."

I didn't think it prudent to tell her that I hadn't even seen her until I stepped on her. No need to assign my name to any of her bruises. She had probably been lying there a while before I found her. Not that she looked like it now. Her brown hair was back in a professional bob. There wasn't a single crease in her reapplied makeup. Even with a hidden bump on her head, she played up-and-coming better than I ever would. She cared and it showed.

I sighed and sat up straighter. "I'm going to go for a swim later. Want to join me?"

"Didn't bring a suit." Her lightly plucked eyebrows came together in a frown.

"They have some in the shop at the front."

"Look, Sedona." Her pale brown eyes glanced towards the outside patio where several men were lounging. Almost everyone except Kathy had changed out of their business suits. She cleared her throat and whispered, "You don't want to go around in your swimsuit. Trust me. The guys will talk."

I stopped chewing. "I wasn't going to tour the place in it, just swim!"

She shrugged. "You don't want to be seen in it, even under water. They'll talk."

I didn't bother to tell her it was too late. We finished our dessert out on the patio in relative silence and then went our separate ways.

Chapter 18

Tuesday was the same hell, only this time I kept food nearby and didn't skip lunch. By the time the day was over, I was almost used to the schedule. I thought I had things pretty well in hand until the phone rang that evening.

It was Turbo. He was back in Denton.

"I thought you were here," I said, surprised.

"I got a phone call from Sally telling me to come back on Monday. She said something about Strandfrost not wanting to pay my way for the entire week. I wasn't too worried until this morning."

"What happened?" I asked.

"I found out they flew Bruce back too. I thought they called me back because someone decided we both didn't have to be there. But then...not having Bruce there...that's really bad."

"It is?"

There was a long pause. I didn't know if it was Turbo being Turbo or if he was waiting for my turtle brain to come up with the answer. Finally he sighed, and I knew that I had failed. "You're on an important case. Don't you find it a little suspicious that they flew back your only protection?"

He probably should have been more concerned that I hadn't even noticed he was gone. Some detective I was. "Uh...when did you leave?"

"Got the call just before lunch on Monday. Sally had my ticket purchased for the afternoon. Basically once the setup was done, I got sent back."

"You went back yesterday?" Though I hadn't seen him or Bruce, I hadn't thought much of it. In fact, I had been looking over my shoulder all day, expecting Turbo to scold me for doing something wrong. If anything, I had been trying to avoid him, not find him.

"Yeah, I ran into Allen right after we finished your setup on Monday. He asked if we had everything done. I said yes, of course. Sally called an hour later and told me I had a flight. I had to go straight to the airport, which is why I didn't get a chance to tell you I was leaving."

I wasn't sure what to make of the situation, but it was too late to panic. "I guess it's okay that you went back. I've been managing okay."

"That's what I figured--until yesterday when I found out that Bruce had been sent back too, just a different flight than mine."

"What difference does that make?"

"I started asking some questions and verified with Sally that the order for us to come back came from Allen, not Gary."

Turbo made Allen's very name sound sinister. "But you don't really work for Allen anymore."

"Exactly. Even if Allen thought it was a waste of money, he should have told you to send us home, not just had Sally arrange it."

"Allen doesn't know that you're helping with the investigation, right? Or that Bruce is undercover?"

"Damn right, he isn't supposed to know. But he knows he was caught red-handed bilking Strandfrost. Even though he didn't get arrested, I bet he knows he's being watched."

"Well, okay. But why would he be suspicious of Bruce? Or you?" Allen didn't act on the ball enough to have gotten suspicious. Then again, he didn't look bright enough to try and cash checks either.

"Bruce is new. He's the most obvious candidate to be watching him. And there's someone else I bet he thinks is watching him too, and I don't mean me."

It was a thin hint. "You mean me?"

"You're a threat to him whether he thinks you're watching or not."

"I am not--"

"You've been promoted. You've taken over his people and projects. You're now the competition."

"Okay fine," I agreed. Chewing on my lip, I had another idea. "Maybe Gary told Allen to call Sally and arrange for you guys to go back. Maybe he thought it looked funny to have you guys at the conference." There weren't any other engineering specialists at the conference unless you counted me, but as a lab rat technician, I had been even lower on the totem poll before my promotion.

"You need to be more careful."

He meant I needed to pay more attention. He was probably right, but the plan was for someone to approach me, not for me to go looking for trouble. "I think things are going fine." I ignored the sweat on the hand that held the phone. "Kathy has been giving me tips on where to be and what to do."

"Maybe you should spend more time with her. You know. Don't eat alone."

"Turbo, don't be ridiculous! While it's possible someone could shoot me, it's not likely that they'd hit me in this crowd."

"Just be careful," he reiterated. "I'll see if I can figure out if Allen was sending us back to make sure you didn't have technical help or if he has some idea that Bruce is undercover. I'll be in touch if I learn more before you get back. Gotta go."

"Okay." We hung up. I pinched the bridge of my nose and went in the bathroom to brush my teeth. There was only a couple of days left anyway. I could probably live through it. Right?

Chapter 19

Wednesday went by in a blur. I wanted to ask Kathy how she was doing, but we were both swamped all day. I kept glancing over at Dan's partition too, wondering what deals he was up to. I noticed he didn't spend very much time doing demos. He seemed to reel in customers and then walk off with them. Once he was in motion, I couldn't keep track of him, but his booth was empty a large part of the day.

Any old customer could walk back behind his table or his partition. I rubbed the back of my head. Something about the bump on Kathy's head bothered me, and not just the fact that it had happened at all.

Thursday morning, I tried to be extra cautious because it was the last day of the show. No one had so much as suggested I steal a pencil for them. If they were going to make a move, maybe they would do it today.

Turbo had made me nervous. His ominous tone made me wish I could see Allen's booth from mine. Did he spend as much time doing demos as I did or was he like Dan, drifting around going wherever he pleased, meeting with...unsavory individuals?

By lunchtime, the crowds were already thinning. Some people had headed home, but the rest of them weren't wasting the last day looking at demos. They were at the pool, the golf course, the mountains.

I knew I wouldn't be missed at my booth, but instead of changing into shorts right away, I slipped behind the partitions. It wasn't any easier to see than the first time, but I knew where I was going and what to watch for. I placed my feet carefully. I listened.

Dan was long gone and any voices were muted pieces of conversation.

I found the boxes of equipment. I walked around two boxes and tried to remember where Kathy was when I found her. It wasn't immediately obvious, but it didn't matter. Nowhere that I looked could I find anything sticking out that was at shoulder or head height.

The bump on Kathy's head was at the back of her head. Had she hit the partition? The only hard part to the partitions were the supports. They went straight up about ten feet. Pretty hard to run smack into one--probably even harder to hit it hard going backwards. They had some give to them too.

Of course, I had backed up myself when I heard Dan's voice. Maybe she had backed up for some reason and hit...what? None of the boxes were piled head high and she had been closer to the real wall than the partition frames.

Maybe she had fallen backwards and hit her head on the way down.

Maybe I was losing my mind. If someone had been back here, they obviously hadn't been stealing the equipment. The boxes of hard drives were all piled as I had last seen them, next to extra servers and other stuff. In fact, it looked to me like several more boxes of equipment had been added to the pile.

I took a last look around, but nothing made any more sense than before. Obviously I was just being paranoid.

It didn't take long to return to my booth. Since I had been behind Dan's area, I knew he was gone. I was sure I should be also. If I started breaking the equipment down...even if Turbo didn't hear about it, it wasn't a good idea. Allen had sent Turbo back. Perhaps it was his way of making sure I stayed in my place--my old one, rather than the new one.

I wandered around the resort, watching for Kathy. I wasn't sure what I could ask her that would make me feel better. If she had seen anyone else back there, she would have said so.

Eventually, I drifted outside and found myself at the golf course. I didn't have to play, but that didn't mean that I couldn't make myself available to some creep wanting to steal from a charity.

I inquired about lessons, but thought I had lost my hearing when the guy told me the prices. At last, I had found some thieves. Maybe not the ones Huntington was after, but certainly candidates. "You want how much for a half hour lesson?"

"Seventy-five dollars. Normally it's a hundred and fifty, but since you are a guest of the resort, we give you a discount." Mister "TV-dreamboat" smiled smoothly, flashing perfect teeth. He looked to be in his twenties with a blond crew-cut short enough that it had to be real hair. He wore a green resort shirt that made his brown eyes stand out.

"How many lessons will I need before I can play?"

"Don't worry," he said, giving me an encouraging up-and-down look. "Couple of lessons, you'll be out there tearing it up."

"Isn't golf kind of a hard game?"

"Oh it is, it is. That is why we are here."

I had a feeling he was here more to play up to rich older women that wanted a thrill. I didn't remember any of the golfers on TV having biceps that looked like overgrown tree limbs. "What exactly am I going to learn in a half hour?" At seventy-five dollars a pop, even on my new salary, I would be broke in a couple of months if I took golf lessons.

"The basics. Do you have clubs or do you need to rent them?"

I gave him a "get real" look. "I think I'll inspect the course. See if it looks beginner friendly."

"Our resort has five tee boxes, which encompasses every skill level in golf. If you like, as part of your lesson, I can grab some clubs and show you the basics out on the course. Although in that case, you'll need to pay for the round of golf in addition to the lessons. I assure you it is well worth it. Our resort was designed and has been played by some of the most famous names in golf. Would you like me to bring around a cart?"

I wasn't going to embarrass myself by asking if there was a charge for the cart because there had to be. Besides, I needed the exercise. He frowned as I started towards the first hole. "Uh, Miss?"

"Yeah?"

"You, uh, aren't going to just walk around?"

Since that was precisely what I intended to do, I nodded.

He looked ill-at-ease, kind of like the doorman back at Huntington's condo whenever he saw me coming. "You need to watch for golf balls. It isn't safe out there. Perhaps you should take a cart." He emphasized the suggestion rather more sternly this time.

"Fine." Dan was probably playing anyway, and if he saw me, there was no doubt in my mind that he would aim right for me.

Joe Trainer didn't have any lessons scheduled so he drove me around and explained that I needed to be quiet and stop the cart when someone was hitting. I was right about Dan; we got to the second hole, and there he was with Gary and a couple of other guys. Gary waved his golf hat and gave a shout, "Come on over!"

I had never seen the man in such a good mood. Since he knew about the plan, I could only assume he suspected one of the guys he was playing with, and he wanted me in attendance.

With a rather weak smile, I stepped out of the cart and joined them on the tee box.

Gary's golf cap, now back on his head, took ten years off his profile. The gray ring of hair visible on the sides of the hat made it appear he had a full head of hair rather than a rounded, bald top.

"Do you golf?" He had asked me that before. The answer was still the same.

I noticed that Autumn was in one of the carts. She looked pretty interested in her nail polish, so I strove for a more intellectual approach. "I'm a student of the game."

"Did you see that shot I just hit?" Gary asked. "I hit that ball so hard I about came out of my shoes!"

By staring very hard, I could see a golf ball on the short grass about halfway to the hole. "Wow." Okay, I was no expert, but it seemed to me that there wasn't any water or hazards or even a particularly threatening tree line in his way.

"We could use an extra cart, ride along with us," Gary suggested.

That helped clear up the question of his enthusiasm. With Autumn along, one of the men must be walking.

"Sure." If my own enthusiasm was lacking, no one seemed to care. Joe Trainer knew his business. He hopped out of the cart with his forty-dollar-a-month tan and gave me a quick salute before jogging off.

The other three men hit their shots and none were quite as far as Gary's shot so he continued to beam. Thank God Autumn was along; she got stuck with Dan in the cart.

Gary jumped right into the driver's seat after moving his clubs to my cart. He drove like a man obsessed. "You should have seen my shot off the first tee. The thing was like greased lightning."

"Mm." He didn't seem to require my opinion so I kept it to myself. It was probably a good habit, because his next shot to the green was way over and in a sand trap to boot. He hacked it out of there, and then took three putts to get it in the hole.

Okay sure, off the tee box he hit it farther than any of the other guys, but he spent a lot of time making up for it around the greens. Tiger Woods he was not.

I started wondering if the other guys were letting him win. With nothing else to do, I kept track of the scores. The guys seemed to spend a lot more time trying to out-drive Gary than on overall scoring. Leave it to a bunch of guys to turn golf into a muscle game.

I waited impatiently for the famous business discussions to start. With all the money companies spent on these conferences, when were they going to talk about sales? Samuel and Rupin, the other guys playing in the foursome, were from a Denver company. Neither had talked about buying any equipment or services from Strandfrost, unless Strandfrost had started selling Ping Irons yesterday.

By the end of the ninth hole Autumn hit her limit. She popped out of the cart like a genie from the bottle and yodeled, "I've got a massage treatment at three!" With a dainty hop, she scooted back to the clubhouse. To say I was tempted to follow would have been an understatement.

"Three, already?" I bounced out myself. No one noticed, primarily because while they were waiting for the group ahead to finish up on the tee box, Gary was talking about the evening before.

"Can you believe that old biddy asked me to dance? Like I don't have a wife at home and need entertainment outside the office." He took off his cap and rubbed his bald pate with a towel. "Gimme a break. I've had far better offers to stray."

Rupin and Samuel both laughed. Dan didn't even wait to see if Autumn was out of earshot. "Oh, but it's nice to have a warm one that travels."

"Hey Sam, I think that Kathy babe looked pretty interested in you," Rupin added his two cents.

I would definitely be missed, as in forgotten. Unbelievable. Not one word of business. Furthermore, Kathy was not likely to be interested in any of these old farts. She was afraid to even show skin in bathing suit form. I doubt she had given Rupin, or anyone else at the conference, a second glance.

I snorted. No one heard; they were still busy making up stories. By tomorrow Gary would have an audience believing he set a new course record, and that I accompanied them with a belly dancing routine.

Slapping at an insect in disgust, I returned to my room. The conference had been a complete waste of time.

* * *

Friday morning I flew home. As an up-and-coming executive, I probably should have put in an appearance at the office, but from what I had seen at the trade show, it was more in character that I act like I was too busy to show up. I got a taxi from the airport and headed directly to the condo.

I should have known from the look on the reception guy's face that something was wrong when I passed him on my way to the elevator. Thinking he was still miffed at me for answering the phone funny on the first day I ignored him.

"Ms. O'Hala?" he called after me. The kid walked towards me as if he had hemorrhoids. He handed me a slip of paper. "A...ahem...a Ms.," he coughed in his hand, "Harrison came by to see you. Claimed you offered her a job." The cough and his mannerism told me that he didn't believe the story. "What shall I tell her if she returns?"

"I don't know a Ms. Harrison. What did she look like?"

He sniffed. "A rather...well." His job didn't allow him to say whatever distasteful words he wanted to use.

"Cut to the chase here." I scanned his badge. "Michael. Was she blond, tall, short, fat, what?"

He ahemed again. "A rather beat up looking woman," he finally responded without meeting my eyes.

"Beat up?" For a moment I couldn't imagine what he meant, and then suddenly the scene in the bar downtown came to mind. "You mean bruises?"

He nodded, still without looking up. "Rather large cut on her face. I was certain she was making the story up about the job offer." He turned to march his way back behind the bellhop desk.

"Michael?" He turned, a half-cocked ear facing me, as if he couldn't expend the energy to get his whole body back around. "If she returns, send her up immediately. Oh and here, take this." I rummaged for scrap paper and scrawled my cell phone number on it. "If I'm not here and she shows up, call me on my cell."

He stared, now positive I was diseased. He could barely muster the courage to take the scrap of paper. I didn't care. If Marilyn showed up again, I'd see her. If she was still alive.

I was worn out from my trip and glad to be back. I really wanted to go straight home to my own bed, but it seemed important not to blow my cover. If anyone checked my expense report, the taxi receipt showed me coming to my lovely new condo.

When I opened the door, I found that Huntington had been busy in my absence. Hanging in the kitchen were brand new pots and pans. The bedroom now had a gorgeous white embroidered comforter, including the skirt. Giant fluffy pillows with matching throw pillows finished it off.

I zipped into the study and was grateful to see a new desk. He hadn't replaced the ridiculous chair, but at least I had a desk that wasn't lopsided.

Grinning, I checked the balcony. Sure enough, he had filled the place with plants. "Woohoo!" I felt like it was my birthday. My mood lifted, I changed clothes and went out to get some groceries. Someone had to put those pots and pans to use.

Chapter 20

Saturday morning, I headed to my karate class. I felt guilty because not only had I not practiced, I hadn't even shown up for my first scheduled lesson. Luckily, the dojo was over on Eighth Street near Angela's shop so I could go for a massage later if I needed one. While I was there, I could pester her for more information about James.

I bowed to Abba from the doorway. He hurried across the smooth wooden floors, gliding like the master he was. "Seedona!" He clapped me on the back. "It is good that you have come at last."

"I was out of town," I explained.

"Mm, yes. Your name was in the newspapers. This not good." He shook his head as he looked me over. My karate uniform wasn't ironed, and it wasn't very worn either.

The shiny wooden floor was cold as I shuffled my feet back and forth, guilty as silently charged.

"I think we start you in Aikido this morning, yes?"

"That would be excellent." I hurried over to start some warm up exercises.

After about fifteen minutes, Abba let his helper take over leading the class and took me aside. "I think you need evaluations," he confided. "I work with you myself this morning to see if you fast enough. We make sure you ready for the next fight."

"But I'm not planning on any more fights!"

"Yes, of course." He kept it simple to start, but then he brought out the knives. "Now, I hear in the newspaper that you catch the knife. This not good. I don't remember that you had this training. You know you should not try these karates without proper training."

"Well no. It wasn't my brightest move."

"Here." He took my arm. "We learn to disarm instead of catch."

It was no use pointing out that the guy who had thrown the knife wasn't close enough to disarm.

Abba was hard on me. Apparently the newspaper story had frightened him. He came at me holding the rubber knife over my head. I blocked his arm, twisted it behind his back and forced the knife out of his hand. He let me do it several times before he got more serious.

By the time I left, I was wishing for the hospital rather than Angela's shop, but she was closer. She was also busier than I hoped, but I was very good at looking pathetic. She bustled her bright pink self right over to see what I needed.

"I just got out of karate and wondered if you have someone available to do a massage," I asked, pulling back the sleeves of my uniform to show her the red spots where bruises were likely to form. "I have to take the class," I whispered. "What if they attack again?"

She looked down at the counter. "Well, they probably won't."

"I hope not." I sighed, lowered my eyes and looked as sad as possible. "Karate probably won't do me any good anyway, but it makes me feel better to take the class. I can't stop thinking that they might be back."

"I don't have anyone available today," she said regretfully. "What about during the week?"

"I have to work. I figured I'd stop in and hope someone had canceled. I know Friday and Saturday are your busiest."

She nodded. "Look, Sedona." She hesitated, glancing around the shop. It was loud today with two hair dryers going and lots of chatting. "After you left the other day, one of the girls told me that Emma's nephew is only fourteen and lives in Colorado Springs, not Denton. I'm not saying he is or isn't, but I guess maybe he doesn't know squat about those thugs that attacked."

"Fourteen?"

She shrugged. "Like I said, it ain't something I asked Emma about. Next time she comes in, I can verify for sure, if you want. I can ask his age or where he lives, but I'm not gonna go asking what he was in for!"

"Okay, okay." I patted her shoulder. "You let me know. And how about you put me down for a massage on the next Saturday where you have a slot?"

She checked the schedule and found a slot in three weeks.

I couldn't complain. I had come more for information than a massage anyway. If the kid was fourteen and didn't live around here, maybe he wasn't involved. Still, I called Derrick and left him a message. Maybe Derrick could track James down and make sure he wasn't a threat, because I was pretty sure that karate lessons weren't going to be enough to save me if someone came after me again.

Chapter 21

Turbo had an annoying habit of being very cheerful on Mondays. Usually people were energetic on Fridays, but not Turbo. He was at his best on Monday mornings. When he stopped by my new office, he was actually humming.

I glared at him as he stood in the doorway, but it didn't remove his smile. "Oh, just come in already and tell me what you're so happy about."

He did, surveying my new office as though it hadn't been there all along. The only difference was that it was now mine. Turbo took the visitor's chair. He bounced a couple of times, testing its softness. It was a much fluffier chair than the one in my old office. Finally, he got down to business. "I was right about it not being Gary that suggested Bruce and I come back early."

"You know for sure?"

"I asked Gary. He said he had no reason to call us back. And let's face it, if Gary pulls this investigation off, he stands to be promoted."

I blinked. "He pulls it off? I'm the one undercover here. All he does is let Huntington run the show. How does that mean he is qualified for a promotion?"

Turbo shrugged. "Since when do people get promoted because they deserve it?"

Good point. I tapped my pencil on the desk in irritation. "Let me make a guess here. If I screw this up, not only will I get demoted back to my old job, that is what will happen if I'm very lucky. If I just happen to pull it off, Gary will be the one that gets a great promotion out of it."

Turbo suddenly looked a lot less happy. I hoped it was because he was going to feel bad for his part in involving me when I lost my job. "I could be homeless within six months." Maybe I should have pocketed the money Huntington had provided for new clothes.

"You won't fail," he reassured me or maybe himself.

"Yeah, I'm getting lots of interest in my new status." I looked at my watch. "Speaking of which, I have staff in ten minutes."

"Let me tell you what else I found out," Turbo said. He leaned forward. "From what I gather, Dan saw you mucking with the equipment at the show and decided it was obvious you were still willing to do that job."

"What?"

Turbo crossed his arms in disapproval. "He said you were crawling around the back just like you used to. No need for us."

"Who told you that?"

"Were you?" he countered.

"I had to fix a hard drive!" Dan must have noticed me popping in and out of the back space.

"Aha!" Turbo sat back. "Then he was right. You gave him the perfect excuse to suggest to Allen that we go home."

"Nonsense," I argued. "You said Allen told you to go home before lunch. I was back there after lunch started." It was possible that Dan had run straight to Allen after seeing me, but I doubt they had waited for that excuse to send Turbo home.

"You shouldn't have been fixing it at all," Turbo said.

"Come on, Turbo, that's ridiculous. The guy sees me fix a single hard drive and tells Allen to send you back? Gimme a break. He didn't have the right to do that anyway."

Turbo shrugged. "No, but he had the excuse ready just in case anyone asked."

"And you asked?"

"Not him," Turbo assured me. "I did some investigating."

I rolled my eyes. "Sally? Or one of the other guys?"

"Don't you have to go to staff?"

I glanced at my watch again. "I'm going to ask Sally. I bet she told you what Allen said about getting the tickets."

"It wasn't Sally." He sniffed. "Be nice to the guys in staff, Sedona. You need them on your side, even Dan. You never know who might approach you for a deal."

"I am not putting up with ass-grabbing." I walked out the door ahead of him. "And brown-nosing would be too obvious, right?"

Turbo glared at me.

Apparently, I should have considered the brown-nosing strategy. Strongly. Gary's staff consisted of Dan Thorton, Allen Perry, Patrick Toll, and Ross Canton. Ross was the marketing and program manager. Patrick was like Allen and myself; a technical-type manager. Dan had to be satisfied with being a finance expert since his people skills were in the Neanderthal camp. I'd worked with them all before, but I was the newbie on the block and the only woman.

I did not fit in.

"I think the conference went well," Gary started out in a self-congratulatory tone.

"Absolutely," Ross agreed. His head was rectangular, a little like Frankenstein without the knobs on the side. It didn't help that he kept his hair ultra short on the sides, but topped with longer, wavy brown locks. A tuft or two was often sticking up because he frequently ran his fingers though it. He talked in rapid-fire bullet points as he flicked copies of data across the table. "Check this out. So far the new sales total one point five percent better than we expected. I'm working with the team to get the new projects scheduled."

Looking down at the sheets, I dared ask, "Who, uh, is going to handle new projects?"

"Not a problem," Ross said heartily, straightening his tie.

I refrained from pointing out that his projects were chronically late. He always excused schedule problems by saying the customer added requirements as the project wore on. I was usually privy to the customer requests, and I could state unequivocally that new requests were not the problem.

The spinning of his tall tale began as he ran down the project names. The sheets had less than half the information actually needed in order to scope the work and time required to do the job. Ross had taken the liberty of filling in a "completed by" date anyway.

"Has Turbo seen this? Or Paul?" I asked. I knew they hadn't, but what was the point in sitting here if I couldn't point out a few of the injustices that I suffered down in the ranks?

"Sure."

An out and out lie. Turbo would have marked this up in so much red ink the Feds wouldn't have been able to read the original with their best microscope. "Oh, that's great. I'm surprised Turbo didn't mention the P&R project. My special team is booked on that through August or September. I'll check with him and make sure he gets back to you."

See now, a smart man would have let it go. But Ross was a spinner, not a thinker. "I'm sure your group can handle both of these projects in that time frame."

The old fart put it back on me as the failure. "Not a problem. We can handle those two without suffering any quality problems. Patrick, I assume your group will be taking over Mamba?"

Patrick drew his beetle-black eyebrows into an ominous line. "Uh..." he glared and peered over his impressive eyebrows, looking for a victim. There was no one lower on the totem pole besides me, and since I was the one to toss the assignment his way, I was no longer available.

"And these next three..." I ran down the sheets. "What are your plans for those? We'd love to help, especially on the one you coded as Treker." I flipped the page. "I think my team could help here after September."

Ross stared at me with his mouth open. "We've already told the customer these dates," he sputtered. "Look." He grabbed the sheet from me. "Let me show you how this can work."

I lost track of what he was saying, but he counted October at least six times in the next five minutes. I'm pretty certain he invented months, he just didn't give them actual names.

Gary's frown got steadily darker. "This doesn't sound like it is going to work. I want you guys to meet and have a new schedule for me next week."

Ridiculous. I huffed out with the rest of them, not saying another word.

Back in my office, I started my desktop, but there was no mouse. "Argh."

It had been missing since the move. I went into the lab to try and find it.

"Hey Tam, have you seen my mouse?"

He looked up blankly. He had a network card in one hand and a piece of casing in the other. "No, do you need me to order you one? How about one of those wireless ones?" He set the casing down and zipped over to a row of catalogs. He flipped through one of them. "It won't work well on a laptop because they are radio controlled, but if it is for your desktop, well, these are the best." He showed me a picture. "It's kind of expensive..."

"Over a hundred dollars? You've got to be kidding."

He grinned. "Ah, comeon! You're an important boss now. You gotta look the part."

"Look the part?" Did he know I was a fake? Did everyone know?

He continued blissfully, "I have been wanting to get one of these babies in. We could use some in the lab. Of course with all the emissions in here I'm not sure how well it will work. So then I'd have to take it to my office." He looked very hopeful.

I scratched my head and thought about this. "So if I were to sign off on this very necessary purchase, you are suggesting that you'll need one for yourself?" I was greatly relieved to discover his comment about blending in wasn't because he was aware of my duplicity. He was just hoping to gain from my new position. Not exactly an offer to cash in charity checks, but it was a start.

Tam grinned and looked like a four-year old with a new fire truck. "Be most happy to assist you with yours when it gets in. I'll install them both."

"I don't suppose you lost mine on purpose?"

He looked confused. "What?"

"Never mind. Just order whichever one you think will work best."

"You need anything else?" he asked quickly.

I looked back. He was grabbing catalogs and paging frantically. "What else do I need?"

"Flat panel monitor. There's this new one out." He held up a picture and pointed.

I waved my hand. "Fine. Better get a couple."

"Cool!"

At least someone had found a use for my new position. I went back to my desk to stare at the impossible schedule and look up new curse words on the web.

Tam had an order form filled out and on my desk before the end of the day. I signed it and stared at my signature. Just like that. A few thousand dollars, and all I had to do was sign. No wonder Tam thought it was so cool.

As I turned the paperwork in, I hoped no one needed the network card Tam had been working with when I walked in to ask about a mouse. I vaguely remembered it disappearing under a tall pile of catalogs. Unfortunately, before I could go back to the lab to remind him about it, my mother called. Abba wasn't the only one that had seen my face in the newspaper. Of course, I was pretty sure that my brother had something to do with my parents looking in the newspaper, but that wasn't the point.

"We decided on a surprise visit," Mom informed me. "We're staying with Sean."

My parents usually stayed with me rather than Sean, but who was I to complain? "Oh, that's...great!"

"I know you're at work and very busy, and we got in early, so we'll just stay here with Sean where we'll be out of the way."

I wasn't fooled. Parents never have a problem inconveniencing their children. "I didn't know you were flying in."

"We're just driving through. Your father wanted to make a trip up to Denver. We're planning a nice, relaxing dinner for tonight, here at Sean's. Can you make it?"

I was pretty sure the trip was all about finding out what had happened at Strandfrost. No wonder they stopped at Sean's house. Without me around, Sean had likely told them everything he knew and also thrown in a few suppositions. "Of course I'll be by for dinner."

"Good. We can't wait to see you."

Now I had to get home on time because I had dinner plans. "Great." I raced through a "suggested" version of the schedule, knowing it didn't matter anyway. I mailed it to my illustrious colleagues and headed home to whip up a cake for the "nice, relaxing dinner."

Chapter 22

By the time I trundled over to Sean's house, I felt like I'd been through the wringer. If my mother weren't such a great cook, I'd have stopped and gotten a store cake, but she would have noticed.

Letting myself in, I yelled "hello" and headed for the dining room where I found my mother. She didn't look her regal self. Her reddish-brown curls were completely untamed. Her face looked pinched around her eyes.

"Hello, dear."

I immediately felt guilty as she hugged me tight. There were actually tears in her Irish green eyes.

I would quietly kill Sean later.

Dad was in the backyard crawling around on the grass, not unusual since he was an agricultural scientist. From the look of concentration on his face and the tweezers, it was likely that Sean's lawn wasn't up to snuff.

Without greeting my treasonous brother, I hopped out to the back porch, letting the screen door slam so that Dad would possibly notice my presence.

It took a while to register, but the banging did the trick. He looked up, blinking into the bright setting sun. "Well, hey!" He brushed his hands off and stood. "Did you know that your brother has a grub problem?"

I shook my head and grinned. "No, really?" I enveloped Dad in a hug, at least as much of him as I could get my arms around. He stood six feet tall and was as big around as a giant oak tree. He built a lot of muscle moving plants around, mixing soil and digging. His hair always looked slightly unkempt and out here in the breeze, the black strands with just a hint of gray danced to their own tune. "Heard you were in a bit of a spot, but you look just fine." His coal-black eyes sharpened on mine for a moment. "I expect next time maybe you'll be a little more prepared."

"Dad, they don't let me carry a weapon at work!"

He smiled. "No, I expect not. But Sean wasn't particularly happy with your self-defense. Beef it up next time." The worry was there behind his eyes, but Dad trusted me. He knew I had done what I could. My mother and brothers made up for his perceived leniency.

Brenda came out onto the porch, drying her hands on a dishrag even though she hadn't been in the kitchen a few seconds ago. Unlike my mother's flushed kitchen cheeks, her face was perfectly relaxed. Her short haircut barely stirred in the light breeze. She announced happily, "Dinner is almost ready.

Sedona, thanks so much for the cake! You know I love that recipe!"

My mother watched us from the kitchen window. Her strawberry curls bobbed up and down rather frantically. Sean came out and Dad launched into a discussion of beetles and proper lawn care. It would have been easier to just sit on the porch, but Mom looked like she needed company so I went back inside.

"Could you boil some eggs?" she hissed.

"What?"

She looked fugitively through the back screen door. "She made deviled eggs." Mom's face blanched. "Lord knows what she put in them. I didn't ask. But we can't serve that! Sean invited his friend over!"

Brenda had my recipe for deviled eggs. I looked into the fridge and had an inkling of what had gone wrong. The recipe called for bacon. She apparently misunderstood or ignored the part of the instructions that specified that the bacon must be chopped very, very small. Her eggs had huge lumps of bacon with some of the stuff actually draped over the sides of the eggs. The paprika was so heavy, it looked like a burial.

I sighed. No wonder my mother had nearly been brought to tears. "Does she have any more eggs?"

Mom nodded and pointed to the pot of water she had set to boil. "I sent Sean." She rolled her eyes. "I got lots of other extra stuff. Sean is going to grill some steaks, and I made broccoli cheese soup and Caesar salad. You didn't tell me you were interested in Sean's policeman."

I nearly dropped the eggs. "Sean didn't tell me I was."

She turned and caught my tightly drawn lips. "You did know he was coming, didn't you?"

Of course I hadn't. I should have brought a date. That would teach my conniving brother. Being my brother though, he assumed I was too much of a loser to have a date. Of course, only a completely desperate daughter would bring a date to meet her parents on such short notice, knowing full well that said parents would leap to all kinds of false assumptions.

I started the eggs and the bacon while Mom arranged a veggie tray. Being me, I stole some celery filled with peanut butter. "Sedona! What will your date think?"

Nearly choking on the celery, I looked up to see that Sean had come back in. Very succinctly, I said, "I don't have a date." Hadn't I said that before just recently?

Sean chose to ignore my challenge. He stole his own handful of carrots before retreating, carefully remaining out of knife range the entire time.

Mom ignored the mutual glaring.

Derrick showed up before Sean put the steaks on. I managed to avoid everyone while introductions were made. It was pretty obvious that no one had told Derrick he was my date either.

Sean and Derrick went out to get the grill ready and Mom arranged the vegetable tray within easy reach. We finished the eggs and brought them outside too.

Brenda helped herself to the eggs. She didn't seem to notice that half a pig was now missing. "Do you like the eggs, honey?" she asked Sean coyly.

Sean nodded. "These are great. Taste just like Sedona's." He spoke around a mouthful.

Brenda beamed. "They are her recipe."

My mother looked pained. She offered Brenda a glass of soda and poured it for her, taking ice from the outside cooler. It was the last of the two-liter bottle. Dad noticed and frowned. "You don't need that soda jug, do you?"

Mother looked wary. "No."

Dad took it from her. "I can use it. I'm working on new slug traps. Drowning them in beer doesn't work, but I found that if I put slug bait in the bottom of a plastic bottle with a small hole in the side, slugs go right in. Birds can't upend the bottle because I bury it to the level of the hole. The bait would kill the birds if they ate it," he explained to a slightly goggle-eyed Derrick.

Dad stepped around us to go into the kitchen to wash his soda bottle.

Mom smiled self-consciously. "Sedona's father is a farmer, and he is always inventing new contraptions that are friendly to the environment. He hasn't been happy with beer traps for a while, so I'm afraid in his enthusiasm he forgot that we are eating."

Derrick stared rather suspiciously at his frosted mug of beer.

Dad popped back out on the porch. "Don't put salt on slugs to kill them either," he continued as though there had been no interruption. "Salt ruins the soil."

"You want us to start the steaks now or should we wait awhile?" Sean asked.

Mom shrugged delicately. "We have plenty to snack on, and we haven't even started on the salads. Why not sit and let's all get to know one another." She beamed at Derrick in that mother-in-law way.

Derrick caught my eye and coughed around a carrot. He either finally got the fact that we were the only single members in attendance or my dad's slug lore was bothering his appetite.

Dad ignored the change in topics and continued with his own concerns. "The salt does kill slugs, sucks the juice right outta them, but in the process you ruin the soil too. You can't mess with the pH of the soil like that. Before you know it, you won't have anything but deflated slugs and useless soil." Dad took a drink of his iced tea. "Whooee, and you can imagine the smell too. Dead slugs ain't nothing to be proud of all over a garden. The things are nothing but decayed material anyway, and that's before you kill them. Try drowning them in that there beer of yours, and the smell is worse. The beer ferments, and the slugs weren't too good to start with."

Mom sighed. "Dear, don't you think we should talk about something else?"

Derrick set his beer down.

"Can I get you a soda?" I asked politely. "Maybe some iced tea?"

Brenda popped out of her seat. "I'll get you some. I need a refill, and I've had enough soda."

"Don't worry," I told Derrick. "There aren't any tomatoes in the salad today so you won't have to hear about hornworms. Unless you ask, that is."

Dad glared at me. "I wasn't going to talk about hornworms during dinner."

Right. Not now that I had mentioned it wasn't suitable.

Mom tried for normalcy one more time. She addressed Derrick with a cheerful little chirp. "Sean tells me that you and Sedona are working on a project together for abused women. I think that is wonderful."

Derrick smiled weakly. "Well, there was one such project."

Leave it to Sean to beef up reality. I decided to clarify. "Derrick was hoping to get a particular woman some help and have her turn state's evidence. It didn't work out," I said. "Of course, we're both still hoping that she will get some help with the abuse."

Derrick didn't look very comfortable, but he quickly agreed. "Her husband has a bad track record. Getting her away from him was our number one priority. Giving up evidence that might have helped us would have been nice too." He shrugged. "We are quite desperate."

"No luck with watching Larry's Body Shop?" Sean asked.

Derrick shook his head. "We've been at it like hawks, but there's too much business for us to catch anything specifically. Apparently the owner just got a new maintenance contract with a trucking company. There are more trucks in there than a gas station. Without searching them all, we're going to have a hard time figuring out which ones Ted is using for illicit drug deals. If we get a search warrant at the wrong time, it will kill the case."

"It sounds dangerous." My mother glanced at Sean, her happy chirp dialed down more than a notch.

Sean shrugged. "He's a policeman, Mom. He helps people just like I do only at a different level. If he could have gotten the lady to step forward, believe me, I would have been happy to act as her attorney."

Dad might be interested in watching grass grow, but he wasn't slow to add two and two. "So where did you fit into all this?" he asked.

Sean looked worried suddenly. I considered telling my parents that he had sent me in to protect the big bad cop from a possible rape charge. Of course, I didn't want my parents to visit too often. "I was the example of independent womanhood. You know, the type that doesn't need a man around to do every little chore."

Mother, knowing she was losing control of the conversation again, stood. "Why don't we start on the salads? Brenda?"

The three of us trooped off like proper little wives. Brenda dropped one of the salads on the tiled kitchen floor. Not even my gracious mother could keep an impatient sigh from escaping. Dressing ran down Brenda's leg, and the shattered bowl was in millions of pieces. Without a word, I took two of the bowls out and handed them to Sean and Derrick.

Dad leaned over and asked, "What kind of lettuce is that?"

"Romaine and something else mixed in."

He nodded approvingly. "Iceberg lettuce has the least vitamins in the family. Of course it is a vegetable so there isn't a problem with eating it, but a lot of the other greens are better for you. Sean, when are you going to put a garden in?"

"When the devil wears a parka," I muttered and went back inside to get Dad his salad and help Mom clean up.

From the floor, Mom whispered, "Do you know that she made cookies?"

I shook my head. Mom didn't look up from where she was crouched as she wiped up the last of the mess. "The cookies melted all over the pan. They were stuck on there so hard, we had to scrape them off with a knife."

"Too much sugar?" I surmised.

"I can only guess. And she forgot to spray the pan."

"They probably tasted okay."

My mother glared at me. "That is what she said."

"It happens."

"When they have children, my grandchildren are going to starve!"

"Nonsense. And Sean looks good now that he has lost weight. I bet her kids learn to be excellent cooks." They would have to just to survive.

Mom rolled her eyes at me.

The rest of the meal went well. Sean grilled a mean steak, and Derrick was a pleasant addition to the usual banter of family discussion. He and Brenda, old friends, argued over the edibility of the cookies. My mother was horrified that Brenda actually presented them. Always worried about my marital status, it took a superhuman effort for her to swallow back the words that would make it super clear just who had made them.

I grinned. "Mom did you want to serve the cake also?"

She jumped up and fled to the kitchen, glad for the respite.

Tomorrow was a work day so shortly after a piece of cake, I said my goodbyes. On the way out the door, I hugged my brother rather close and whispered, "You know it isn't wise to give your sister a gun and then start arranging her dates..." I let it trail off. He squeezed back hard enough to hurt.

"Someone has to help you."

I grunted and shoved away. My dad had some shopping to do up in Denver the next day; a new strain of buffalo grass he wanted to look into. With my parents thus occupied until the drive back through, I was off the hook for the week, at least on the personal side of life.

Of course, my life might be better and safer if I was more like Dad and just learned to have fun shopping for grass and tomatoes.

Chapter 23

I should have known that after the Monday staff meeting some of my new peers were going to have a couple of problems with my bulldozer approach. For one, as a team, we were supposed to be putting together a schedule that we agreed upon; for two, it was due in a week, and unless half the projects were dropped, there was no way we'd get a real schedule.

First thing in the morning, Dan sent me the financial impact statements for the new customers. Much as I disliked the little weasel, he was good at his job. He had a very good grasp from past projects of just how much equipment the test team was likely to purchase in order to prove a concept to a customer.

On the other hand, Ross and Patrick weren't ready to accommodate reality. Patrick was furious that I had tried to pass him the buck on some of the extra work. He didn't see why he had to be dragged into an argument that in his opinion should have remained my problem. I got wind of the trouble when Sally stopped by to warn me that Patrick was in Allen's office bitching.

"I guess Allen is happy I am failing on my first task," I said.

Sally shrugged. "He figures that Gary will ask him to step in and save things or at least help you out. The way he tells it, if he has to help you, he deserves to be promoted back above you."

The logic was breathtaking. If Allen helped me, he would only be doing his old job, not a higher-up one. "Maybe someone should remind Allen that these projects used to be his. If he hadn't taken on so much in the first place, it wouldn't be so difficult." And if he hadn't cashed charity checks he'd still have the job, but I didn't know just how much Sally knew so I wasn't about to bring that up.

"You won't stop trying, will you?" Sally seemed genuinely concerned, but she was also good at extracting information. I had to be very careful.

"What makes you ask that?"

She leaned in and whispered, "That is what Allen told Patrick. He said you wouldn't last more than a month or two, but it's been nice...having someone that I can talk to."

"It isn't as though if I don't succeed at this job, I'll leave the company," I said. "Not unless they fire me. But I can't do this on my own. If Patrick, Ross, Dan, Allen and Gary don't want me to succeed, I don't see how it is possible."

"Oh, Gary loves you. He thinks you're doing a great job. I've heard him tell Allen."

I knew it was probably a false endorsement from Gary, but Sally didn't. It might be enough to keep the others from out and out lynching me, but not much else. Dan already hated me, and now I had made sure Ross and Patrick hated me also. Allen couldn't even muster the energy to feel threatened by me. He sent people home that supposedly worked for me.

The whole situation was depressing and rang too much of what Huntington had talked about--if someone like me really did find themselves with this opportunity they would have to claw desperately just to hang on. Huntington thought it would work in my favor, but I disagreed. If I didn't start looking a little more like I might succeed there would be no reason at all to approach me. If I didn't start succeeding a little bit, I might get out-and-out fired.

With that in mind, I set out to find Ross and try to smooth things over. There probably wasn't any fixing the problem since I had no idea what the hidden rules were, but I could try.

Patrick found me before I found Ross. "Do you have a minute?" His beetle-black eyebrows made a vee on his forehead. He looked like he was trying not to puke on my shoes.

"Sure. I was going to talk to Ross about the schedule, but we can chat first." Patrick sat in the office next to Ross. I could just go from the fat to the fire. I stepped into Patrick's office. He shut the door behind me. Slammed it was more like it.

He stepped around to his side of the desk and then sat facing me. Stubby fingers drummed the desk while he stared at me. He was in his forties, but had a full head of hair and only a small paunch around his middle. "I wish those thugs had just shot you. Then I wouldn't have to put up with a smart-mouthed woman in this job."

I didn't know if he was mad because I had passed the buck down his way, or if he had a problem because I was a woman, or if he was truly angry because I was alive. "Look," I said, "we all know my group can't handle all the new work that Ross is passing around. The Mamba project fits into your group--"

"Like hell!" he exploded. "I have all of my projects lined up. I worked it out with Ross beforehand! You can't go suggesting that I take on more work in front of Gary. That isn't the way it works."

I thought about what he said for a minute. "So the way it works is that I go behind your back and get Ross to assign it to you before the meeting? Then when you walk in, you don't have any idea what is going on?"

"What?" He scrubbed a hand back and forth across his bushy hair. The man appeared to have no idea that I was merely restating, in my favor, what he had already done.

"You prefer that I manipulate the cards before the meeting rather than during?" I repeated.

"Don't be a fool, Sedona. They gave you this job because you scared off some scum. You're hardly management material. You have no idea how to get this job done. There is no reason for Gary to be impressed with you."

"Why is he impressed with you?"

That stumped him for about fifteen seconds, but the man was good at angry responses. He stood up and leaned over the desk into my face. "Because I know my job. I do my job. I get my work done on time," he bellowed.

"Sure, as long as you and Ross have an agreement. But then that just makes me the loser in all this."

He snarled, "I don't care who loses. You fight your own battles and stay out of my way."

There was no point in sticking around to get yelled at so I stood up and shrugged. "I take it that you and Allen got along just fine because Allen never protested the extra work?"

It was a question, but he was breathing too hard to answer. I opened the door and walked over to Ross' office. "Hey, Ross."

He waved me in. "Sedona! I got your message. Here's a new schedule." He tossed a presentation my way before grabbing a lunch sack and dumping its contents on the desk.

I stared down at the schedule. Ross mumbled around his sandwich, "Took your suggestion about Mamba. See if that helps." He started typing with his free hand.

It didn't take me long to figure out that he hadn't changed much. "Ross, you still need to move some of these dates out."

He shook his head. "No can do, my fair lady. I'd like to you know, but the customer." He shrugged. "I can't tell them we can't make that date. I already promised."

Grinding my teeth seemed like the right action. "But Ross, we aren't going to make the date."

"Sure we will." He licked mayonnaise off his fingers and took a huge gulp of a soda. "We always do." He winked. "Come on, Sedona. You make the schedule, we both get a terrific bonus."

"And we get fired if we don't make the schedule?"

He coughed on his soda, startled. "Shit no. Look, I can move the dates out a week or two if that makes you happy."

"Are you asking me to walk into Gary's next staff and lie about making the schedule?"

Ross was not prone to spending a great deal of time on anything, especially something as mundane as logic. He shrugged. "Lie? I don't know if I would call it lying."

"Well, if I tell Gary I can make this schedule," I pointed to it, "and I know that I can't, wouldn't that be a lie?"

The confusion cleared. "Shit no! You're really new to this aren't you? I forgot. Look, Gary wants a schedule. He wants one that agrees with what the customer wants. That's all we are doing. We're just giving him what he wants."

He finished his soda, crushed it and tossed it towards the trash. Since his office was only ten feet by fifteen it wasn't much of a shot, but he leaned back in his chair, dress shoes in the air and cheered. "Hey, I'll move them out a couple of weeks, but no more than that, okay?" He grabbed his suit jacket from the back of his chair, checked his square head in the glare from the computer monitor and walked out of his own office while I sat there trying to figure out a way to make my point. He clicked his finger back at me, fake gun style. "You and me, we're going to work just fine together."

I stared after his retreating back. And why shouldn't he think we were in total agreement? His version of reality was so far from mine, he flat out wouldn't notice if I turned into an alien and started gobbling up his desk. He might even offer me his sandwich if he figured hunger was the problem.

Turbo's office wasn't far. I didn't bother to knock. I slumped down in his guest chair and proceeded to tell him what happened. "I am willing to steal from a charity, Turbo, but lie to the boss? Isn't that going a little far? I'll be giving them an excuse to fire me!"

Turbo looked at the open door. He started to speak, but then he just stared at the open door. With a loud sigh I leaned over and closed it.

"Uh..." That was all he managed to get out before I continued.

"Turbo, Gary doesn't seem to have any idea how poorly things are run around here! Shoot, I don't think I had any idea. I mean, I knew we were always trying to make ridiculous schedules, but I didn't know that was just because it is the way it is done." I thought of something. "Wait a minute. Does Gary know we're all lying?" That confused me more. "So if we're all lying, and he knows we're lying then...what is the point?"

Turbo blinked at me.

"Have you ever attended Gary's staff meeting?" I asked suspiciously. He nodded. "Was it full of lies?"

He thought about it for eons. "Well. I don't think the people thought they were lying."

Leave it to Turbo to turn a poker game into philosophical argument. "Turbo." I closed my eyes so that I didn't scream at the look of concentration on his face. "If we are all lying, then why do we have schedules?"

When I opened my eyes, his face was much happier. He knew the answer to this one. "Politics," he declared happily. "It has something to do with that."

Great. My fearless mentor didn't get it either. I gently banged my head down onto his desk and tried not to cry.

"Well," my brilliant friend advised, "look at the bright side. If people know you lie, maybe they'll think you'll steal from a charity, and we'll find our man!"

I removed my forehead from the desk and glared at him from over the stacks of paper cluttering it. "But no one is going to know the difference between a lie and reality, remember?"

He frowned. "There is that."

Indeed. I banged my head down again.

It didn't help.

Chapter 24

I was still tired and frustrated when I got home. After my late night on Monday, I could have used three or four days of sleep, but Michael interrupted my plans per earlier forgotten instructions.

He called up to announce that Marilyn had showed up.

"Send her up," I ordered, afraid he might run her off.

Michael promptly escorted her to my door. No doubt, he didn't want to let her run the hallways on her own, although she was probably in better shape than when Michael had seen her before. Michael didn't look at either of us, but waited for further instructions after I opened the door.

A cut on her face had been stitched closed. She had made an effort with her clothes too. I wondered if she had showed up bleeding on the carpet the last time before she finally made her way to the hospital. "Marilyn. What a surprise!" I grinned at her like we were long lost sisters. Her eyes slid to Michael, not sure if she was supposed to play a part. Immediately her eyes went from wary to hopeless.

I threw the door open and waved her in. "Thanks Michael. If Mr. Harrison shows up here looking for me or Mrs. Harrison, you are not to show him up. You are to call the police and have him removed from the property immediately. I don't care if Ms. Harrison tells you it is okay, you are never to let him up here or anywhere on the property, especially my property. It is completely out of Ms. Harrison's hands. Understood?"

His eyes flew to my face, an action I am sure he promised himself he would never do. Never look the insane in the eyes. It might be catching. "Uh, yes, ma'am."

"Never," I repeated firmly. "I don't care if someone is dying, and he says he's a doctor."

He nodded rapidly and backed away. He wasn't certain what to make of the situation, but with Marilyn standing next to me with a jagged scar forming down her cheek, he probably wasn't too eager to run into her husband.

"Well," I said turning to my guest. "I won't bother to ask how you're doing. It's quite obvious your life stinks."

I backed myself into the living room and waved at the couch, but instead of sitting, she stood next to it. I retrieved a couple of sodas from the fridge and handed her one. The fridge was running low again. I sighed. "I hope you're here about that job I mentioned."

She nodded without looking up.

"Good." I had thought of the perfect thing. "One of your jobs is going to be groceries. And cleaning. Have you ever cleaned homes before?" I wasn't looking forward to teaching someone how to clean. It didn't just come naturally to women as some men might assume.

To my surprise, she nodded. "Sure."

"Okay." I was still doubtful, but willing to make the best of it. "Here are rules. If you ever steal anything or find a way to let your husband up here, you're fired. No second chances. I am not interested in getting my face bashed in by a lunatic husband. If you keep going back, that's your business. You let him in my life, it becomes my business. If he breaks in here, be warned. I will shoot him."

Violence was not new to her. She nodded without looking up from the floor.

"Can you do this job?"

Another nod.

"I'll pay you eighty dollars for each cleaning."

That got her head up where her eyes met mine for a fraction of a second. "How often," she swallowed, "do I clean?"

I wasn't a messy person, so I figured I could get by with twice a month. On the other hand, she could probably use the money. Since it was Huntington's money, I was generous. "I can use you every week, but if you can't do that, try for every other week. I'll give you money for the cleaning supplies. Do you have a car?"

She shrugged. "Sometimes."

"Well on those times, get supplies and groceries. I'll make up a list of the staples I like to keep on hand, and then depending on when you're working, there may be additions."

Now the worry was back. I could tell by the slump of her shoulders. "What day do I have to be here?"

"That's up to you."

Up came the head again. "What do you mean?"

I took a seat on the couch even though she hadn't sat down. "Marilyn, you haven't been able to hold a job because your husband doesn't want you to have a job, right?"

She didn't answer. She just looked at me like a doe waiting to be run over by a large truck.

"I need you to show up every week to two weeks. Check the groceries and clean the place. You can come here anytime if you need a place to sleep or get away. At the moment, I only have this couch, but it'll have to do for now." Maybe I could get Huntington to put a bed in the study. I thought of another problem. "You don't have to call first, but if you need to go to the hospital, go there first and then show up."

She watched me warily. "How am I gonna get in?"

I went to my backpack. I really did need to get rid of it and carry only the briefcase. Huntington had given me two keys. "Here." I handed her one. Her eyes flew wide. She backed away.

"Don't mark it. Don't tell your husband. Like I said, one chance. You can clean this apartment out of furniture and every scrap in it, but then you'll be where you are today. No job, no safety. Keep the key safe, and maybe it will be worth it."

"I ain't no thief."

She probably wasn't allowed out of sight often enough to be a thief. "I am trying to convince you that it isn't worth it to become one. I gather your husband does enough illegal stuff for the both of you." I had about a hundred dollars in my backpack. I took it out. "Here's some money. You must have the car today. Let's get the grocery and cleaning supply list going, and you can use the money for that." There was an ATM in the building. I would have to get more cash to pay her for the cleaning. "You get the supplies today. Do you have time to clean?"

She looked panicked.

"Never mind. Get the supplies. Come clean when you have the time. I'll pay you the eighty as an advance on the cleaning."

"I...I don't know when exactly I can come," she spit out hurriedly, ignoring the money. "But I'll be here. You just don't make me go to no counselor or cops or nothing, okay? Every time I go to one of those, he gets mad. Real mad."

I shrugged. One step at a time. "I can't fix your problems, Marilyn. If you want some kind of help, ask me for it. Right now all I can arrange is this. Maybe someday you'll clean enough houses you can make your own future."

Her eyes shut down again. The future wasn't a place she visited often.

Chapter 25

The rest of the week was one big muddle. We still had projects due, and now that I was boss, I had to write up the final reports. Turbo was an excellent engineer, but his reports were lengthy and almost impossible for anyone non-technical to understand. Truthfully, I don't know who had cleaned them up before. It certainly wasn't Allen because he wouldn't know what to cut and what to leave in. Or maybe he hadn't bothered to do any progress reports.

On Wednesday afternoon, Paul stopped by with his report. It clearly said that he was turning his stuff in on time, but when I pulled Ross' original schedules, they showed the project was supposed to have been finalized three months earlier.

"Hey, wait a minute." I stopped him from leaving. "Your report says you are on time, but the original--"

"Note the questions that were added after the project was assigned." He stepped back in, flipped a few pages and handed the report back to me.

The test requirements and questions on the list were basic. "Paul, anyone with half a brain would know we had to answer these questions when it was first assigned."

He shrugged. "Not my problem. I didn't do the schedules. That would be your job." He stomped out.

On Thursday, Ross left me a message wanting to know if I had cleared the schedule because we were going to have to talk about it in staff on Monday. Patrick sent no less than four notes trying to get out of the Mamba project, all of which I politely replied to, making sure that he knew I wasn't taking it. After the fourth note, Gary sent an irritated reply asking to be removed from the email trail. Implicit was the warning that we have it settled by Monday.

"Impossible," I muttered. We had fourteen projects scheduled in the next six months. It was already the end of June. The team would barely be able to finish the six already assigned if all went well--and it never did. I sent Ross a message and told him to sell one of the customers on getting something extra, but having to wait for results. I also copied Patrick on the seven projects not yet covered. Then I sent a message to Gary and told him we needed an entire new team, and mentioned that I would be glad to head it up and handle the budget for it.

When I got fired, I would teach a class on the most effective way to get noticed and summarily dismissed.

Marilyn showed up to clean in the evening. The place needed it so I wasn't going to complain. The arrangement wasn't ideal, however. What if I needed her not to come? What if I really, really needed the place cleaned? I didn't have any idea how to reach her unless I asked Derrick where she lived. I may as well arrest myself for harboring a witness and save him the trouble.

"Looking good," I told her when it became obvious she knew what she was doing. I retreated to the study rather than follow her around. Maybe Marilyn's mother had taught her how to clean before Marilyn ran off with Ted the loser. I still feared that one day I'd come back and half my stuff would be missing. Luckily it was mostly Huntington's stuff. I didn't know if I would have been so generous if it was my real home.

That made me wonder how she had found me in the first place. "Hey Marilyn," I called out from the study, "How did you find out where I lived?"

She didn't answer for a minute. I went to the doorway to find her dusting the kitchen bar.

She didn't look up, but said, "County tax record."

That was interesting. And of all the people that Huntington was trying to fool when he "sold" me the condo, Ms. Harrison wasn't even in the running. "How did you know to look there?"

"Used to work in the courthouse."

"Oh. Guess your husband didn't like you working there." She didn't answer. I shook my head and went back to sorting my bills. How did one go from having a job to letting some freak run your life? Since I didn't expect her to say anything else, I almost missed what she said next.

"I was only sixteen. Wasn't supposed to be working there when I met him. My mom lied so I could get the job."

I was twenty-six. She looked older than me. Just how long had she been putting up with the beatings? I went back to the doorway. "Your husband made you quit?"

"He said I didn't have to work. He would take care of me." She glanced up. "I didn't want to go back home. Mom had enough problems."

I didn't want to know what they were. "Did he hit--did he always treat you like he does now?"

"Nah. He didn't hit me until a couple of years ago." She moved around to the kitchen table and checked it for dust and then began sweeping. "Only a little and not like now. Hardly at all, you know?"

No, I didn't know. Just an occasional slap here and there that had over the years turned into a life-threatening situation. I was saved from an answer when the doorbell rang. It wasn't the buzzer from downstairs, so it had to be Huntington. Michael or one of his cohorts always announced all the other visitors. Huntington just popped up of his own accord.

Trying to act nonchalant, I answered the door. "Huntington." I didn't get out of his way.

He waved Chinese food at me. "I brought dinner. We need to discuss our lack of progress."

It wasn't my fault I looked so wholesome no one had crawled out of the woodwork and offered me illegal deals. "Oh. Well. Now isn't a good time." There was probably no real harm in Huntington meeting my cleaning lady, but we couldn't sit and chat business with her around.

He moved forward. I had no choice but to make a scene or back up.

"Did you bring enough for three?" I asked. "Marilyn is here today. Remember, uh, we talked about cleaning."

He paused in the living room. "I think Michael mentioned you had a visitor. There's plenty."

Marilyn stood in the dining area, looking like a trapped animal. I gave a mental sigh. "Can you set three plates?" I asked her. "Grab whatever you want to drink. I'll get a diet soda. Huntington likes that mineral water stuff that's under the bar."

Huntington put the takeout on the table. It was from the same place as before. It was good stuff, and they weren't shy with the portions. I wasn't certain that Marilyn would eat a thing, but that wasn't going to stop me from offering. She was skinny enough to be classified as anorexic.

She set the table, all the while stealing looks in my direction, begging me to let her out of this. No way. I smiled at her and took my seat. "Do you like Chinese?"

She shook her head in instant denial.

"Oh," I stood up, "then I'll make you a sandwich."

For a moment, she stood in indecision. I thought she might run for the door, but then she sat with a whoosh. "No, no, I like it."

"You sure?"

She almost got up enough nerve to glare at me, but dropped her eyes to the plate instead.

Huntington ignored us both and served generous portions of steamed rice and stir-fried vegetables with beef. There was also a container of hot pepper shrimp that was delicious enough to put any woman off her diet. "Where do you get this?" It was hard to talk around my mouth full of food.

"Happy Family Chinese. It's two blocks over on Tinnet."

I grinned at Marilyn, and then had to nudge her under the table to get her to look at me. She jumped. I thought she might go for the door again. "Make a note of it. I might add it to the grocery list."

She stared at me without answering. I doubt she had heard Huntington at all. Maybe she was worried about dropping rice on her lap. Maybe she just lived in fear all the time.

Dinner was less than entertaining. Marilyn sat hunched over waiting for disaster. When I was finally more than full, I dragged Huntington towards the study. I shooed him into the other room and bounced back into the kitchen. "If you need to stay here, just hang out until he leaves," I whispered.

She shook her head. "No, no. I'm going now. Soon." Her face hadn't looked that great when she showed up. Now it looked a little green and quite panicked.

"Marilyn." I waited until she looked up. "It isn't a big deal. Just hang out if you need to."

Her unease kept her still. She didn't have any nervous habits, at least not visible ones. "I don't really need to stay here tonight." Her eyes darted to the study door, but it was still securely closed. "Is your boyfriend going to stay?"

I nearly choked. Granted, I had been friendlier with Huntington than ever before, but I was trying to make everyone feel at home. "No!" More quietly, I repeated, "No. We just have some work stuff to go over."

She nodded with her eyes back on the floor. "I don't need a place. I'm almost done."

I hoped she meant with the cleaning, not her life. "Take the leftover Chinese food if you want it."

She didn't bother to answer.

Instead of putting her through the agony of making an excuse, I scurried back to the study before Huntington could get too suspicious. He ignored me when I entered. He had taken the only chair, the big leather one at the desk. "We're going to need more furniture if we're going to be working in here," he said.

Cool. I had been wondering how to broach the subject. He had walked right into it. "Yeah, I was thinking it could use a bed." If Marilyn ever did decide to trust me enough to stay, she needed a better place to sleep than the couch.

He obviously wasn't pleased with the trap because his mouth worked a few times before he managed, "A bed?"

"Sure!" I flourished my arm in my best Vanna White imitation. "A bed over in this corner and maybe an easy chair to sit in." I bounced over to the spot for the chair. "And I hate that chair you're in. Something a little less ostentatious and practical would look better. Then the recliner and bed will fit into the room and be comfortable and cozy."

He blinked and opened his mouth again. His face got red, a total over-reaction to a relatively inexpensive shopping request. "If you just buy a double bed, there will probably be room for a dresser too. A twin would work though if you want to save money."

"Were…you planning on us discussing business in the cozy bed or the comfortable chair?"

My mouth fell open. I reviewed the conversation. Maybe it hadn't been such a great time to bring up my plans after all. "Uh…" My face flamed, almost matching his reaction.

He swiveled around in the chair, his blue eyes studying me and then the room. "Then again, I can see where it might improve things."

The room was suddenly way too warm. "Uh--"

From the kitchen, Marilyn turned on the dishwasher.

"I could be persuaded to your way of thinking." There was a definitely happy sparkle in his eyes. I wasn't sure if he was teasing me or just laughing at the situation.

"I was actually planning a sort of guest room look," I squeaked out.

He stroked his chin, focused on me completely now. His eyes were very blue. "Really."

"Really," I said. "To, you know, perk..." I stopped breathing because I was just making things worse.

For a moment I think he was holding his breath, but then he spun the chair back to the desk.

From the kitchen, the pantry door closed.

I was very quiet. Speechless in fact. He looked up at me after a moment. "Maybe a queen bed." He smiled, a cat thinking about a mouse. "Maybe all this shopping of yours will take my mind off the fact that we just lost another load of equipment."

I sucked in much needed air. "Equipment?" I was at a distinct disadvantage, not sure about the strange tingling in my fingertips that was probably due to lack of oxygen. I stayed in my spot way at the other end of the room.

"Of course a bed isn't likely to get stolen. We could keep a close eye on it." He glanced over at me and laughed out loud. "I'll see about the bed. Never hurts to be prepared."

I rolled my eyes heavenward and prayed for deliverance.

He dug papers out of his briefcase. "I came over to let you know that more equipment went missing after the conference. Equipment that was supposedly ordered for demonstrations that wasn't needed. Turbo happened to notice there was enough stuff to give about five extra demonstrations."

It took me a minute to change my train of thought, but it didn't take me long to figure out the equipment he was referring to. "It can't be missing! I saw all that stuff..." I thought hard. "It was still there on Wednesday...no Thursday." I had gone back to check. There had been lots of boxes back there.

"You saw it? What about Friday?"

I shook my head. "I don't know. The break down was scheduled for Friday. I left Friday morning, but I didn't go back to the ballroom before leaving." I raised empty palms. "I saw no need to. I only went back there the second time--"

He waited. I stared at him, wondering if it mattered. There was no reason not to tell him. "I was back there the first time on Monday." I told him about Kathy's accident. "I went back because I couldn't figure out how she hit her head, but there was nothing suspicious back there. I heard someone else back there on Monday, but it could have been anyone looking for replacements. I thought at the time that it was Turbo, but it couldn't have been because he had already been sent back. The boxes were still there on Thursday."

Huntington tapped a pen against the desk. "Those stacks definitely disappeared. There was enough extra stuff for five or six demos."

"Are you sure it's those specific boxes? Maybe it was other stuff that went missing, things from the actual demonstrations."

"I gave Turbo a copy of everything that was ordered for the demonstrations. Since he and Bruce were setting things up, I figured they could keep track. Most of the missing stuff was the stuff that was unused, and there was a lot of it."

Turbo was good with details. He probably counted the screws. "So where did the stuff go? How did someone get to Allen?"

Huntington pulled more documents out of his briefcase. "I don't know. My guess is that Allen isn't the one still stealing from the ballot box."

"It could be Allen," I said, thinking of him sending Turbo and Bruce back. Then, I shook my head. "Or anyone, dammit." The extra equipment had been stacked behind Dan's partition. He'd been wheeling and dealing, but in all fairness, I couldn't see him hand-selling heavy boxes of hard drives to someone willing to slip him some cash. He certainly could have told someone where the equipment was waiting--but for that matter, even Kathy could have supplied that information. Anyone that walked behind the partitions could have seen it. But how did they get the stuff out of the conference without anyone seeing?

Huntington handed me a sheet that listed equipment.

I found my own demo equipment on the list easily enough. Two servers were circled and fifty disk drives. I hadn't needed that many disk drives. I never would have known there were extras at all if one hadn't died. I scanned the other demos while Huntington explained the bad news.

"Looks like the folks behind this scheme have already found another contact, and it isn't you. They managed to pad the equipment order without any trouble. Maybe they were working on finding a replacement for Allen before we got wind of the scheme."

"But Allen or Gary or someone still has to sign off on this stuff!"

Huntington shrugged. "Allen is in this thing up to his neck. He was getting a cut from the charity thing already and even more money once he started cashing checks on his own. His signature or lack thereof doesn't mean a thing unless we can prove he is pocketing the money."

In disgust, I looked through the expense report, adding up numbers in my head. I didn't know exact prices, but there were thousands of dollars worth of equipment marked as missing. The end of the list contained line items for other conference expenses. The conference itself was an enormous cost with the hotel fees, food, travel expenses and extras. My eyes nearly popped out of my head when I saw that a big decorated cake with Strandfrost's name, logo and miniature candy computers had cost seven hundred dollars. The missing equipment money was simply swallowed inside the sheer number of items.

I almost skipped over the miscellaneous section, but one of the items caught my attention. "Who is Debra Honel of Signs Inc?" I asked. All of the signs had to be done long before the conference--not at the conference like the charge implied. That fact probably wasn't obvious to Huntington, but I recalled the banners. Most of them were heavy-duty plastic and large enough to stretch several feet. Those things didn't get done overnight.

He pulled the papers back from me. "Her?" he found the listing. "I have no idea, why do you ask?"

I answered slowly. "No big deal." I didn't want to sound paranoid, and I'd already looked like an idiot quite enough. Still, I was curious. I got a pen and paper from my backpack and wrote her name and business down along with the cake company, "Catering for You." There was another one called, "Superior Presentations" that looked funny to me. As far as I knew, every one of us did our own presentations, so I couldn't imagine why Strandfrost might be billed by an outside company.

Luckily, I knew just the person that could tell me about these services and probably in more detail than I actually needed.

Chapter 26

First thing in the morning I went to visit Sally. I had to wait until she got off the phone, but when it was my turn, I asked, "Do you know a Debra Honel that does signs for Strandfrost?"

"Signs? I don't know about that, but she sits down on six, I think."

"Marketing?"

Sally laughed. "No, silly. She's an admin, like me. Why?"

An administrative assistant. What was she doing charging for signs? Maybe there was a mistake. Maybe she had ordered the signs and her name was down for the business. "I dunno. Do you ever use "Catering for You" or "Superior Presentations?"

Again she nodded, but this time she leaned forward. "I think Debra uses that caterer." She wrinkled her nose. "And I'm pretty sure Superior Presentations is run by a buddy of Dan's. You know those good old grabby boys hang together."

"The guy from Superior Presentations grabbed you?" I was aghast. Just how many pigs were running through these hallways anyway?

"Oh no. I've never met him. I just know he works with Dan. I get requests from Dan for their work all the time. They do some sort of setup for the conferences."

"What about the catering place? Have you ever used them?"

"I can look it up." She pulled up the expense reports. "I've heard the name before...I think I did get it from Debra...Here it is." She smiled. "Yup, looks like I set something up for the Tamarron conference."

"Do you remember what you ordered?"

"Frankly I don't remember ordering this stuff at all, but I did a lot of stuff for different people." She thought about it. "The hotel could have called it in. Or they could have needed something and just tacked it on the end. Allen signed it. Maybe they had him sign it at the conference."

Yeah maybe. Maybe not.

I wandered down to the sixth floor and scanned offices until I found Debra.

"Hi, I'm Sedona O'Hala. I was wondering if you could help me order some signs."

"Sedona? The one that beat up those intruders? Cool!" She was younger than me by several years, probably just out of high school. She was shorter and rounder also.

"Well, uh, I guess."

"Signs? What kind of signs?"

"Oh well, I saw that you did some ordering for the Tamarron conference. I thought maybe you could give me the contact name." The paperwork actually said she was owner of the business that got paid, but I didn't think telling her that was a good idea.

She shrugged. "Sure. But you have to order at least six to eight weeks ahead. These people are not fast." She pulled out a folder and extracted a sheet. "Let me run a copy. These are all in town, and the first two will expedite."

She walked to the copier with me and gave me a copy. "Do you want me to look up the Tamarron stuff? See who did the stuff?"

I scanned the list she gave me. There wasn't anyone close to a Debra Honel on there. "No, that's okay. For some reason, I thought there was a sign company that we used that had your name on it. Thought maybe you were related or something."

She grinned. "Nah, not that I know of. That first guy is the best one as far as I'm concerned. If any of my relatives go into the business, I'll let you know!"

I hurried out before she could ask me any more questions.

Back at my office, I left Huntington a page. He called me back, but since talking over the phone wasn't a good idea, he said he would stop by the condo again. I could have complained about the intrusion, but in all honesty I didn't have plans. That kind of annoyed me. I needed to beef up my private life. As in, get one.

This time he didn't bring dinner, but Marilyn had gotten groceries, so I started browning hamburger for a casserole. I was going to miss her when this was over. Having her around to do the shopping was a fabulous perk.

Since Huntington was getting impatient, I explained while I cooked. "That sign company on the list you showed me looked out of place so I asked around. I actually found a Debra Honel, but she doesn't do signs. She's an admin at Strandfrost. A couple of other businesses on there don't make much sense either." I set the table. "Do you have that list you brought with you last time?"

He got up and grabbed it out of his briefcase.

I showed him the names of the companies. "Superior Presentations might be legitimate. Dan could be using them to do his presentations. I didn't want to dig too deep there because Dan wouldn't tell me if the building were on fire." I pointed to the next one. "Sally didn't actually order any catering. Even if she had there is no reason for the resort to have sent a separate catering bill. If they hired an outside caterer, they would add their own slice to it and bill it so it would be a charge going to the hotel expense, not to an outside caterer."

He stared at the list. "Any of the others?"

I shrugged. "Those were the only ones that I noticed. I have no idea what all those businesses are or if they are real. All I know is that an outside caterer doesn't make sense and, hang on, I'll get you the list of the companies that Strandfrost really uses to do signs."

I dug out the list while Huntington grabbed his cell phone.

He was already talking by the time I handed him the list. "There's a quick way to check on these," he informed me.

I wandered back and forth between the kitchen and the table. The casserole was done long before he was, so while I waited for him to finish checking his sources, I started eating.

By the time he got off the phone I was almost done. "I could ask around some more at work," I offered.

He started shoveling food into his mouth. Around his dinner, he explained, "Yeah, but I wanted to do some additional tracking." He continued eating, attacking his food in place of an invisible enemy. "There is a Debra Honel, just as you said, but she is the only one that even remotely exists. There is no sign company anywhere in the United States named after her."

I got up, cleared my plate and started making cookie dough while he talked.

He kept eating, but worked his way down a checklist. "There is a business listing for a Catering for You, but I talked to the manager at Tamarron. You were right--they don't bill for outside caterers. If they do have to use an outside source, the manager assured me that I would never know it as a customer, unless I asked."

"Wow. So who billed Strandfrost?"

Huntington rubbed his chin, watching me mash butter and sugar together. It looked like cooking therapy would do him good, but I was worried about my bowl getting smashed so I didn't ask for his help.

"It gets worse," he grumbled, crushing one of the papers in his fist and throwing it at the balcony door. "I went over the conference charges with the Tamarron manager. There were several things listed that don't look legitimate. I'm going to have to check every single vendor listed as part of that conference." He looked at me like it was my fault.

"Hey," I protested, "I just thought I'd find out whether Miss Debra did signs."

"Why in the world would anyone use her name in the first place?"

I dumped flour into my mix and stirred vigorously. "Looked to me like anyone studying the bill would just assume Debra ordered the signs. Her name in the company field would look like an innocent typo. Of course with her name in the wrong spot, it would be hard to figure out exactly who got paid." I patted out a few cookies and put them in the toaster oven.

"My question for you is, if you're so good at noticing things, why didn't you notice this at the conference when it might have done some good? For that matter, you might have noticed that equipment for several demos just disappeared!"

I dusted flour off my hands and glared right back at him. "The equipment was there. I saw it. So did Kathy. Maybe not all of it, but a lot of it was still there on Thursday when I checked."

Huntington began pacing. "They order it ahead of time. It shows up, but no one needs it. It gets piled out of the way. Someone very helpfully takes it out of there. When everything comes home, no one even knows it is missing because they never needed it in the first place."

"Maybe whoever I heard behind the partition wasn't someone taking a hard drive or two like I was--maybe it was someone rounding up the extra equipment not in use. Put it all in one place for easier stealing." I frowned. "But that doesn't tell us how they get it out of the conference, no matter where it is. Maybe they haul it out at night?"

Huntington shook his head. "They can't get it out at night. The place has security."

"They can't walk it out of there one hard drive at a time!" I thought about it. "But there are guys coming and going all the time. I saw a couple with small dollies, but I think they were caterers."

"Did they have boxes?"

I hesitated. "I saw them bring boxes in. They unloaded boxes of donuts every morning. I don't think I saw anyone go out and certainly not with anything as large as a server, but I was there doing actual work--watching my own stuff, getting ready and so on. It's possible they took some things out during the conference."

Pacing back into the living area Huntington asked, "So just how much money are these people making off of us?"

The stacks of boxes behind Dan's setup represented a healthy amount of equipment and there easily could have been other stacks around the perimeter. "My guess is a lot. And my guess is that Allen figures you haven't found all the areas he's been milking. Or," I tapped my foot quickly, "he isn't the one that is milking this particular cow. The only time management pays a whole lot of attention to attendees is when money is running short. Then they cancel people like lab technicians, not actual demonstrations."

Huntington stared at me. "They cancel people like you if you had been in your old position."

"Well, yes." I turned back to check on my cookies, but they were still soft and gooey in the center.

"Seems to me that since you know so much about how this all works, you could be a little more useful in finding evidence against the culprit," he said. "You get the perks out of the company, and you can't even con a single thief into approaching you."

"Hey, this wasn't my idea! And frankly, nice as this place is, I'd still move back to my own. I don't really care about all your--"

"Right!" he shouted. "That's the reason you wanted to add furniture. Not enjoying yourself at all." He stomped to the door and flung it open. "Don't get too comfortable."

"I'd leave, believe me," I yelled after him, even though he shut the door before the words were out.

He was just mad that Strandfrost had been taken for a bigger ride than he knew.

Chapter 27

Abba was expecting me Saturday morning. I lived through it and had bruises to show my parents on Saturday evening when they came through on their way back from Denver. They slept at my place, and we all trouped to church together on Sunday morning.

Mom beamed at Derrick the entire Mass. I didn't get in trouble for sighing, not once, because I was too exhausted. Between my various appointments and running between my real home and the condo, I was turning into a raving lunatic.

Monday's scheduling nightmare got a reprieve because Gary decided that we needed to discuss last minute preparations for the next company event. It had been in the works for a while, but no one had mentioned it to me.

I considered kicking Allen under the table, but what good would it do? Even though he was supposed to help me transition into the position, he was a man that under normal circumstances wouldn't care if I succeeded. Given that his ethics code allowed for pilfering from a charity, I was lucky he hadn't hired someone to run me over with a bus.

I scrambled to take notes and pretended I knew about the event, but my guts churned. Not a single person had bothered to copy me on a pertinent email. Looking around the room, it was obvious I didn't have any friends. Ross might have emailed me if he needed something specific, but Patrick, Allen and Dan excluded me on purpose. Gary would probably have told me, but when? Once the conference was set up, he probably answered individual issues, but he wasn't detailed enough to think about his new manager needing information about a project that had been on tap for a while.

I tried not to panic, but it was hard. Even if this job wasn't quite real, I didn't have any desire to look like a complete idiot.

Luckily the event was in town, held at the Whispering Pines Resort. After all day presentations Tuesday, the sales and marketing teams would handle personal customer meetings the rest of the week for any of the guests that wanted custom demos or specific financial negotiations. Of course Strandfrost would be helping them enjoy Denton the whole week by making sure they had golf passes and other amenities.

I counted my blessings that at least I wouldn't have to travel.

Dan spoke up. "I think we should offer that chauffeur service from the airport that I told you about last week. Maybe meet a few of the clients either in the evening for dinner or for breakfast depending on when they are flying in. This is our territory. Let's show them some VIP treatment, let them know we are glad they came out."

That would take care of his meals for the week and possibly the weekend. Good ole Gary just nodded his okay. "How many are we expecting?" Gary asked.

Dan ran through the numbers and the sales necessary to cover the expenses. He had already assumed the limo from the airport would be covered. I wondered why someone couldn't figure out that without the chauffeur service the company could keep more of the money it earned, but my job was to blend, not to point out waste.

I kind of wished that Huntington attended some of these meetings. If Huntington put a stop to the all the skimming, Strandfrost wouldn't even have to catch the bad guys to come out ahead.

After the meeting broke up I went in search of Sally. She was on the phone, but waved me in. First thing I spotted when I sat down was a box tucked behind her filing cabinet. The top was opened and t-shirts peeked out. "For the conference?" I mouthed so as not to disturb whoever was on the other end.

She nodded. If no one was going to help me, I'd just have to help myself. This time I'd have freebies to hand out. Since Sally looked pretty planted on the telephone, I took as many shirts as I could carry and left a note asking for an extra pass to the conference in Suzy's name. Suzy would get a kick out of attending. Her husband was an engineer at Strandfrost, so he probably could have gotten her a ticket, but he tended to forget about these things, and he rarely attended himself.

I called Suzy and told her about the conference. "Free meals. Swimming. You can probably bring Jimmy."

"Are you kidding? It would be wasted on him! We're talking a day in the sun!"

"Great. See you there." I hung up with a triumphant smile. I could throw favors around at company cost, just like Dan. Well, almost. One extra conference pass wasn't going to cost Strandfrost very much, and no one had asked me to do the deed. Real thieves wouldn't be too impressed.

My happy moment disappeared. I had a conference to prepare for. At least we had the proper equipment for the demo. Unless it had been stolen.

I marched over to Turbo's office to make sure we had what we needed, and that he and Bruce could help with the setup. I felt marginally better when it became apparent that he hadn't known about the event either.

"I can't believe no one said anything to you either. Who is going to set up all the marketing and financing equipment?" We looked at each other for a heartbeat.

"Patrick," he said.

"Patrick's team," I said. "Allen and Dan must have asked him instead of me. I've been dealt completely out again," I moaned.

"I better call Huntington," Turbo said. "If Bruce and I aren't doing all the setup, it's going to be harder to keep track of the equipment."

I nodded. I hadn't ordered anything because I hadn't even known about the event. It would be interesting to find out whether anyone else had a special order. "We'll have to see what stuff shows up and whether it all gets returned." This time, I wasn't going to miss any fat piles of equipment, no matter what happened. And I'd do the demo too, just to prove to the fat, happy suits around this place that I could handle the job.

Chapter 28

Since the conference was in town, I was able to take my time the next morning. According to the pass card and rule sheet that Sally had given me, I could have stayed at the resort, but I was already losing my identity by trying to live in two places. I managed to squeak into the conference in time for free breakfast.

Bruce was already at my booth, struggling with the setup. Since Turbo wasn't around, I helped.

It turned out that the pins on one of the cables was bent, and without a proper connection, the external storage was flashing like a frantic Christmas tree. This was not the type of reliability that customers wanted to see, so Bruce went off to find a cable that wasn't damaged. It would give him a good excuse to look around for extra equipment.

Unfortunately, that left me with a half working machine, which made me more nervous than I already was. I reminded myself that my first job was to put on a front. I decided to read through my notes to settle myself down.

Fretting about the conference all day yesterday must have destroyed my brain, because when I turned to locate my briefcase, I saw my backpack. The old me had no need for a briefcase, but the new me did, and that was where I left my notes--in the condo, in the briefcase. "Uh-oh." I looked at my watch. If I left to get my notes, I'd be late and completely miss giving the first presentation. If I didn't have the notes, I'd have to bumble through it, and the setup was already hanging by a thread.

I tried calling Suzy to see if she could run by the condo on her way here, but she didn't answer her phone.

Right before jumping into the SUV, I remembered Marilyn and the fact that she had a key. I didn't have her phone number. I had no right to call. But she could be planning on coming by to clean or deliver more groceries, right?

Probably not. It hadn't even been a week. Well, it had been a week since the grocery trip. I thought long and hard about it. In a lot of ways it would be easier to just leave her to her own decisions, even if her life was a mess.

I called information. They had a number for Ted Harrison.

If she didn't answer or worse, if Ted did, I'd act like a solicitor. I wasn't far from being one anyway.

She picked up after two rings. "Marilyn, it's me, Sedona. Can you talk?"

"Ye--es." Her voice was just as tentative over the phone as in person.

I explained rapidly about the briefcase. "Do you have the car today? If you run it by here, I'll throw in an extra twenty," I promised.

The bribe probably wasn't necessary. She was such a nice person, she would have done it without any pushing. "I was going out to run errands anyway," she said.

"Excellent! If I'm not out front, leave it with the front desk." If she didn't make it in time, I'd still be free to fake my way through the first presentation and collect my notes for later.

I checked my watch on my way back into the conference room. Marilyn should just make it. Things didn't really get started until nine-thirty. I could probably delay even a little longer.

I looked up in time to see Autumn arrive on Dan's arm. I couldn't imagine why she bothered to attend the conferences, but maybe it was her only chance to see Dan. More likely than that, it was a chance to hobnob with the bigwigs. She headed straight for Huntington, flying past Bruce as if he didn't exist. Apparently she had figured out that Bruce was only hired help.

Rather than watch her bat her eyelashes at the various fish in the ocean, I wandered over to the buffet table. At the donuts, I found Suzy. "Hey, couldn't you have come to see me first? I just tried to call you."

Suzy had a smear of chocolate on the corner of her mouth, which she enthusiastically licked off. "I checked my purse in at the front desk so I can swim later, and I forgot to get my phone out. I was getting a donut to bring to you."

Since she had two in her hand, it was probably true. Whether she would have been able to actually find me before eating them both was another story.

I helped myself to the one on top and grabbed a plate for extras. "I need some for Bruce and Turbo when he shows. Want to see the booth?"

She shrugged, not all that interested in high-level technology. Her interest started and ended with resort amenities and maybe some of the booth freebies-- not unlike a number of conference attendees come to think of it.

We wandered back to my booth anyway. I started to give her one of the free t-shirts I had snagged, but couldn't decide on the size.

She laughed. "Make it a large, and I'll give it to Robert. He can always wear it. If I keep eating like this, I won't fit in it even after the pregnancy." She beamed, the thought not bothering her overmuch.

Huntington walked over our way with Autumn trailing along.

I eyed the other chocolate donut on the plate greedily. Autumn wasn't nearly as slim as I, but she made up for it by hiding any sign of fat underneath her boobs. If men never looked past your cleavage, you didn't have to worry about a few extra pounds. Since I didn't have that large a benefit, I left the donut.

Huntington didn't actually speak to me; he just checked out the booth and Autumn. She gushed about some company or other and, to my surprise, it sounded like she might be working the sale of a printing service. That would explain her enthusiasm for attending these events.

"--individual deals, individual attention--nothing but the best," she told Huntington. "Come by my office. I'll have some free samples printed up--business cards, announcements, whatever you need." She pointed to a small logo on her shirt, right over her left boob. "This is one of my designs--notice how clearly it printed even on cloth."

Huntington caught me rolling my eyes. He grinned.

I picked up the donut and considered how much toilet paper I might need in order to look as "printable" as she did. The good news was that I wouldn't have to unroll the paper. I'd need the whole roll, so I could just shove two up my blouse without wasting any time unwinding.

Turbo showed up. He managed to greet me before Autumn, but just. Autumn smiled at him like he was a hundred dollar bill. I wanted to make a snipe about overdressed, needy women, but her make-up was minimal and her blond tresses looked natural too. She had a vulnerable quality about her, like she needed Huntington's business and wanted Turbo's help.

I took a huge bite out of a second donut and pushed around Bruce. There was no point in manning the booth at the moment. Turbo could answer any technical questions and Huntington, if he could peel his eyes from Miss Congeniality, could answer any company questions. One of them might notice a server being carried out, if we were lucky.

I beckoned Suzy and was almost free of the tangle when Huntington called after me. "Sedona, things are looking good here."

"Uh-huh." I still had part of the donut in my mouth and used it as an excuse to mumble. "I'll be back. I gotta go buy some Nerf balls."

Turbo must have heard me because he frowned.

Suzy grinned. "Pregnancy works too, you know." She waved at the boys and pushed her chest out as far as she could without toppling over backwards. She slipped her arm through mine and giggled. "I didn't know you had a new employee."

"We don't. She's dating one of the financial guys."

"Shouldn't I have guessed that?" She batted her eyes playfully. We headed back to the buffet table for juice and coffee. The crowds were picking up. I got nervous again.

Suzy noticed the milling people about the same time that I did. "Hey, I have to go start signing up for the freebies at the other booths. Are you coming?"

"No, I should get back to the booth. I'm supposed to start presenting at nine or so, but lots of people show up early to get the t-shirts. Sign me up for the free trip to Paris though." Technically I wouldn't be allowed to win, but that had never stopped me from entering.

Suzy waved as she started away. "I've got a date with the pool as soon as it warms up outside. I'll check back with you later."

It was a long day after that. Marilyn got my notes to the front desk sometime after the first hour. I was grateful because I could stutter less. When Gary stopped by the booth, I tried to talk him into getting some fluffy, baseball-sized balls with the company logo on them as free giveaways. He thought it was a fine idea. I didn't tell him the logos wouldn't show up under my bra, but hey, I was catching on to the management thing. The idea was to suggest things that somehow benefited me personally, like Dan and his free restaurant meals.

When the crowds thinned at lunchtime, I popped behind the partitions. I promptly ran into Turbo.

"What are you doing back here?" he asked.

"Looking for equipment. What are you doing?"

"Watching the equipment. Don't worry. We've got it staked out. No one is going to take it without us catching them. We've added some extra stuff to see if it gets moved anywhere special."

"Mm." The large box of equipment behind my partition must be one such item, otherwise he wouldn't have been making the rounds to check on it.

He waved me back to the front of the booth.

I went, but not for the first time, it occurred to me that Turbo had the better end of this job.

Luckily, Suzy came back by. She dragged me outside to the pool. I went willingly since it wasn't likely anyone was going to be interested in a demo for at least another hour. There was no point in going hungry.

"I just spent a hour out here swimming. Do you think I lost enough weight to eat lunch again?"

"You already ate?"

"Mm. Someone came by with snacks. Does that count?"

The pool really was a dream. There was a buffet table setup outside, and we showed our badges and sampled the goodies. Down another level on the lawn, there were BBQ pits. The smell of grilled hamburgers was very tempting. Suzy settled for picking through the various pastas, and I got myself a grilled chicken sandwich.

No one had bothered to approach me with any suggestions of clandestine meetings. I did have three offers for dinner from various male clients, which I went over in great detail with Suzy.

Gary found us poolside before I was finished eating. "Can you take one of the limos and pick up a couple more clients at the airport?" He looked at his watch. "They were due in at one, but I've got something else going."

I was disappointed that I couldn't chat more with Suzy, but she ushered me off good-naturedly. "Don't worry about me! I've been to these things with Robert before. He never has time to say boo to me. I'll just help myself to the buffet again and probably still be here later."

Feeling sorry for myself, I headed to the front of the resort. Dan was just getting ready to go to the airport. I watched with avid interest as the breeze tousled his hair. It was really hard to tell it was fake. Sadly, there was only one limo waiting outside. Since the limo driver was holding the door for him, I helped myself to the other side and slid into the car. He never said a word, so I didn't bother to make small talk either.

At the airport, I noticed with relief that there were two limos with drivers holding up signs for Strandfrost. I went over to one of the drivers, a short guy that looked about twelve years old. Hoping he really had a license to drive, I asked him about using the car for the return trip. "Hi, I'm Sedona. I'll be picking up some suits. Can we ride back with you?"

Solemnly he shook my hand. "Just call for Pablo. I'll be right here."

Good. I didn't want to ride back with Dan the schmoozer. He would probably do something illegal or unethical. Oh yeah, I was supposed to be watching for that.

Shrugging, I zipped into the baggage area and found Gary's clients. To my surprise, I recognized one of the guys standing with them. Gary had asked me to pick up Tony Preston and his partner, but Tony was talking to the head of Baxtell Solutions, our biggest customer.

I introduced myself, and we shook hands all around. The Baxtell guy was tall and distinguished with peppered hair. "I didn't know you were coming, but we're glad you could make it," I welcomed him.

Baxtell was completely at ease. "I wasn't coming in until next week. I had a personal demo set up, but my flight to Toronto got canceled. I was in the Atlanta airport when I ran into Tony and remembered the conference, so I grabbed the flight here with him."

"Excellent," I murmured. No way would Gary have sent me if he had known Baxtell was going to show up, but it worked well for me since I was supposed to be scrambling to get ahead. "Glad to have you."

Baxtell smiled in that executive way, as though his mind was on other things. Tony was a little more down to earth, but he was using his time wisely by discussing business with Baxtell.

I wasn't the only one that had spotted Baxtell. Dan practically ran over six people trying to get to us. "Timothy!" His long stride almost beat his welcoming hand. "What a surprise. We didn't think you were coming this week!" He slapped the older guy on the shoulder. "This is excellent. I've got a limo. Do you have reservations at the hotel already or do I need to set you up?"

"We took care of it from the air," Baxtell replied with a broad smile. "I brought Sissy with me. She's freshening up." He looked towards the club lounge door. "She'll be out in a minute."

"Great! Maybe she can ride back with Sedona, here. Sedona, how about you ride with Mrs. Baxtell and give her a line on what to do while she is visiting?"

"Sure, I'd love to." Dan the Weasel obviously wanted Baxtell all to himself. There was no point in starting a skirmish over it. I had little to say to the man unless he asked me a technical question and at his level, he would want to talk numbers.

We gathered the bags and stood around until Sissy finally sashayed out of the lounge. There was no doubt she was Baxtell's wife. The woman shouted money from one jeweled earring right through her upscale coiffure. I was surprised she was able to shake hands since the diamond on her left hand looked like it might weigh several pounds.

"I'm ready, dear. So sorry to keep you waiting." The apology was the equivalent of the absentminded patting of a poodle.

"I'm going to ride back with Dan and Tony," Baxtell informed her. "Sedona is going to give you all the info on the local color and make sure you have something to do. Where's dinner?" he asked Dan.

"Ah, I think the Cabin by the Woods is in order here," Dan replied, stepping up quickly to the automatic doors. He made a ridiculous show of holding them opened.

I didn't mention the huge expensive buffet being served at the resort. Apparently that wasn't good enough for Baxtell. Or maybe it wasn't good enough for Dan.

"Isn't that the restaurant that has all the wild game?" Baxtell looked pleased. "I like that place." He turned to his wife. "Don't worry Sissy, they have a wonderful seafood selection."

She sniffed. "We're out in the middle of the desert. Anything will do. I'm sure they'll have a simple Chicken Milanese or salad."

I had a feeling that Dan would be making a phone call to the restaurant to order the chicken Milanese and several salad choices.

As we trouped out to the limos, I felt bad for the guys that Dan had originally been sent to pick up. A Bob something or other and another guy named Ralph had almost been forgotten. Names weren't my strong point, but we chatted on our way out.

Bob asked me where I was from and I said, "Colorado, all my life."

"I like it here. Pretty."

"Yes, it is. The air is dry and clear."

"Doesn't the dry air bother your skin?" Mrs. Baxtell wanted to know. "You must have to hydrate more than once a week!"

I blinked. "Uh, sure, just part of the territory." If you included swimming, I guess I hydrated. I was pretty sure the resort had a full spa facility, but I was thinking of calling Angela, my hairdresser, and asking her where to find the best spa for Mrs. Baxtell. Dan seemed ready with all that kind of information, but he had been doing this a lot longer.

At the limo things got confused. There was a guy standing around talking to the limo guy I'd made arrangements with so the driver didn't immediately start grabbing bags. Dan used the opportunity to help load the luggage and before I knew it, I ended up in the car with Mrs. Baxtell, Tony and Ralph. Tony looked vaguely annoyed. Ralph didn't seem particularly bothered by the shuffle.

"How about some mineral water," I offered everyone. "The air in Colorado really is dry and plane flights don't help any."

"Oh, that would be lovely." Sissy took the bottle I handed her and helped herself to one of the glasses. Somewhere in the exchange, one of her fingernails got dinged. Part of the paint chipped the tiniest bit. "Dammit!" she exclaimed, inspecting the damage. "I told Margie this new paint wasn't very good. I wish she would be more careful in her selection." She glanced down at my hands.

Despite my new role, I had never painted my nails. "Oh dear," I mumbled, tucking my fingernails into hiding.

Ralph grinned.

Smart-ass. To change the subject, I brought up my own demo. "I'll be giving--"

Sissy wasn't done with her complaints, however. "My goodness, you need some powder, dear. Your face is a bit shiny, even in this light."

Okay, I let people have their shots now and again, but she didn't need to make it any more obvious that I was dirt. I put my own nose in the air and said, "Oh, after my modeling days, I just couldn't stand to wear powder. You know, it gets so caked on. Especially in the sunlight, powder makes it so obvious that you're wearing all that makeup. I'm lucky I don't really need it most of the time." I smiled my sweetest smile and stared right through her over-powdered face.

She didn't miss a beat. "You were a model too? I don't recall ever seeing you! I can't believe it." Her look conveyed her double meaning.

"I did most of my work in Canada," I lied. "Maybe if you traveled to Toronto a few years ago?" I had had my picture taken when in Canada, and it even made the paper. Never mind that it was because I took a wrong turn looking for a bathroom and ended up on a stage where some half-failed band was showing its stuff. The local paper just happened to be taking shots for the entertainment section.

"Mm, no I don't recall." She looked down her nose at me, the street urchin. "It's amazing that you wear your makeup the way you do, considering all the training models get. It hardly covers those fine lines."

"Yes, that's always been a problem. I laugh too much," I admitted more to Ralph and Tony than to her. I added enthusiastically, "I can't see any lines on your face at all, and at your age too. Did you have a face lift? Who did you use?"

Her face, lines and all, froze. She straightened her shoulders and shifted her perfect size thirty-six bosom out. "Hardly. I didn't need one. Although, if you need a recommendation for your nose, I can certainly ask my husband. One of his best friends is a surgeon." She smiled. "Maybe you could even model again if you had it scaled back a tad. Some people just get bigger features as they age."

"True. Will you have him work on your chin do you think? Do you like his work that much?"

Ralph looked like he might suffer from apoplexy any minute. Tony coughed and decided to help himself to some water after all. He swallowed a healthy slug of it and asked Ralph how things were in Maryland. "Weather still good?"

Ralph nodded and then looked kind of sly. "Yes, it's perfect. Not too humid and not too dry. We don't get too much direct sunlight so we don't have to worry about premature wrinkling."

Tony looked shocked and turned to the window either to choke or laugh.

Mrs. Baxtell didn't bother to answer my question. We had arrived at the resort anyway. The limo driver let the animals out of the cage. Dan must have called ahead because Huntington and Gary were waiting as well as the two other board members I had met before.

Mrs. Baxtell headed straight for her husband with her claws still out. "Oh dear," she called, giving his arm a quick squeeze in greeting. "Can you imagine? Sedona was a model. I couldn't believe it myself." Her sugar-coated voice didn't fool anyone. Ralph could have followed Tony up the steps, but he chose to stay and mingle. Might as well get his money's worth.

Baxtell was an important client. But I had learned a thing or two from watching the lovely Autumn. Men like women, and they like to be helpful. "It was so long ago, when I was just a teen," I said wistfully. "It was really nothing." I looked at Baxtell with all the hope of an abandoned kitten.

In obvious confusion, he looked from his wife to me and then magnanimously offered, "You are still stunning. I can see where the camera would have loved you."

I blushed, actually embarrassed at my own duplicity, but he couldn't have known that. "You're too kind. You're very lucky to be married to such a beautiful woman. I hope you have a lovely time."

Miss Sissy pressed her lips together. It looks really petty when you're bitchy if no one else is playing.

Huntington watched me much like a man might watch a time bomb.

"Let me know how you like the spa," I called after Sissy and made my exit up the stairs into the conference.

Ralph was grinning from ear to ear. He whispered, "Bravo," as I swished by. Tony hadn't even stayed to greet Huntington or Gary. I was guessing that he wasn't going to be a very good future customer after being summarily ignored and dumped by the wayside.

I got back to work at my booth. The afternoon flew by in a sea of faces and questions.

By the time I was ready to leave the conference, the limos were gone. Cinderella's ball looked a tad shabby. Instead of the carriages for the fine gentlemen and ladies, all that was left were dirty trucks and burly men waiting to take the equipment back to Strandfrost. Turbo had showed up for the breakdown. Bruce had disappeared. I hadn't seen Suzy again.

I wandered across the room and looked for leftovers on the buffet table, but the resort was thorough. They had already taken the magic tablecloths that never ran out of food. Underneath was nothing but scarred cafeteria tables.

I waved at Turbo and yelled, "Need any help with any of that?"

He glared at me, but I sashayed over and said much quieter, "Did the equipment get taken?"

He growled. "No."

"Do you think they know we were watching?"

He straightened from where he was undoing a cable. "I made sure no one would notice me." His answer was rather stiff. I guessed he was not only disappointed, but also wondering if his plan to sneak around hadn't been sneaky enough.

"I'll see you tomorrow."

He gave a half grunt.

I headed for home. Outside, the sunset was just fading, bouncing off all the trucks pulled up to load computers to take back to Strandfrost. I cooled my heels on the steps waiting for the valet to get the Mercedes. Out of the corner of my eye, I saw someone moving in my direction, almost jogging. Hoping it wasn't Gary or Huntington with some last minute chore, I turned.

When I got a clear look at the man, I panicked. "OhmyGod." Even though I had only seen him once, I knew who he was. *How had he found me?*

I ran, barely waiting for the automatic door to open before scooting inside. My morning, eons ago, came back full-force. I had called Marilyn.

Her husband, Ted, wife-beater loser that he was, must have followed her to the hotel. "OhmyGod." What had he thought? He must have staked the place out, watching the businessmen milling about and waited, trying to figure out whom she was meeting with. Instead of finding a lover, he got me. Unfortunately, he was bound to remember me from the meeting with Derrick and draw the loony conclusion that his wife had come here to give a statement.

"I'm dead. She's dead. Oh, bad, bad." Like a busy executive, one that was clearly deranged, I fled. I scurried through the lobby, looking over my shoulder as I turned the corner. Ted pushed past the doorman and stood still, waiting for his eyes to adjust to the dimmer light. Taking advantage of the unexpected boon, I zipped back into the ballroom. No one took much notice of me, except Turbo. He stood up and started over for the door right after he saw me slam it closed.

Most of the equipment movers were carting stuff out the back way. I peeked through the doors.

No Ted. There were several other doors along the ballroom wall that led into the room. I could close them all, but not before Ted, if he figured out my location, caught up.

"What are you doing?" Turbo asked.

I peered around Turbo's shoulder looking for escape routes. Would Ted follow me in or just wait for me to come back out? "Can you go check and see if my Mercedes is out front?" I squeaked.

Turbo opened the door wide. He looked out into the hallway. "There isn't anyone there. Oh wait, looks like the bellhop just went towards the elevator. Who are you running from?" He looked suddenly disapproving. "Remember," he whispered, "you're supposed to remain approachable by unsavory types. You never know who they might send to recruit you."

While that was true, and Ted was certainly unsavory, he was a wife beater and a drug dealer. He wasn't likely to question me about the latest computers on the market.

Turbo took my arm. "Do you want me to escort you out?"

I shook my head. "No. No, the car should be there by now. Thanks." I hurried back out, dawdling in case Turbo decided not to watch out for me.

When I checked over my shoulder, he was still watching patiently. He got an eyeful of me stepping behind a potted plant and peering into the lobby.

No Ted that I could see. Turbo followed, doing his own watching from behind the plant.

Like a little mouse, I made my way along the wall to the door. The damn doorman opened the door before I could peek out into the parking lot, but my Mercedes was right in front, so I sailed through and hopped in. The windows were tinted, but not enough that someone couldn't see through them. I didn't waste any more time.

Just as I drove off, I saw Ted in my rear view mirror running out the front door of the hotel. He looked both ways, but I pulled around another car that was waiting for its owner. I would have stepped on it and been gone, but a resort catering truck and one of the moving trucks blocked the lane out.

The doors were locked. Unless Ted got out a crowbar, I was probably safe. He hadn't seen me get into my SUV. At least I didn't think so.

I let out a huge breath as the bottleneck cleared. I eased into traffic, keeping an eye on the mirror the whole way, just in case.

Chapter 29

My hands had mostly stopped shaking by the time I opened the door to my apartment. Sadly, instead of a quiet, soothing peace, I found Huntington pacing in the condo. He reminded me of my father in some ways, bigger than life and full of energy. But where Dad's energy was focused internally, Huntington's was like a laser, centered wherever his eyes went, testing the walls of the condo, me, the air.

I wasn't afraid of him anymore, but that didn't mean I was happy to see him making himself comfortable at my temporary home. "Could you wait until I get home to barge in?" I grumbled. "Shouldn't you be with Baxtell and his lovely wife?"

He pivoted away from me, completing the circuit back to the balcony door. "Vic and Christopher have it covered. If anyone should have been at dinner with Baxtell, it would be you. Since you decided it wasn't worth your time, how could it be worth mine?"

Except he really was supposed to keep the customers happy, while I was just pretending. Baxtell needed people that could truly influence decisions. Huntington had set me up in a good position, but I still didn't have a real role.

"Baxtell probably isn't involved in the scam," I said.

"That's the problem!" Huntington paced back my way, his long legs making short work of the living room. He stopped in front of me. "Who is? No one has even attempted to bribe you. Why not? You're young, obviously vulnerable," he looked me up and down with the blue lasers of his eyes, "and...pretty. Why wouldn't they approach you?"

I sucked in a confused breath. Had he just called me pretty? "I don't think anyone has noticed me."

He reached out a hand and almost brushed back a lock of my messy hair. "Impossible."

I stared up at him, my briefcase suddenly too heavy. His eyes were a mixture of emotions; frustration, maybe a bit of anger...and a glint of...curiosity.

I was willing to bet my own eyes were pretty curious too. The backpack weighed me down from behind. It started to slide. I had to set my briefcase down to lower it. Our eyes broke contact, but my breathing was still shallow. I really didn't fit in his world. It was all just make-believe.

Without daring a glance back up, I headed for the kitchen. There was frozen cookie dough in the freezer, and boy was I in need of comfort food. I popped a set of four cookies into the toaster oven. "There's no reason for anyone to approach me. I don't have anything they want."

He stayed on the other side of the bar, but I could feel his eyes following me. "We've given you access to money, people, company assets. What are they waiting for?"

I licked dough from my fingers, until I noticed Huntington staring. I stopped, leaving my hand pressed against my lips. His eyes finally raised up to meet mine. Half of me wanted to step forward; the wiser half wanted to run.

"Are you done with that cookie dough?" he asked softly.

"Uh...um." I kept my eyes on his while I used the spoon to scoop some dough out of the container. Tentatively, I handed it to him--without going around the counter.

He took the spoon without breaking eye contact. Our fingers didn't touch.

I put the rest of the dough back in the freezer, and tried to remember what we were talking about. It had to do with work, I knew that. I had been hired to do a job, something to do with slimy Allen. "I might be a threat to Allen, but he's avoiding me entirely, hoping I don't get too many of his perks. Dan doesn't need me for anything. Since I can't do anyone any favors, essentially I'm powerless. Why would anyone buddy with me? They have nothing to gain." I rinsed my hands and dried them off while Huntington began pacing again.

"Whoever is looking to make money off of these deals doesn't know that. They should see an up-and-coming woman desperate to get ahead that is ripe for corruption!"

I didn't think now was a good time to tell him I hadn't been looking especially desperate. Eager to please might even be a stretch. "I haven't done anything corrupt. I haven't tried to fire anyone or get to the next job level or oust Allen or give anyone any reason to believe I'm in over my head."

He stopped and stared at me. "Why not?"

In confusion, I checked my cookies. They weren't done. "Well...because I guess...I haven't been. In over my head that is. The worst thing that has happened so far is that Allen has tried to make my life more difficult by not telling me things or sending people home. But I know how to run my own stuff so it isn't a big problem. You've made sure I have what I need. I haven't had to bargain or, uh, look desperate." This wasn't going well.

"Did you just ask me to yank your support?"

Even he couldn't believe my stupidity. I was having a hard time believing it myself. "No, I'm pretty sure that isn't what I said." But it was. Executives counted on owed favors to get what they needed. Huntington had created a high level position, but he handed it to me with everything I needed to get the job done: people, equipment, a budget and a salary. No one was going to come to me to get payback or favors. I didn't owe Gary, and I didn't owe Allen. While I probably should have tried harder to bargain with the other managers on the work that needed to get done, I hadn't bothered because I really didn't need to.

"You're unbelievable," he muttered. He opened the oven, tried to grab a hot cookie and burned his fingers. He cursed, yanked on the towel hanging by the stove and snatched the cookie again. Juggling the broken pieces, he slammed his way out of the condo.

Chapter 30

I was tired, confused and light-headed from a jumble of emotions, but the second Huntington left, I headed for the phone and started dialing.

Marilyn answered on the second ring. I barely had time to explain that her husband had seen me at the hotel before she muttered, "I'm fine," and hung up.

Sleep did not go well. If I had known where Marilyn lived, I'd have driven over there and kidnapped her. Plots to do just that mingled with dreams of people chasing me and me chasing something I couldn't see.

In the morning, Marilyn was still alive when I called before work. She hung up on me after telling me to quit calling.

With no real choice, I stopped calling, but I checked the internet at least five times when I got to work, looking for any domestic violence deaths.

I hadn't even gotten organized or interested in my real job when Huntington phoned. Lucky me, he caught me before the meeting to discuss the schedule of old clients and possible new clients from yesterday's event. Like a sitting duck, I was available to respond to his latest idea. Apparently he had spent the night thinking up plans for making me look like a bigger idiot.

"You need to throw a party. Invite the group, but specifically get Gary's staff to attend. I have a list of other people to invite too."

"A party," I repeated flatly.

"You have the place for it now. Let everyone see that you're living it up and that you need some extra money to support your new lifestyle. I picked up the Dodge Viper yesterday. At the party, you'll have to act like you're not sure how you're going to pay for it. Someone is bound to approach you to make a deal under the pretense of helping you earn extra money."

He made it sound like he had picked up a loaf of bread, and I was supposed to do something as simple as make turkey stuffing. "A Viper, as in the car."

"Exactly. But this is my personal car and not covered by the fees from Strandfrost so don't think you can drive it to work everyday."

"Wouldn't it be easier for me to just shoot myself and leave a suicide note claiming I couldn't pay for it all?" At least then I could benefit since I would be out of this situation.

He paused to give my suggestion serious consideration. "No, that wouldn't work," he decided. "No one could approach you after that, and we still wouldn't know the identity of the perpetrators."

I didn't mention that maybe I should shoot him instead. "So let me get this straight. The condo in Alpine Hills isn't enough debt. Walking around in fancy new clothes isn't enough. Now you want me to throw a party and drive a set of fancy wheels into the middle of the living room."

His reply was cautious. "It would be better if you left the car in the garage and casually showed it to some people."

I didn't reply. After listening to the various phone clicks and silence, he added some encouragement. "Look, with the party we can show people how desperate you are for extra money. You're young, you got promoted, you spent too much."

"This isn't misspent youth, it's insanity."

"I've already hired the caterers. With the Fourth of July coming up, it will be a good excuse to get people out. The car will intrigue them enough that they won't dare miss the party."

I should never have told Huntington that people didn't think I was desperate. "Wouldn't it be easier to take a bunch of these guys out golfing?"

"Probably, but that would only get you talking to three of them at a time. And even if you drove the Viper some of those guys wouldn't--"

I knew what he was going to say so I finished for him. "Won't play golf with a woman." Dan came to mind, and I was betting Patrick wouldn't play golf or come to the party in spite of the Viper.

"Which night is it?" I asked with a sigh.

"Saturday."

"You should move it to Friday night." Men didn't know anything about parties, not even one as smart as Huntington. "The Fourth is on Monday and on a long weekend like that people might be traveling on Saturday. A Viper isn't going to have a lot of pull with a wife trying to get dad and the kids over to Aunt Melba's in Tennessee."

"Aunt Melba?"

"Yup. Or Uncle Edward."

"You have to visit your Aunt Melba on the Fourth?"

I prayed for patience. "It was an example. I don't have an Aunt Melba."

"Then why the hell did you bring her up?"

"Just move the party, Huntington. You have a better chance of getting people on Friday."

He grunted. "Okay, I'll change it. Do you think that lady that you hired to clean can perform butler duties? The caterers will handle the serving and food, but you need someone to answer the door. Tell her you'll make it worth her while and get her size so that I can order a uniform."

Butler duties. Oh boy. Marilyn wasn't going to like this news. I wasn't even sure she would still clean the condo anymore never mind greet a room full of strangers. "Uh. I'll have to check."

He didn't notice my hesitation or didn't care because he spit out some other details about the food. After reminding me to get the invite out pronto, he hung up.

With less than a week, it would take a miracle for me to be ready. I needed a second miracle to live through it. I snorted. A Viper. With all the power it had, I would probably plow it through the building the first time I drove it.

Huntington's call made me late to staff and that was hard to do since Gary liked to stroll in ten or fifteen minutes late himself. I arrived breathless and foolish. Since I had already interrupted and everyone was staring at me, before I lost all possible friends and enemies, I announced the party.

"A getting started party," Gary mused. He looked like he might be trying to think of a way out of it. "I think that would be great. Good way for you to team-build with your new peers." He nodded, getting more enthusiastic as he politically commanded his troops to go, all the while working on excluding himself.

"Well, yes, that is certainly one reason." I hesitated and looked shyly over at Dan, the most easily manipulated male in the room. "I uh, well, I bought a new car...last weekend...and I'm sort of having problems with it."

Predictably, Dan's eyes widened as he sensed a vulnerable female. He wouldn't want to miss a chance to point out his superiority or in my case, use any opportunity to show I was an idiot and unfit for my job.

Patrick, on the other hand, looked pained. Ross was busy ignoring the entire thing, and Allen hadn't bothered to stop picking at his fingernails.

Before Dan could run with things, I added, "It has this kick. I can't figure out how to get it going, like from stop lights, without stalling it. I'm just learning to drive stick." I hadn't asked Huntington if it was stick. It had better be.

Patrick actually snarled. Ross didn't look any more interested, but he did comment. "Why not just get a friend to give you a couple of driving lessons? Shoot, couldn't take much more than an hour. What are you going to be serving?"

I didn't know what kind of food Huntington had ordered, so I stuck to the car. "Oh, you know how Vipers can be difficult to control. The salesman warned me it wouldn't be like driving other stick shifts even though I sort of already know how."

At least that ended the discussion on food. The grimace on Patrick's face eased into slack-jawed amazement. Dan choked on his coffee. Gary perked up immensely.

"I don't think there's anything wrong with the car or anything like that," I added hurriedly, "but you know, it would be nice if a few guys could drive it and check it over for me."

It was probably Ross' marketing background that gave him the agility and speed to step in ahead of everybody else. "Shoot. I'll be more than happy to show you how to shift that thing." He sat up straighter. "Shouldn't take more than a few days. Maybe a once a week lesson for a month or two. Be happy to bring it home and check it out for you too, if you're really worried something might be wrong."

"Sounds like you need your team, and we'll be there for you," Gary announced.

Dan and Allen nodded automatically when Gary looked around the room. Patrick just continued to look stupefied, but he wasn't scowling anymore.

Huntington had been right. They would show up, if not for the car, just because all the other guys were going to be there to see the car. Amazing.

Gary was so pleased with the party idea that he barely paid attention to the schedule discussions. Even Patrick's occasional attempt to whine was brushed aside. Gary gave me partial okay to go ahead with hiring the new group, approving half of the people and all of the equipment. That made no sense because without people to run it, why order it, but I was learning not to argue.

Allen was overjoyed at one more sign that instead of replacing him, I was just a new regime. He put in a request for people too "in order to start building a special team" but it appeared rather spur of the moment. Probably to be politically fair, or some other reason I didn't understand, Gary gave him permission to hire a technician and order a couple of servers. Allen went from nearly shutout to a startup up team in a heartbeat--for no good reason at all.

I scurried out of the meeting and sent the hiring requisitions with Gary's signature to HR. Then, before I could pretend it wasn't happening, I sent out a proper invitation to the party. Depressed, I stopped by to talk to Turbo. He had already begun to hear rumors, but he was ecstatic when I confirmed the story about the Viper. He completely ignored me when I mentioned that Gary had approved the fifty thousand dollar analyzer he wanted to purchase.

"What color is it?" he asked.

"The analyzer?"

"No, no! The car!"

I took a deep breath. It would have been easier to guess the color of the analyzer because most computer equipment was beige or gray. "Uh...probably red." I remembered my earlier car discussion with Huntington and figured that now that he was trying for attention, it was probably red. "Or black," I considered, changing my mind. If Huntington was stuck with the Viper, he might not want red.

Turbo looked at me askance. "Probably?"

I shrugged sheepishly. "I guess I should have asked." For a moment, I think Turbo had forgotten I was playing a part because he looked rather chagrined. "It isn't as though I picked it out."

"Oh. Yeah."

"It was Huntington's idea, of course."

He nodded. "Absolutely. You, uh, might want to do some research."

He was right. "I guess I'll go do that. I told the guys it was stick shift. I hope that Huntington ordered it that way."

Turbo looked pained. He closed his eyes. He did that whenever he was about to tell someone bad news or in my case when I did something particularly dumb. "It has a six-speed manual transmission. That type of vehicle does not have automatic transmission. Ever," he emphasized. "That would be pointless. It has at least 450 horsepower and can go nearly two hundred miles per hour."

"Oh." The ability to go that fast seemed rather wasteful since I hadn't seen a speed limit that high, but I was supposed to own the car, which meant I had to be impressed with such things.

"Did you get the coupe or the roadster?" he asked.

I just stared at him.

"Does it have a soft top or hard?" he clarified.

"I haven't seen it."

He looked terminally wounded.

"I think I'll go do some research." I kept my head high during my escape, despite feeling more than a little stupid.

The condo was quiet and peaceful when I got home. Half-heartedly I looked at cars on the internet, but when I put my laptop next to me on the bed, somehow I fell asleep.

Michael woke me from a hard sleep. "I am bringing her up," he said into my ear.

My fogged brain didn't figure out he meant Marilyn until I opened the door.

"OhmyGod!" I ushered her inside. She was badly bruised, but no cuts this time. "This is all my fault!"

"The potatoes," she said around an ice pack.

"What?"

"He was mad about the potatoes."

"He saw me! At the hotel yesterday--"

She shook her head. "It was the potatoes at dinner. I thought I had all the lumps out, but I didn't."

I had nothing to say to that. The good news was that Huntington had gone ahead and ordered a double bed for the study. I only had sheets for the king bed, but we made do. There weren't any extra blankets, and I had no idea what had happened to the old bedspread.

"You'll have to go in the morning and see about buying some sheets and a blanket or two," I said, as if her face didn't look like that of a bloated corpse.

"Couch would work," she mumbled.

I didn't think she was much up to arguing, so I let it go. "I guess Ted followed you to the hotel and saw me later and figured we were plotting. This is all my fault." I was ready to cry.

"No. He was at the bar before dinner. He gets real picky when he eats snacks there before dinner. It was my fault. I didn't get the lumps out."

"But he--"

"I promised him after the last time when he brought his friend and his wife over that I wouldn't ever serve lumpy potatoes again." She swallowed noisily.

I had no idea what she was talking about. "Get some sleep. Make sure you eat something in the morning. I'll leave some cash so you can get some sheets and things tomorrow."

There were tears in the corners of her eyes. They started to spill before I left and closed the door. I didn't know how to help her so I didn't try.

Chapter 31

Back in the main bedroom, I paced before calling Sean. I asked him about counselors. He yelled at me a lot and wanted details, but I told him he could answer my questions or I'd go somewhere else. He knew me well enough that he stopped pressuring me and gave me some names.

Just in case Marilyn asked, I ought to be ready. If I could have forced her there...ah, but then force was the problem in the first place, wasn't it?

In the morning, she was up before I was. She had tea brewing and breakfast made. She must have heard me in the shower. Unfortunately, she hadn't brought any extra clothes. I went back in the bedroom and found a clean pair of sweat pants and a t-shirt. "Help yourself to the shower."

She didn't look up. Her face hadn't improved over the night before. Her short brown hair looked as though she cut it herself; shorter on one side than the other. With a good cut that framed her face, she might even be pretty, but Marilyn had a lot more to worry about than a haircut. "There wasn't any coffee," she said.

"Grab some at the grocery. The pot is somewhere." I vaguely remembered seeing one. I set two places. She stared at the plates, and her mouth set in a firm line.

"I don't need charity."

"Yes, you do, but I'm not going to sit and argue with you about it. You'll need some food in your stomach before you go get sheets. Might as well eat here."

"No one else eats with the hired hands."

"How would you know? Isn't this the only job you've had in a while?"

She pressed her lips together. "My grandma cleaned houses. I used to go with her."

"So this house is different. Pull up a chair, get yourself full and then you can see if you can do some of the shopping. Just get the one set of sheets for now. I'll have to ask Huntington about getting a dresser." The last was said more to myself than to her, but she heard it.

She sat. "Are you his whore?"

I nearly choked on my eggs. I didn't even like eggs that well, but at least these were scrambled, and she had put cheese all over them. "What?"

"His name isn't on the apartment. Why do you have to check with him? I guess even rich women have some man that runs things."

I was appalled and without a satisfactory explanation. I stuttered for a while, burned my tongue on the hot tea while trying to decide how to answer and finally managed, "No, I am not his...anything. He...picks the furniture, that's all." I rolled my eyes at how stupid I sounded. "Fine. When you're at J.C. Penny's looking for sheets see if they have any dressers."

She looked doubtful. "Penny's sells dressers?"

I had no idea. My dad's friend, Hal, made most of what I needed. I still had the same dresser he had made me when I was teenager. "Maybe we can have something made. How about you just get a suitcase, and then you can leave clothes here in case you need them?"

She stirred her eggs. "Why are you helping me?" She made it sound as if help made her hurt somewhere.

"I need a housekeeper."

She looked like she might argue, but it wasn't in her nature, at least not anymore. "Thanks."

I barely heard it. "You're welcome. Looks like you could use some more ice."

She shook her head. "Won't help now. Maybe some heat."

Assuming she knew best, I offered her the tub. "There's a whirlpool jacuzzi off the master." The master bath was almost as big as the study and in my opinion, more luxurious. She could have used the very nice bath off the study too, but it didn't have jets in the tub like the master did. "Take yourself a bath. Pretend you're someone else. I gotta get to work."

She looked panicked as I got up to leave. "What sheets do you want? What color?"

"Get sheets. I don't care what color. Not pink. They are sheets."

She watched me stuff things from my backpack into the briefcase. "You don't know much about being rich, do you?"

Our eyes met. I held my breath before finally asking, "Do you?"

Her eyes fell and then rose again. "I guess not."

I shrugged. "We'll both make it. Who needs to understand it anyway?" I had my hand on the door, when I remembered the party. "Uh, Marilyn?"

"What?"

I had no right to ask, and I wasn't sure that having her continue to work for me was the right thing to do. Then again, no matter what I did or didn't do, Ted would keep on beating her. "I'm having a...party Friday. I kind of need someone to get everything ready so it's really good that you showed up." She looked like she thought I was lying just to make her feel better. I hurried along hoping she might not even notice the word "party" and the implied "people." "I was wondering, I kinda need someone to, uh, answer the door." As if I wasn't plenty healthy enough to answer my own door.

She stared at me without blinking. "Answer the door? Downstairs, like the guy that lets me in?"

I felt even more foolish. "No. Up here. During the party." I waved my hand. "Oh, never mind."

I was almost gone when she called out, "I guess I'll be free Friday. I don't guess I need to rush right back. Usually I go to my mother's for a few days after something like this anyway."

I paused and looked back. "Really? You'd have to deal with a lot of people."

She shrugged. "I guess."

"I might need you to not only answer the door, but take coats and help serve food."

She nodded. "I can do that."

"You sure?"

Stiffly she replied, "Of course."

"Obviously I'll pay you for more than just the cleaning. It's going to be a tough crowd." Her eyes started to flick back and forth as though looking for an escape, so I rushed on, "not a mean crowd, but they are…well, some of them are sort of demanding sorts." That was as accurate as I could do on short notice. I could just picture Dan asking her for hors d'oeuvre sixty times. And Lord help us both if he pinched her on the ass. I'd kill him on the spot.

"You mean people that really are rich are coming to the party." She filled in my lame excuse with scary insight. "I can serve. No one notices the hired help. I used to waitress when," she looked down at the dishrag. "A while back."

"You sure you won't get into any trouble for not showing back up at home?"

She didn't answer. After the silence went on a heartbeat too long, I left and hoped I wasn't making things worse for her.

* * *

Once at work, I called one of the counselors. Without giving too much information I told the guy I was trying to help a friend, and I needed to know what to say and what not to say.

"Be there for her," he told me. "If she calls, get her out of trouble. If she asks for help, send her to me."

"Okay, but is there any way I can make her get help?" I pleaded.

Chuck, the counselor, advised against pushing her. "Abused people think they deserve to be pushed. They expect it and almost beg for it because it is the only way they know how to act."

I wasn't sure that was true about Marilyn. "At some point in her life she wasn't like this."

"That's even better. If she responds to you, it might be because you remind her of someone positive that was in her life. She may be nearing the point where she realizes if she doesn't get out she could die. She might be trying to decide whether living is worth it or not."

I thanked him and hung up. His words weren't all that reassuring because I wasn't a very good influence on her. The life I showed her was nothing more than a lie. It might not be abusive, but as she had already discovered, it wasn't a real life lived by a real person. She knew I didn't belong in the world Huntington had created.

Of course, the more worrisome thing was that if she could spot it, others probably could also.

In fact, the rest of that day, I was pretty sure I was making it painfully obvious that my life and history were totally bogus. Turbo quizzed me about the car again, and I still hadn't gotten around to asking Huntington about it. Gary also stopped by my office and struck up a conversation about the Viper. The only thing that saved me from looking a total fool is that the man loved to talk more than listen, so I just let him rave about all its great features. Things in my life were heavily out of control. I needed help.

The number Huntington had given me made clicking noises as though it was being forwarded before he answered. "Huntington."

"I'm not sure about the butler thing. We probably need a backup," I told him.

"The cleaning lady?"

"Yeah."

"Okay, what else?"

I sighed. "It would probably be a good idea if you brought the Viper over. People keep asking me questions about it."

There was a much longer pause before he answered. When he did, his patience was gone. "It's already in the garage. Didn't you see it?"

Parking spots were assigned in the condo. I had two permanent ones and the use of several temporary ones. The valet parking guys usually parked guest cars, but if they didn't I was supposed to direct my guests to use the correct ones. "Uh..mm."

"I take that as a no." His voice was strained.

"Well, I don't have the keys." It wasn't much of a defense, but rack my brains as hard as I could, I didn't remember a car being next to my normal spot. I was so jittery from Marilyn showing up late on my doorstep, I could have driven the wrong car into work and not thought twice about it.

"I'll stop over." He hung up as usual without saying goodbye.

I was not functioning at full power.

It took a lot of effort to force myself to finish the order for the new equipment. After that, I read through a few of the resumes that human resources had sent over. The first three were not harbingers of hope. Human resources had obviously used a word search program because they equated my request for "operating system experience" with "operate large, complex equipment." People who drove bulldozers weren't likely to be very interested in setting up computer database systems.

Maybe it was best that I didn't actually hire anyone. After I got fired, I didn't want Strandfrost to let the new people go for lack of remembering why they were hired in the first place. Without an empire builder to defend their cause, the poor souls might end up on the street with me.

When I got home that evening, Huntington was waiting for me. Given the activities of the day, I was late. He was doing his caged animal dance across the condo, dressed in his usual casual business attire. His eyes glittered with an anger that reminded me of the attack.

"Oh come on," I complained. "It's just a car. I saw it on my way in." It was right where he said it was, next to the Mercedes' parking spot.

"Very funny!"

"It's a nice looking car." He had probably gone to a lot of trouble to get it and paid a huge sum of money. "I like black." I tried to sound hearty and enthusiastic, but at the moment I was more concerned about food than any car. Hopeful, I looked in the kitchen for Chinese, but there wasn't any. The refrigerator was sadly lacking also. Maybe I would make some cheese and broccoli soup.

I started mixing the flour and butter to make a paste for the base. "Since the car has a hardtop, I assume it is the coupe. That is good. I was never much for having to take a roof on and off. Too much work."

That was not the answer he was hoping for. "Somehow I could have guessed that cars weren't your thing considering that you didn't even notice it in the first place. Forget the car. The problem is that we are not getting very far solving the real problem."

"Did something else happen?"

Huntington ground his teeth together and paced back into the living room. He stared out the balcony door. "He cashed in another charity check!"

"Allen?"

Huntington snarled, "Who else?"

With the way Gary continued to let him participate, I wasn't surprised. "So he thinks all is forgiven."

"How would I know what the man is thinking?"

I shrugged, watching my mixture thicken. "Can you grate some cheese?"

There was a funny silence that went on for too long. Sighing, I got the grater out and tried to stir and grate cheese at the same time. The cheese had to go in very slowly or it would curdle.

After a minute of this routine, Huntington came over and took the grater from my willing hands. His culinary attention mashed the block of cheese, but some of it did come through in small pieces.

"Do you think whoever is working with him is just going to keep working with him?" I couldn't decide if I should be grateful it was almost over or sad because I hadn't helped any.

"Near as I can tell the idiot cashed it on his own. You'd think between being questioned by the Feds and getting his ass kicked around the office, he would wise up."

I doubted it. It must have shown on my face.

"What?" he asked.

I tried to think how to answer. "They are still letting him do essentially the same job. No one has acted any differently except maybe right at first. Why should he change?"

"He's been caught!"

"He didn't even get his hands slapped, at least not by anyone at Strandfrost. The man is making an awful lot of money, and if he wants even more, why should he stop? Nothing truly bad happened when he took the first few rounds." I finished stirring the soup and moved to toast some bread.

"He knows we're on to him!"

"And he knows that you didn't do a damn thing to him."

"He could go to jail! I could lock him up tomorrow!"

"Yeah, but he didn't go to jail. When they didn't fire him I think he took that as a sign that what he did was okay. No one has really grilled him because the Feds are after whoever started this scheme. I think he believes his little part in the play was actually so minor no one cares."

Huntington let out a huge breath of air. "He thinks he is getting away with it?"

"More than that. I think he believes he didn't do anything really wrong. It's as if a few charity checks were just no big deal. He's one of the boys and they will just...overlook his scandal. At first he seemed worried, but now he is back to rambling through his day. The way he looks at it is that you guys don't have enough proof or there just isn't that much wrong with it."

Huntington stared at me for a long moment. "He got off easy. He shouldn't even dare to get a speeding ticket."

"From what I've seen, most of the people on Gary's team are men not used to being tracked. As long as they turn in an occasional report, and the company makes money, why should they worry?"

"You're saying they're all bilking the company?"

That was a little too close to what I thought of the group, but what I had observed was not illegal, it was just carelessness. I ladled the soup out and sat down to eat. "I'm saying that Allen is one of them, and he doesn't seem to be aware he crossed over a line. So he just keeps right on doing what he was doing--and that may or may not include the equipment thefts."

Huntington looked incredulous. He stood there, not using the paper towel he had torn off to dry his hands. After a short while, he sat down and helped himself to the soup.

We ate in silence, my spoon much quieter against the bowl than his.

Apparently he wasn't in the mood to help with dishes, because when he was done eating, he set his bowl in the sink and grabbed his jacket from the living room. "I can't even believe this mess."

On his way out the door, he nearly ran poor Marilyn over. He grunted. I froze, watching from the kitchen over the top of the bar.

Marilyn gulped as he towered over her. She dropped two shopping bags in the process of trying to rescue the package of sheets that had skittered down the hall when Huntington opened the door and startled her.

"I'll get it," he growled impatiently, grabbing one of the bags and tossing it towards the couch.

Marilyn scurried inside, holding another of the bags up higher to cover her obviously damaged face. I nearly leaped over the counter to take the sheets from Huntington. "Thanks."

He glanced back into the condo at Marilyn, but she had scrambled out of sight. Even though he couldn't possibly understand what was going on, he was a gentleman. He did not ask awkward questions.

I was grateful.

"Is she going to do the butler stint?"

I nodded. "Yeah."

"Good." He stomped away.

Chapter 32

As if I needed a reminder of my double life, Suzy stopped by work on Thursday. I hadn't seen her since the conference. She didn't look so good. Her face was red and beaded with sweat.

"What are you doing here?" I rushed around the desk and offered her a chair.

"I wanted you to be there again."

I stared at her flushed face and licked my lips nervously. "Be...there."

"You were," she paused and took a deep breath or two. "Late, last time," she gasped out. She collapsed into the chair after getting out this less than pertinent information.

"Uh, Suzy." I twitched. "Are you...are you in labor?"

She nodded proudly. "Started this morning about four o'clock."

I gulped. "You went into labor at four o'clock this morning and you are sitting in my office now?" My voice rose to a near shriek.

She looked to be in pain again and started to breathe funny. "Don't-- worry! It took thirty hours last time, remember?" A few more pants and a pitiful groan. "I...didn't...want to go...too early!"

"Did your water break?"

She nodded, quite unable to talk. I reached for the phone. It took me a moment to remember the emergency number. We couldn't use nine-one-one from inside the complex. With shaking fingers I dialed and then yelled into the phone, "I need an ambulance. My friend is in labor." And from the look on her face, it didn't look like she had thirty hours to go.

The guy on the phone started asking all kinds of questions. I interrupted. "Can you get me a doctor, a real doctor on the phone?" I eyed Suzy. She didn't look good. In fact, she leaned back and started to gasp harder. Then, she screamed.

I thought the wall was going to cave in. The phone fell from my lifeless grasp, and I clutched my ears. "Suzy!" I made shushing motions.

It was too late. The entire hallway erupted as people poured out of their offices to see what was going on. Even if the entire floor hadn't heard the first shout, the next three screams that ripped from her throat would have done the trick.

Warily, I edged around the desk, trying to stay away from her flailing arms. I remembered her doctor's missing beard with a clarity that lent me the caution of a trainer handling a wild tiger. "I think you should lay on the floor."

I reached to close my office door just as Turbo burst in. He brandished a long piece of bent metal that looked as if it had been ripped off one of the server racks--not an easy feat considering the things were generally strong enough to hold about eight hundred pounds.

Before I could say a word, Suzy let out another screech. Bruce came in behind Turbo, knocking him sideways into me. "Omph." I went down hard. Turbo crashed on top of me and nearly took my head off with the rack pipe.

Bruce had his firearm pointed at the window above Suzy's head. Luckily her pain had taken her to the floor where she lay panting and groaning.

Bruce stared wildly at the scene.

"What is going on?" Turbo demanded, rolling awkwardly to his feet.

"She's in labor!"

I could hear other voices in the hallway and feet running. The stairwell door opened and slammed twice.

"What?!?" Bruce blinked rapidly and then, like a shadow, his gun was gone. "Labor?" he repeated stupidly. "You're not being attacked?"

"In a manner of speaking. We are about to be assaulted by a baby." To bring the point home, Suzy screamed again. The phone squawked.

"Ambulance," I shouted at it. "Turbo, I called one. Can you organize people to direct the help when it gets here?"

He stared down at me and blinked. He nodded but didn't move.

"Bruce do you know first aid?" He was an agent. I was hoping they taught him something about saving lives.

Turbo finally got the message to his brain. He whirled around and, still carrying the metal rail, he tripped over Bruce and disappeared. I heard him shouting that everything was okay, it was just a birthing.

I closed my eyes for a moment. Just a birthing. No problem.

When I opened my eyes again, Bruce was backing out of the room. "Bruce," I threatened. "I need help in here. I need towels and lots of them. The guy that sits next to me works out at lunch." I pointed in the right direction. "He'll know who else might have towels."

Bruce shook his head mutely.

Bruce," I warned as he looked around wildly for a place to run or hide, "Get me towels or I'll blow your cover!"

As if it wasn't totally gone. The man had run down the hall, probably with his gun drawn and acting as if he was ready to stop a war. He better get himself together and help me with this baby because I sure wasn't going to deliver it on my own.

I picked up the phone and worked my way around the desk again. "Did you find a doctor yet?" I asked the phone.

"We, yeah. What is going on there?"

"Just a little bit of excitement what with the labor and all." Suzy wasn't acting any better than she had the first time. She screamed for her husband, trailing off around another contraction.

"Yeah sure," I told the voice when it suggested I try to keep things calm. "Suzy, we need to get you undressed." At least the bottom half. Thankfully she must have been expecting to go to the hospital sometime today because she had worn a tent dress.

Sally stuck her head rather timidly around the corner of my door. "Is it really just a pregnancy?"

Just a pregnancy? What was wrong with these people? "Yup. No cause for alarm." What was I going to do? I couldn't deliver a baby!

Sally crept in the room. "What can I do to help?"

"Can you get behind her and support her head or something? Sort of give her something to rest against?"

Sally started towards Suzy. I yelled, "Watch her hands!" Sally leapt backwards and hit the desk. She tried to get her balance, but tripped over my leg and landed on her butt with a loud, "Ow!" Papers floated down around her head.

I groaned and tried to explain. "She's got this problem with tearing things apart when she is in labor."

Sally looked like she was going to faint. Gingerly she stood back up and edged around Suzy. "There, there," she tried, wiggling down between the wall and behind Suzy.

My friend was weakening and grateful for Sally's folded legs under her shoulders. There were tears in her eyes. "I want my husband to be here!"

I didn't think I'd earn any brownie points by telling her that she could have arranged that had she gone to the hospital like a normal person.

Bruce showed up and shoved a handful of towels in my general direction. He immediately turned away. "Bruce, her husband's name is Robert. Get him either here or tell him to make his way to the hospital."

It was time. I could tell. I had seen this before. The contractions were fast and heavy. I relayed the information into the phone and when I could hear, I did as I was told and measured her diameter and looked for the head and tried to remember to breathe through my mouth.

Birthing is a messy and smelly business. It is not a process that I recommend at all. When I get to heaven I have a few questions about the whole design process. In fact, leaving to ask some questions right now sounded like a pleasant alternative to telling my best friend to "push!"

"I am," she screeched back at me. "Aaaaagh!"

Sally used one of the towels to wipe up the sweat, and I used another to wipe off the other stuff.

When the baby finally made its entrance, I was panting nearly as hard as Suzy. "Turbo, if you don't get that ambulance here pronto I'm going to--" I couldn't think of a vile enough threat. "Turbo!"

The baby was breathing. I followed the doctor's orders, orders I could now hear since Suzy had stopped screaming.

God must have heard my prayers or the combined screeching, because the ambulance attendants arrived. One of them stood over me and helped with the baby. There were two others with a gurney in the hallway, waiting for me to get out of the way. I gladly gave up my bundle and backed around the side of the desk where I could do no harm.

Efficiently, the attendants helped finish the process, got Suzy loaded and moving. Turbo peeked around the corner. He took one look at me, and his eyes widened. I shut mine and reminded myself to breathe through my mouth. I smelled. The room smelled. Sally looked disheveled, but she had been on the other end of the mess. She was crying.

"Isn't it just wonderful? A miracle. An absolute miracle," she boo-hooed into the one remaining clean towel.

"Try it from my side next time," I muttered, a tear or two coursing down my own cheeks. Okay, it was kind of special. Even if it was messy.

"Uh…" Turbo cleared his throat nervously. He leaned over and handed me a handkerchief. "You okay?"

I looked down. I looked almost as injured as when the thugs had attacked me. "Yeah." Getting cleaned up was going to be a chore. For once, Turbo didn't offer advice. In fact, he scooted out rather quickly, as if he was afraid I might get goop on him. I didn't blame him.

"Didn't you see your own kid's birthing?" I called after him, moving his way, my hands out.

He realized he had been retreating and stoutly stopped. "Yes. It was… interesting. I'll call a cleanup crew." Abruptly he turned down the hall. He didn't run, but it was close.

Sally and I made it to the ladies room, but my clothes were ruined. I cleaned up as best I could and told her I was going home. She was still teary-eyed. "I've never seen anything like it. Wasn't it wonderful? Makes you want to have some of your own, doesn't it? Well not at first, not when she was screaming, but then that little helpless ball just came out and it was real and breathing and--" she sobbed some more. Normally I would have put my arms around her and let her cry it out, but once she calmed enough to see all the resulting smears of gore, she wouldn't appreciate my comforting gesture.

"Sally, I have to go home and change and then to the hospital to see how she is doing. Can you make sure Bruce called her husband?"

That thought gave her pause. "Oh my! He'll want to know right away!" Like a little bullet, she sped away, intent on bringing the wonderful news to the father.

I slunk through the hallways, trying not to be seen in my latest condition. Turbo must have hidden in his office because he wasn't anywhere around. Neither was Bruce.

Chapter 33

Friday, the day of the party, I woke up fat and ugly. This, as any female can tell you, was a very bad thing. These days happen and they are not controllable, but you should avoid any woman having one of these days.

I showered and decided that I had a headache. To make up for my fatness, I wore a skirt instead of the usual pantsuit, and for the ugliness, I wore extra makeup.

It didn't help.

Marilyn was awake and up before I left for work.

"You'll make sure the caterers get in and setup?"

She nodded.

"I think you dusted that already," I told her.

She ignored me and kept at the furniture.

I did my best not to ram into anyone on the way to work, but started wishing I had by the time I read my fourth email. Today of all days, the new equipment had arrived. Usually, receiving logged it all and then sent notification for us to come and get it as we needed it. Since the order was for my new group, it was too large to leave piled downstairs in receiving.

I called Tam and Jerry and asked them to help cart the stuff upstairs. "Can you get it into the lab and unpacked?"

"Racking it will take days," Tam pointed out.

"I know. Just get it in the lab or hallways for now. We'll set it up later."

Turbo showed up and handed me a clipboard. "So that you can track it," he offered helpfully.

If it had been any other day than an ugly day, I would have happily done as he suggested. Instead, I handed the clipboard back to him. "You track it. It will take every one of us helping to get this done before the end of the day." I led the way with my ugly little nose in a twist.

Downstairs, I started signing for boxes. Turbo checked items off of the list. There were two delivery trucks still in the docks so I went outside to see how that was progressing. The deliveries came from various companies into a hub run by Strandfrost. Since our company handled setting up equipment for various locations, once orders arrived in the hub, it was delivered by local movers to businesses or in this case, to Strandfrost. One of the trucks was from Pilgrim's Moving and the other, much smaller truck was from Three Boxes and a Man.

Pilgrim's moving truck was an almost empty eighteen-wheeler. Two guys were sliding things onto dollies and moving things back and forth. They were moving very, very slowly.

There were so many people walking around, I almost didn't notice the extra guy sulking about the corner of one of the trucks, coming towards me.

I took a few extra steps in his direction, assuming he wanted to waste time by asking a question or otherwise stall in getting the trucks emptied. I was halfway between the truck and the building when I got a good look at his face. "Ohboy."

Even with the cap on I finally recognized the enemy. The movers probably assumed he was part of the other trucking crew. There was no reason for anyone to know better, but I did.

I spun back for the building so fast, I nearly lost a shoe.

With Marilyn not showing up at home, Ted had come looking again and stupid me, I had completely forgotten to make sure I wasn't being followed. Maybe the hotel had told him where I worked. Or maybe he had followed Marilyn to my condo and then followed me here. For that matter maybe he caught up with Marilyn, and she had given him the information in order to save herself.

However he had managed it, Ted had just gotten lucky and found me without even having to break into the building.

I backpedaled up the dock, but it was too late. I was the only woman near the loading docks, and he spotted me just as I dodged behind the larger truck. Out of the corner of my eye, I saw him whip his baseball cap around and exchange the slinking walk for a run.

I stepped up the pace, not paying any attention to the hooting catcall when I lifted my skirt and jumped up onto the ramp. The moving guy could see me stark naked for all I cared. I was pretty sure that standing out in the parking lot and getting beaten to a pulp by Ted was not a good alternative.

Turbo smiled at me as I rounded the corner.

"I have to leave!" I shouted on my way past.

He stopped smiling and looked outside. "They giving you--"

I dropped my share of the paperwork onto one of the boxes. "You sign for the stuff."

Ted moved into view, clearing the ramp like a greyhound let loose to catch the rabbit.

Without further ado, I pelted into the hallway and hit the stairs at a full run. Where was Bruce? I needed to borrow his gun.

It didn't take me long to find him since most of the group was downstairs, and he and Paul were the only ones in the lab. "I want your gun," I demanded around heaving breaths.

"What?" He looked around the lab rather worriedly, his hand unconsciously moving towards his lower back before he caught himself.

"Do you remember the day I came in looking like hell?"

He stared at me and then coughed nervously.

"Besides this one," I clarified. Loose strands of hair floated across my face. My skirt was askance. I couldn't see myself, but the extra makeup was bound to be worse for the wear since I had just completed a run up fourteen flights of stairs. I wiped at the sweat.

Bruce must not have understood what I was trying to say because he just mumbled, "Well, uh…"

I waved aside his uneasiness. "Let's cut to the chase, here. You talked to my friend Derrick and found out I had been with him on a stakeout the night before I came in looking like hell. Remember?"

Bruce rolled his eyes. "Derrick mentioned you blew his cover," he said pointedly, eyeing Tam, who was just coming back into the lab. Tam stared at us with obvious interest.

"Yeah well, if idiots in wet suits try to be alligators don't expect the alligators to be fooled."

"What?"

Apparently, Bruce had conveniently forgotten about running through the hallway with his gun out, or maybe he figured that his own mistakes didn't count. I moved on. "Look, the guy that I went to talk to, well actually, the guy that Derrick was trying to get a confession from or actually it was his wife." I stopped talking. On days that I am fat and ugly, I am also mean and incoherent. In frustration, I stomped my foot, yanked my skirt halfway straight and started over. "Okay, what I mean is, the guy is downstairs now. He has followed me once before."

Bruce stood up, understanding the urgency at last. Then, in a cowardly move, he sat back down. He moved his hands up and then back onto his knees. Finally he managed, "Let me get this straight. Derrick, your cop friend, is following you?"

I didn't have time for this. "Could I just have your gun?"

His eyes bulged. "Uh, no."

"No?" I was feeling really mean now. "Fine. Just remember that I was forced to kill him with my bare hands because of you." With each word, my finger dented his shirt above his cold heart.

I spun on my heels. Ted wasn't going to intimidate me. That was Marilyn's role, not mine. And if Bruce wouldn't let me shoot him, well I'd just tell old Ted to get off Strandfrost property.

I took the elevator down to save my strength. By the time I made it to receiving, some of my anger had deflated, replaced by caution. I opened the door and peeked into the dock area.

Turbo looked around the ends of his longish hair without taking the pen from the clipboard. He sidled up to me and whispered, "He's gone."

I tried to see around him. "Are you sure?"

Turbo jerked his head towards the wider, outer doors. "That the same guy that whistled at you?" He puffed out his chest. "I told him to get lost. I told him he wasn't going get away with anything around here, not with me around. He'd have to go through me before I'd let him get to you."

"And he just left?" Unbelievable. I peered around carefully. Sure enough, no Ted.

"Oh." I smoothed my skirt again and tugged at my hair. There was no help for it. I sighed. "Sorry I ran off. And, uh, thanks."

I turned around to find that Turbo wasn't paying attention to me anymore. He was busy frowning over the rest of the boxes. The eighteen-wheeler backing away made conversation impossible for a minute.

Before I could thank Turbo properly, he beckoned me over and pointed to an empty space. "They are gone. An entire crate of hard drives, an analyzer and a load of ten high-end laptops."

I looked at the list. "You have them checked off as received."

He nodded. "Exactly. One of the movers brought me the paperwork for the laptops. I signed off. They were right here. The hard drives hadn't been unloaded, but the loader was getting them off the truck. I personally watched one of the movers carry the analyzer over."

I shrugged. "So Tam or Jerry took them upstairs." Or Tam had misplaced them on the way upstairs.

He shook his head stubbornly. "No, I haven't checked this box. If the delivery people or Tam or anyone takes something upstairs, I check here."

I could see the various check boxes he had created. "Well then, where did they go?"

We both looked out the wide doorway. There were only Strandfrost receivers and a couple of UPS trucks out there now. "Did you look in the trucks to make sure they were empty?"

Turbo's face was red. He hadn't. He probably hadn't had time. What with checking boxes going upstairs and those being unloaded, he hadn't been able to keep track of it all. On top of that he had to defend me from a scum wife-beater since I hadn't stood my ground.

"I checked outside once or twice after you told me how slow they were moving, and I looked in the small truck when they got the last of it out."

"When would they have had time to put boxes back in? Could they be in the UPS trucks?" The UPS guy was moving a lot of small boxes onto a cart. I could see from where I was standing that his truck was pretty full. It didn't look like it had room for the hard drives. "Where else could they have gone? Why would the guys load them back on the trucks?" Was this how the equipment was disappearing? I had assumed that someone was breaking into Strandfrost and waiting for the right moment to roll it away.

Turbo wasn't listening. He moved around the dock, checking other items. I caught Tam as he came back down and asked him about the box.

"Nah, I move from this section. Jerry grabs right after me and then Henry." He pointed to a guy sitting behind a desk. "He takes up a load too about every third round." Tam leaned in close and whispered, "Has other things to do. There's another guy from down here helping too. His name is Alvin something."

Unperturbed by my question, Tam slid the dolly under the next crate. Turbo was there instantly to check it off. After Tam left and Henry got up to take another crate, Turbo showed me his tally. "We're going to be short over a hundred seventy-three hard drives that were sitting on that first crate. I think we're also missing about forty servers that should have been delivered."

"Right under our noses."

He nodded glumly. "No one even had to bribe us to clear the way."

Huntington wasn't going to be very happy when I told him the party, the condo and the car was for naught.

"I'll keep checking things." Turbo looked around, but there wasn't anything to see, at least not now. "The movers must have seen something."

"I'm sure Huntington will be asking plenty questions once I tell him what happened." Turbo went back to ignoring me, checking and rechecking the boxes. It was barely lunchtime, but I was done. "I have to get home. You're coming to the party, right?"

Turbo grunted a reply so I left him to his parcels. Well, they were supposed to be my parcels, but I had decided Huntington could have them all. I needed a shower and a change of clothes before the caterers took over my life.

Chapter 34

I watched my rear-view mirror all the way home, but couldn't detect anyone following me. When I arrived, I checked with Michael, the watchdog guard. He swore he hadn't seen anyone hanging around.

Marilyn was still at the condo. I hopped in the shower, but it didn't really make me any less ugly, although I cut back on the makeup. I dithered in the bathroom, wondering if I should tell Marilyn about Ted finding me at work. If she knew, she would probably run scared. But if she had told him where I worked, I deserved to know that, didn't I?

Before I could make up my mind, the first of the caterers, Jimmy, showed up to arrange the china and tablecloths. He was a portly Hispanic gentleman with a black and white uniform, a very short haircut and penchant for telling silly jokes while he worked. Marilyn helped him set things up. All I managed was pacing. "When are the others coming?" I asked Jimmy.

He smiled. "In about an hour. We'll use your oven to heat a few of the appetizers and then we'll start on the dinner items while people snack. I'll be your barman." He did a little twirling dance while pretending to hold a tray.

Marilyn looked very cute in her little uniform. She dropped her eyes every time I paced by.

Predictably, Huntington showed up before anyone else. He didn't appear nervous at all. He helped himself to a drink, talked football with Jimmy and generally made himself at home.

The rest of the caterers showed up right on time. Marilyn got the door, leaving me with nothing to do. She came back over and nudged me. "Get a drink and stand still."

I went into the kitchen and put some water in one of the larger wine glasses. At least I think it was a wine glass.

I tried to get Huntington into a corner so that I could give him an update, but I couldn't figure out how to tell him everything without dragging him into the bedroom, and that I wasn't willing to do. My God, what would Marilyn and the caterers think?

The first arrivals at least gave me something to do. Ross asked about the Viper. I gave him the car keys. "Test if for me," I told him to make him go away.

Huntington didn't kill me on the spot, but looked like he might later.

Ross didn't waste any time. I wondered if he would come back at all.

Turbo and the technicians showed up about the time dinner was being served. I was impressed that Turbo had talked Tam and Jerry into coming to something so silly. Sally ran around directing the caterers and giggling with Allen's wife. Sometime around nine-thirty, Turbo sidled up to me and whispered, "Balcony. Five minutes."

He skidded through the crowd right away, heading for the open doors. I waited for what felt like an hour and then met him out there. There were a couple of other people on the balcony smoking and watching a few of my neighbors at the pool.

Maybe I should have had the party down there. At least there would be more room. Then again, maybe it just seemed crowded because Ross had kept a steady parade of people coming and going as he showed off my Viper like it was his own.

Turbo complimented the food and made his version of small talk. I could feel my ugliness creeping back in as I got impatient, so I filled in with, "Thanks for your help today. Sorry I wasn't...calmer." I didn't want to bring up Ted by name, especially with Marilyn around.

"No problem. I did some looking into those slow movers." He rested against the railing and watched the two smokers. "I have a theory."

It was all I could do not to groan. We were talking in code since the smokers weren't talking at all, but when Turbo had a "theory" it was time to worry. "I think I'll just have the boss check into hiring someone that works faster." This was my version of telling him to stay out of the mess.

One of the smokers put out her cigarette and waved at us as she went back in. She must have been the wife of one of Strandfrost's employees because I didn't recognize her. As the hostess I probably should have cared.

"I'm not sure, but I think I may have found the tie-in," Turbo said.

Uh-oh. "Don't you think you should let Huntington take care of this?" Just as soon as I got around to telling Huntington that the stuff had disappeared, I was sure he would be happy to arrest someone. Or at least chase someone.

Turbo grinned and looked smug. He got that way quite often when brainstorming computer problems. His ideas were correct ninety-nine percent of the time, but the other one percent were unmitigated disasters. "Uh, Turbo, maybe we should talk about this. This isn't your field of expertise."

"I'm sure if you think about it, you'll get it." He smiled encouragingly.

"I really think this is Huntington's problem."

His smile disappeared into a frown. "The answers are right there for anyone to see. I'm sure if Huntington can figure it out, I certainly am able to."

"Turbo--"

"You need to get back with your guests. Most places won't be open on Monday. It will give me extra time to look into things. I'll give you an update on Tuesday. I'm sure if you thought hard enough about this, you would see the answer too." He sauntered back inside, leaving me to second-hand smoke and a cloud of worry.

As for the rest of the party, it was a waste of time. Once again, no one approached me. They ate all the food and drove Huntington's car until it was out of gas. I had to get Michael's nighttime buddy to tow it back to the garage and put gas in it. Huntington left early, but Sally stayed until the last guest was gone.

"Lovely. It was just fabulous," she told me. "Everyone had such a nice time. How is your friend Suzy doing?"

"She's great. She finally gave in and named the baby Maureen after her husband's grandmother."

"That is wonderful!" Sally cooed. "I'll give you all the reaction to your party on Tuesday." She threw a light black jacket over her ruffled, mini-skirt dress and waved as she made her way to the elevator.

I closed the door and my eyes at the same time. Like the resort, my condo now looked as if midnight had struck. I was left with nothing but pumpkins and mice.

Marilyn cleared her throat.

"What?" I opened my eyes in alarm. It was two in the morning. I was beyond tired.

"Do you want me to clean this up tonight?" She stood there, wilted, with a broom in her hand.

"Are you nuts?"

She actually smiled. "Maybe."

I waved her to the spare bedroom. "Go to sleep."

She swallowed. "It might be better if I went home."

"Now?"

She nodded. "It will be late, and he'll already be sleeping if he's home." She rushed on, "Tomorrow, I'll tell him I'm going to get my things from mother's and instead I'll come back here to clean up."

I wasn't sure why she ever wanted to go back there. Now was my chance to come clean. "Look Marilyn...I'm pretty sure Ted found out about our little setup. I think he's been following me." Her face paled. Before she could run, I continued. "I saw him at work today. I don't know if he followed me from here or he figured out where I worked from the hotel."

She looked confused. "The hotel would tell him where you worked?"

"I don't know." I was relieved that she didn't look as though she had squealed. "He might have figured out I was there with the Strandfrost people or someone at the hotel might have told him that much."

"I had best get home tonight." She set the broom aside and went to the bedroom to get her things.

Her reply defied logic. I had been hoping she would change her mind completely and stay away from Ted forever. But the counselor had warned me that making a difference was nearly impossible.

I watched her leave, wishing I could talk her out of it. The door clicked shut, and I heard her lock it.

With a sigh, I turned to the bedroom. I called Sean. He yelled at me because it was the middle of the night. I asked him to call Derrick and have someone patrol near Marilyn's house tonight in case of a domestic disturbance. He demanded answers, but I hung up. He had gotten me into this. He could darn well help, and he knew it.

I managed to wash the melting make-up off my face before falling into bed.

Instead of a restful sleep, I worried about Marilyn.

Chapter 35

Huntington woke me up long before I was ready. If he noticed I was ugly the day before, this was a real treat for him. I brushed my teeth and came back into the living room. I was still in my pj's.

"You bought all that nice stuff, including the great underwear I saw the other day and you sleep in that?"

I glared at him from my Tigger pajamas. "These are my comfort clothes. I like them."

"No wonder you sleep alone," he mumbled.

"What?" I crossed my arms over my front and tapped my great big Garfield slippered foot. "You wouldn't be insulting my person on a Saturday morning while in my condo drinking my coffee would you?"

"You haven't given me any coffee yet."

I sniffed, but went into the kitchen and started the coffee that Marilyn had bought earlier in the week. I preferred hot chocolate so I stuck some milk in the microwave while the coffee was going. "Listen, Huntington."

He interrupted before I could continue. "Steve. Will you just call me Steve?"

I glanced over my shoulder at him. "Whatever. I think we can stop this stupid charade." I told him in succinct detail about the equipment that went missing. "One or more of the movers either put it back onto the truck or they somehow put the equipment onto some other truck that must have come and then quickly gone."

He nodded. "I know. After the conference last week, not all of the equipment made it back to Strandfrost even though Turbo and Bruce checked off every single box when it was loaded. That is probably how they got the equipment from Tamarron too."

"You knew?"

"I can't be positive until I catch someone in the act, but it's only thing that makes any sense. Strandfrost uses multiple moving companies, sometimes whoever is cheapest, sometimes whoever is available. The moving companies use different guys and a lot of the time they aren't full-time employees, but contractors they call in. I don't yet know if the guilty party is using a particular moving company or one or more drivers. But what you're telling me about the latest theft fits what I was beginning to suspect. What we still don't know is who is the inside person directing the theft?"

"Did you tell Turbo all this?" I asked.

"Not yet, why?"

"He had a theory. I was wondering if he talked to you about it."

"No. Are you going to make breakfast? I'd take you out to breakfast, but you don't look ready."

Huntington could be brutally rude. "I think I'll go shower. Why don't you help yourself? I like my eggs scrambled."

I took myself off to the bathroom and noticed for the first time that my hair, which I had taken such pains with the night before, had mashed up one side of my head into a pyramid shape. The extra hairspray from the party had glued it all together.

By the time I returned, Huntington had managed breakfast. It looked fabulous. He had diced ham, green chilies, onions, mushrooms and cheese into scrambled eggs. He had even found the orange juice. I smiled. "Excellent."

He grinned back. "You look better too." He tilted his head. "But now that I think about it, you were kind of cute before."

I narrowed my eyes and sat down to breakfast. "So what is the next plan? Do you want me to keep playing the role?"

"There doesn't seem to be any point to it. Allen is so afraid of us, he cashed that charity check I told you about. His friends, whoever they were, seem to have dumped that scheme and are sticking with going after the equipment, taking it from right under our noses. All in all, it's been a great success, don't you think?"

"Maybe they don't know that we know the equipment is missing."

He agreed. "It appears that way. They weren't too afraid of coming out in the open and dumping the charity scheme, but they're making far more money off the equipment."

I nodded. "So...I guess I can just move back into my place?"

He smiled. "Not quite yet. I don't want to raise any flags anywhere, and we may need to use you to order more equipment to catch these guys in the act. You're in place, and it would look pretty normal if you did a follow up order. Just keep a low profile. Make sure everything looks the same to anyone looking."

I shrugged, vaguely disappointed. "Okay." I looked around. The place was still a mess. I wondered if Marilyn had lived through the night. I needed to call her.

Huntington took his plate to the sink and rinsed it. I handed him mine. He rinsed it too.

Feeling a little lost, the ringing of the doorbell gave me a chance to escape. It was Marilyn.

"Thank God!" I enveloped her in a huge hug, but immediately stepped back to inspect her face. Her hair was combed, she had no bruises, and her face wasn't puffy. "Are you okay?"

She nodded. "He went off to work at Larry's like always. He's always nicer to me when I first come back."

I ushered her inside.

Huntington grabbed his jacket off the back of the couch.

"She's going to clean this mess up," I said.

Marilyn had gotten used to seeing Huntington around the place, but she still disappeared into the kitchen without more than a mumbled, "Good morning."

Huntington crossed the room, his jacket over his shoulder. He looked me up and down on his way out. "Yup. I like the pajamas. But you clean up nice too."

I didn't know how to reply so I didn't. I had enough to think about what with worrying about Marilyn. Being clever was too much extra work.

Chapter 36

The long weekend did much to restore my good nature. I spent most of it at my real house, mainly because I figured that if Ted was following me, he wasn't likely to find me there. I told Marilyn she could use the condo if she needed to, but as usual, she denied the possibility that the next beating might be right around the corner. I wasn't so sanguine. After all that had happened, I had a bad feeling that Ted had decided I was the problem instead of his wife. I was a new and interesting victim; Marilyn would always be around to beat up. Ted had probably decided that by going after me, he was protecting not only himself, but Marilyn.

Tuesday morning, first thing, without even bothering to read my e-mail I went in search of Turbo. He may as well know that Huntington was going to track down the movers. Maybe I could break the news gently that he wasn't the only one that had figured out what was happening.

He wasn't in his office. Strangely, the door was still locked. He was rarely late.

I went to the lab on the off-chance he had gone there without opening his office. Bruce was already hard at work. "Have you seen Turbo?"

Bruce looked up at me. "You're not going to believe this, but I guess things just got too stressful for him. He quit."

"He won't help with the project anymore?" Since Huntington didn't seem to need our help, that was probably for the best, but it did seem strange given that Friday Turbo had supposedly had all the answers. Maybe Huntington had talked to him, and Turbo was sulking because Huntington had the answers already.

Bruce shook his head. "No, I mean he left Strandfrost. He resigned this morning."

That thought was so mind boggling, I could not even speak. There was no reason for Turbo to ever leave Strandfrost. He loved his job, especially lately, because he was busy playing detective. "That's not possible," I stuttered.

"Yes, he did. He resigned."

I groaned. Something was very wrong here. What was Turbo up to? "I'm going to call Huntington. Have you told him about this yet?" I wasn't sure what was going on, but Huntington needed to fix it, whatever it was.

Bruce didn't answer. In fact, now that I thought about it, he almost acted as if he were trying to crawl underneath the computer rack.

"Well?" I prompted.

"Huntington is, uh, missing."

I didn't even know where the man lived, so missing was a pretty fuzzy term. "Missing? From where?"

"We've tried paging him and called all his numbers. He doesn't answer. He isn't at home. He was working on a moving truck company angle this weekend, but we haven't heard back from him since Sunday morning."

"Where is home?"

Bruce shuffled his feet around and looked anywhere but at me. "Well, technically it's the condo where you're living. He's been in a hotel, but the hotel maid knew he wasn't in last night because the bed wasn't touched. She claims she can't remember whether she had to make it the night before that or not. I don't suppose..." He trailed off hopefully.

"What?"

"We didn't panic. We, uh. One of the agents said Huntington was, uh, at your place, that is the condo, early morning on Saturday. He thought that maybe...well, the party ended late and all."

I started to feel dangerous. "You figured he spent the night."

"It is his condo."

I blushed, a mixture of worry, anger and embarrassment that everyone thought I was playing footsie with the executive. The fact was, Huntington was damned attractive. He had even hinted lately that he was open to being more friendly. There was a part of me that had been considering it, but no one else needed to be speculating about my love life. "Huntington did not spend the night at my condo. Or his condo. On any night."

Bruce looked very disappointed. "That's bad news."

For all of us. It meant that not only was something going on with Turbo, Huntington was gone. If the Feds couldn't find Huntington, who could? He had a way of crawling around where he didn't belong, investigating things his own way. What if Huntington had been downtown again without telling anyone? I wasn't certain what he had been doing down there and..."What did he say last time you talked to him?"

"He was trying to track the missing equipment outside of Strandfrost. The security cameras that we installed in the building have yielded nothing. Since the trail here was cold, he was trying to pick it up after the stuff was stolen and figure out the distribution end."

I waved my hand. "We figured that part out for sure on Friday. They take the equipment before it ever makes it in here. The stuff gets ordered but disappears via one of the moving company trucks. Same thing happens at the conferences."

Bruce stared at me in consternation. "Huntington told you all that?"

I didn't appreciate his proprietary attitude. "Turbo and I figured out the part about equipment not making it upstairs. Strandfrost moves equipment around a lot and apparently the trucking companies are running off with the equipment instead of returning it here. At least that is what happened on Friday."

Bruce grabbed his cell phone and dialed a number. He snarled when he couldn't get a connection from the lab. He headed for the hallway to find a signal.

"There still has to be someone on the inside," I said, but Bruce was gone. I paced. Some of the orders for equipment weren't even real. If it wasn't Allen that created the false orders, there had to be another person who filled out the fake expense reports and the equipment orders. The trucks didn't just show up and take whatever was handy. It was more organized than that.

Whoever it was attended the conferences, had access to employee lists and expenses.

Who had access to the equipment budget?

There was only one person I could think of and since I did my darnedest to avoid the man, maybe I had missed something. Turbo didn't have such qualms. He didn't have to worry about getting his ass patted.

"It's got to be Dan!" I shouted.

Bruce must have heard me because he poked his head back into the lab. I hurried over to him. "Dan is in charge of the department budget information. He knows exactly what I and every other person orders. If Dan needed to steal something, he could peg it ahead of time." He was part of the scenery, privy to a lot of interesting conversations, and he went to every single conference. He was the only one that had access to all the people.

"Dan? The finance guy?"

"How hard would it be for him to add charges to the conference?" I tapped my foot. "Not very. He could pad his own expenses and turn in the expense reports for the non-existent demos. He doesn't order equipment because he doesn't have a team, but he could fill it out the paperwork. Allen or Gary would probably sign it all without paying any attention."

I had stayed as far away from Dan as possible after the little toupee incident, but Turbo wasn't as likely to be wary. And while Dan would never approach a woman--not to ask her to be functionally useful, Turbo was a different story. Turbo had been getting almost as much air-time as I had, albeit for a different reason. "Bruce, when you talked to Turbo this morning, what did he say exactly?" If I knew Turbo, he would have plastered hints throughout the conversation so that anyone paying attention could see how smart he was. Unfortunately his idea of a clever sign was probably so obscure it would be discernible only by an electron microscope.

Bruce walked over to the area where he had been sitting when I first came in. He picked up a single piece of paper and handed it to me. "He left this with his key taped on his door. I never saw him."

I froze. "You didn't see him this morning?"

Bruce shook his head. "Look, this work is stressful. Maybe he just had enough."

I looked down at the resignation letter. It was two lines long. There were no clues, nothing clever, nothing special. "Turbo didn't write this! Shoot, even if he were really resigning, the letter would be three pages long with enough detail to make a court case out of it!" I yanked at my hair. "Dan got to him. It's the only thing that makes sense."

"Dan again? Why Dan?"

I waved my arms frantically. "Because Dan is the most likely suspect. And Turbo found a clue recently, but he wouldn't tell me about it because I told him to let Huntington handle it. I think Turbo may have approached Dan sometime after Friday to ask about the equipment. Dan may have realized that we were onto him. Maybe he thought it was only Turbo that had guessed and now…" I gulped. "And now he had done something with Turbo!"

Bruce looked at me like I was talking in a foreign language.

I tried to explain. "Turbo wouldn't quit, Bruce. Pressure doesn't bother him because he doesn't notice it. He's not normal."

Bruce made a noise that was suspiciously snort-like. "If Turbo didn't quit, you think he is gone because instead of approaching you--Dan--or someone," he stressed the someone rather heavily, "tried to get Turbo to work a deal and something went wrong?"

"Knowing Turbo, he wanted to prove his theory before saying anything. He would have run a test or two first. Maybe Turbo tried to approach Dan and get in on the deal. And Dan didn't like the idea. So, now Turbo is missing." I clenched my fists. What if Dan had hired thugs to take Turbo out? If Huntington had been missing for two days, how long had Turbo been gone?

"He might not be missing," Bruce said. "He left this note just this morning."

"But you didn't see him! Still, you're right--he can't have been gone long, because Irene would have sounded the alarm." I said the last with more hope that I actually felt. "Did you call Irene? To see if Turbo was at home?"

Bruce shook his head. "Irene? Why would we call her? He resigned!"

I ran for the door. "Dan doesn't know we suspect him. That means he'll probably come back to work. We have time to catch him!"

"That's if he's guilty," Bruce yelled after me. "You're just guessing."

I had to agree. But Dan had been at all the conferences. He was around the office all the time and had ready access to Allen's signature or even Gary's signature. Maybe Allen had figured out what Dan was up to a while back and got in on the deal with the charity stuff.

First things first. If the resignation letter had been left this morning, then there was a chance Turbo had only been waylaid this morning. Running into my office, I frantically searched my online phone numbers. It took me three tries to dial Turbo's home number correctly.

"Irene!" I tried to keep the desperation out of my voice. There was no sense in causing her to panic just yet. She'd faint dead away, and I'd have even more problems on my hands. "Uh, is Turbo there? Has he left yet?"

"Oh, hello Sedona! How are you? Feeling a bit better these days, I hope," she said. "No, Adam isn't here, he left early this morning to take the car in."

Irene was the only person that didn't call Turbo by his nickname. "The car?" Was he meeting Dan somewhere and that was his excuse to Irene?

"He probably just got held up there. It's some new place. It isn't even near here, but he went driving around checking out all kinds of places this weekend. Most of them were closed because of the holiday so he had to go this morning." She sighed loudly. "Our little SUV doesn't require anything special, but you know how guy are about cars. I swear he checked every single place that had ever worked on a car. I guess it's taking him a lot longer than he thought."

My mouth dropped opened. Turbo, all on his own, was following up on the companies that had moved the stuff on Friday! "Uh, did he mention where he was going this morning?" I didn't have much hope, especially if he were going to more than one place.

"Oh, I don't remember, but I can find out if you want me to. He takes notes on everything. I think he circled the one he wanted. Just a minute."

My heart couldn't wait a minute. It was near bursting before she finally came back.

"Larry's Body Shop," she said slowly. "There's so much listed on this paper. That man had better not be planning on painting the car. I know men must have their little car fetishes and ever since you got that Viper, he has done nothing but talk cars."

She kept prattling, but I wasn't listening. In fact, I think my brain went completely dead before the neurons started firing. "Larry's Body Shop?" Why did I know that name? It didn't sound like a moving company. Was he really taking the car in? No, that couldn't be, because he had resigned!

"Yes, that's the one he has circled," Irene assured me.

"Did he circle any movers?"

"No, I don't think so. Let me see…" I heard pages flipping. "No, that's the only one circled in red. There's some other ones underlined in different colors."

I thought back to the movers, something about Three Men or Boxes. Ted had chased me off so quickly that…wait a minute. I had an ugly feeling in the pit of my stomach. Both times I had seen Ted it had been around the moving vans. "Larry's Body Shop?" I squeaked out. That was the name of the place Ted worked!

"Yes, that's the place."

"OhmyGod." What if it wasn't Dan that Turbo suspected at all? What if it was someone else I had been avoiding, and Turbo had gone after that someone to find out about equipment disappearing? I knew Ted, therefore, I assumed Ted was after me. Turbo didn't know Ted. He associated Ted with the moving vans!

I groaned. Turbo could be right. Ted had always been around when there were moving vans. Either way, Ted was not someone to be messed with!

I closed my eyes. How in the hell was I going to find Turbo?

I should have made an excuse to Irene before hanging up, but she already thought I was nuts, so I didn't waste the time.

I might not know exactly where to find Ted, but I did know someone that might know--if I could get her to help me.

Chapter 37

It took me half an hour to locate Derrick and get him to call me back. I had no time to mess around. "I need Marilyn's address." I was afraid to call her because I had one chance at getting the information. If she refused and hung up on me, I was toast.

I could have taken the route she had used to find me, but I didn't know if she owned or rented. I suspected she rented, but that was only because her husband seemed like a deadbeat. Having a brother that represented a lot of victims, I knew stereotyping was a dangerous assumption. A lot of well-to-do men beat their wives. Income was not a big differentiator with bullies.

"I am not giving you her address," Derrick said. "What are you up to?"

"Well, how about you tell me where Larry's Body Shop is. I'll just pop in and ask her husband for the address."

I held the phone away from my ear while Derrick exploded. I caught the part about, "I'll take you to her house, but there is no way you are going to Larry's Body Shop."

Unknowingly, he confirmed that Larry's Body Shop, the same place that Turbo had circled, was where Ted worked. I had no intention of confronting Ted at the body shop. Had I wanted to, I would have looked up the address in the phone book. "Fine. Pick me up at my place in fifteen minutes."

I had to drive like a maniac to get to my house to meet Derrick. I changed out of my work clothes and into jeans and a clean t-shirt. I needed to be able to move and suits just didn't cut it.

From the messages on my home answering machine, I could tell that Derrick had called Sean and told him that something was up. I didn't bother to call dear brother back.

I met Derrick in the driveway and hopped in before he had a chance to get out of the car. He wasn't in uniform, but his olive khakis were pleated and ironed as any perfectly as a uniform. His red hair was combed neatly into place.

"Can you hurry?" I pleaded. "I really need to find her."

He drove, asking questions the entire time. I hedged, hemmed, hawed and when that didn't work, ignored the questions and babbled about the weather.

When he finally stopped, I would have bolted from the car had caution not been required.

"It's the house across the street, the white," Derrick said.

Marilyn lived in one of the older parts of town, not far from downtown, but far enough that the house wasn't in the slums. With some fixing up, the house would even command a good price because of its proximity to businesses. "Can you tell if Ted is home?"

"His truck isn't out front," Derrick replied. "But you're going to have to tell me what this about before you go in there."

I couldn't tell if a car or truck might be in the detached garage. The old colonial porch in the front was huge, but swept clean. The grass was cut and there were iris blooms and roses along the raised wooden porch. The one chair that was outside looked a little rickety. I guessed Marilyn sat outside by herself without the benefit of her loving husband.

"Stay here and wait for me," I said. I hopped out of the car before he could argue. Sprinting across the road and up the front porch, I knocked.

It was a long time before the inner door cracked open. Too long. Derrick had plenty of time to join me.

"Go away." She sounded frightened.

"Marilyn, it's me. I need a favor." I continued to hold the screen door opened.

"I don't owe you no favors. That was the agreement." Her eyes darted to Derrick, who loomed off to my left.

"I thought you were going to stay in the car," I complained.

Derrick just loomed. I rolled my eyes and jerked my thumb in his direction. "This has nothing to do with him. He wouldn't give me your address without taking me here himself. Your husband isn't home, is he?"

She shook her head. Something told me that she wouldn't have opened the door had Ted been there. He probably would have just shot through one of the windows and been done with us.

"Marilyn, I just need to ask you something. About my...friend. The one that, uh, you know, comes to the condo now and then."

I refused to glance at Derrick. I was hoping that if I ignored him he would either go away or at least not remember this conversation. "Listen, I'm desperate here. My friend--Huntington--has disappeared. I thought maybe you might have seen him around here." I really wanted to ask her about Turbo, but she had never met him. All I could hope was that Huntington and Turbo had been on the same trail and that by following whatever crumbs Huntington had left, I would find them both.

Marilyn's eyes got big. I almost thought she might laugh. "Why would he be here?"

"I think Huntington might know your husband," I said. Huntington had been hanging around in the same neighborhood as Ted the night I first met Marilyn. Ted was somehow involved with the moving trucks. He had to be. If he wasn't...that didn't bear thinking about. Turbo had definitely been on Ted's trail.

"Ted knows your friend?"

"I think so. Have you seen him around here? Ever?" Marilyn noticed things; like when she mentioned I didn't fit into the rich scene. Maybe she had glimpsed Huntington lurking around. Her next words snuffed that hope. "I don't think I've seen him."

"Are you sure? He wouldn't look like when he was visiting the condo. He looks..." Murkier? Deadlier? More like a thug?

"More like he belongs here?" she asked softly, kindly filling in where I wouldn't tread.

"Maybe." I hesitated, but if she couldn't help me, I didn't know who could. "He changes the color of his eyes. I think he wears brown contacts. Last time I saw him, he had a tattoo. A sword, down one arm."

The sword did it. She stared at me hard right before her face disappeared. The door slammed shut, and I could hear the chain come off. "Why should I help you?" She was looking at Derrick again, but she let us in. "You can't stay long.   Probably the neighbors have already seen you though." She made it sound like a death knell.

"Ted will beat you because you had visitors?"

She just looked down.

"Maybe Derrick can go talk to your neighbor," I suggested darkly. "Do they all tattle on you?"

She looked startled. "No, only Waterbee. She's one of those religious converts that believes in obeying one's husband. Not that she's ever been married." She shrugged. "Eileen, next door, wouldn't tell a soul if I had pimps over here all day. She'd probably come over and join in the fun." Marilyn actually smiled.

I glanced around. Her house was spotless, just like she left the condo. The furniture was a mix of old stuff, the heavy kind that gets passed on through families. The carpet could have been the original that came when the house was built. Not even Marilyn could keep it spotless.

She noticed my perusal. She swallowed and glanced nervously at Derrick. He was trying to appear smaller. I sighed. "Derrick could you go walk the neighborhood or something?"

He glared at me.

"Look," I pointed out, "Ted isn't here and Marilyn isn't likely to beat me up, not yet anyway."

"I can't help you," she inserted hurriedly. "You better leave."

"Hey," I said, "I don't care a whit about your husband's drug operation. I'm just looking for my friends. Huntington disappeared about two days ago. Poof, just like that, no one has seen him. I need to know if he was here or downtown or wherever you might have seen him since then."

She shook her head. "I may have seen the guy with the tattoo you mentioned. I'm not sure if he's your friend or not. It was weeks ago."

I was desperate. I grabbed her shoulders. "Think about it! The guy could be getting himself killed. I've got to find him. They've got Turbo too!"

I would never hurt Marilyn. She didn't seem particularly upset about my manhandling, but Derrick came unglued.

"Hey, take it easy. Violence isn't the answer!" He tried pulling me back.

I gripped harder. "Marilyn, you've got to help me."

Marilyn shook her head, although in her eyes, I could see that she recognized my fear and desperation.

Derrick kept trying to drag me backwards. I grabbed Marilyn's blue shirt when he threw his arms around my waist and tugged. I was about to be torn in half. I clung onto Marilyn for dear life.

"Violence isn't the way to solve problems," he lectured while tugging me.

"Leggo!" I shouted. "Help!" I beseeched Marilyn.

She stared at us both as if we had lost our minds. I still had one of her arms. She had to grab onto the wall to avoid being dragged out of her own house. Derrick was sounding off about being gentle and caring and teaching her about the real world. Marilyn and I looked at each other, silently agreeing that the man wouldn't recognize the real world if it bit him.

"Okay, okay," she said finally. "The guy I'm thinking of goes by Stephen, like your friend, right? But he's, well, I think he's a gang member. He might be a truck dealer. Some of those guys bring their trucks in for servicing at Larry's."

In relief I let go of her. All the air in my lungs came out in a giant woof as I collapsed back against Derrick. He staggered, nearly dropping me.

Marilyn warned, "I don't know if Ted knows him or not, plus asking Ted wouldn't do no good. He tells me what he wants, not what I ask about."

"If you've seen him, why wouldn't Ted know him?" I struggled away from Derrick, but kept an eye on him.

Marilyn shrugged. "The guy I saw, the one with the tattoo, was at the car shop. I think it was a few weeks ago, maybe two or three. I was taking Ted his lunch. He likes for me to do that sometimes so that he has a nice hot lunch." She looked down, but kept talking. "The sword guy was talking to the owner, Larry Shinock, not Ted." She looked puzzled. "I wouldn't have even thought of him except you mentioned the tattoo. But you're right. He does look like your friend, doesn't he?"

Derrick slid into the conversation. "What was he talking to Shinock about? Is he the one that drops the drugs?"

We both turned to him with an evil glare. How dare he insert his business in mine? "Derrick, I told you this was personal. It's not about your case. Do your work on your time."

He gaped at me. "But I brought you here!"

I snarled, "I don't owe you anything for that. I just needed the address, not the bodyguard."

"I'm sure you wouldn't have felt that way if her husband had been here," he said. "Then things would have been different."

Speaking those words was like calling the devil. We all heard the truck at the same time. "Uh-oh."

Marilyn's face went white. I was scared she was going to rip her shirt

again. I grabbed Derrick's hand. "Come on!" I charged through the kitchen.
The back door was locked, but Marilyn was no stranger to throwing a deadbolt
in record time. She had us shoved out the back door before footsteps found
the front yard.

I hit the six-foot high wooden privacy fence at full speed. Derrick was
supposed to be trained to go over fences, but he seemed a bit more hesitant.
Not me. I landed smack in the next yard, right next to Jaws, the rottweiler from
hell.

"Aaah!" Jaws was surprised enough that it took him a moment to charge.
That was good because I just made the side fence. Ted could probably see me
if he looked out the window. Thank God, Derrick was a pace or two behind
me. Jaws couldn't decide which of us looked juicier.

Derrick couldn't follow me because he-of-large-teeth was tearing my pant
leg off. Wisely, Derrick went for the fence on the other side of the yard. When
my jeans ripped, Jaws shook the useless prize of blue material and took off after
Derrick.

I landed in the next yard, and to my great relief, it was that of a friend.
"Hurry," the lady whispered from her back porch. "Stay below the fence and
get in here. He'll hear the dog barking and come out to see what is going on."

Hurry? My feet were wings. They never touched the ground. One leg was
light as air anyway, what with the missing bottom half of my pants. The gray-
haired angel slammed the door behind me and peered anxiously out the back.

"Where did your friend go?" she fretted.

I panted without answering right away. "No idea. How many more dogs
like that are in this neighborhood?"

She shrugged. "There's a poodle in the yard on the other side. Is that
where he went?"

"I think so."

She shuddered. "The poodle is worse than the big dog. Comes up to you
all friendly and then takes a chunk out of your hand."

"Great. I'll probably have to take him to the hospital." At least Sean was a
lawyer. My only question was whose side was he going to be on?

"Do you think I can make it to the car?" We had parked across the street.
I could get there without going through the Harrison's yard.

She shook her head. "You should wait until he leaves."

"When will that be?"

"Depends."

"Oh what?"

"On whether or not he saw you or is suspicious about anything else." She
stayed away from the heavily curtained windows. I would have been frantically
eying the place, but she probably knew best.

"I'm Eileen." She offered a rather frail looking hand that still had a firm
grip. Eileen was almost as thin as Marilyn, but older than both of us by about
two decades. She had on a smart-looking gray jogging suit, and her hair was

combed in one of those styles that women get done once a week.

"You must be Marilyn's friend," I said.

"She needs them more than most."

Eileen's house was neat, but not as precise as Marilyn's. I could see pictures of children and probably grandchildren in the living room. She noticed me notice them.

"My husband passed away about two years ago. That's about the time Marilyn started to trust me. Before that, she just kept to herself." Eileen sighed and sat at the kitchen table. "She was beaten up pretty badly or she might not have even come over here. I called an ambulance."

"You're the one that usually calls in the police?"

She tapped her fingernails nervously. "Yes, for all the good it does."

"Ted threaten you often?"

She kind of half smiled. "No. He is nice as pie when he isn't drinking." She shrugged. "Lately though, ever since the truck shop started making more money, I think he started sampling some other drugs besides alcohol. He hasn't dared say anything to me yet, but he watches me. The only good thing that has happened lately is that Waterbee doesn't take herself over there anymore to give her opinion."

"The tattletale?"

"Yes, that one. That witch used to report on the neighborhood comings and goings any time he'd open the door to her. A week or so ago, she pounded on over there, intent with her news, and Ted scared the daylights out of her. He was so far gone, I don't think he even recognized her."

"Where was Marilyn?"

Eileen watched her fingernails, tapping, tapping against the old oak table. There were a few scars in it and where she sat now, the gloss had worn thin. "She came over here by and by. After he left. Said she was going to stay with a friend." She looked up at me. "Maybe that was you?"

"She's always welcome."

"Sometimes lately, she's had a little more time to herself. Usually Fridays."

"Mm." A lot of conferences ended on Friday. Huntington would probably want to know about Friday, if he was still alive.

"Do you know a guy with a sword tattooed on his arm?" I asked. "He has brown eyes. And brown hair." I had only seen him twice in his disguise and only one of those times close up.

She shook her head. "I don't get out much. I generally avoid men with tattoos."

I smiled. I knew what she meant. We chatted a while and eventually, Ted left. He didn't storm out, so I heaved a sigh of relief, guessing that Marilyn was probably okay. I started to leave, but Eileen put her hand on my arm. "Wait a bit. He usually drives by at least once."

"Oh."

Sure enough, Ted's white Ford pickup made another pass in a matter of minutes. It was a beautiful truck with a front grate and special side rails on the back. He may not treat his wife well, but he kept his truck spruced up. It was quiet too. There was no one to warn Derrick that he was driving by again, but Derrick must not have been sitting out in the open because Ted continued blithely by, stopping the truck briefly in front of his own yard, admiring his possessions.

When the street returned to its abandoned look, I hurried out into the sunny afternoon. Marilyn came out on the porch and took a seat in her chair. I checked the street up and down before going over to her yard. Eileen stayed with me, probably planning on being my alibi if Ted drove by again.

Derrick ruined our caution by charging out of his car and yelling at me. "You idiot! Where have you been?"

With dignity, I mumbled, "Go freeze yourself." It wasn't loud enough for him to hear. I trotted up the porch. "You okay?" I reassured myself that Marilyn was in one piece.

"I told him that the dogs have been barking a lot lately. The neighborhood is very unsettled." She eyed me warily. "He said they'd get quieter if he had anything to say about it. I asked him what he was talking about."

"And?"

"He just smiled and said he takes care of business. He's been out late a lot. That wouldn't have anything to do with your friend, would it?"

Derrick looked grave. I felt a little ill myself.

"I, uh, I asked..." She looked down. "I asked if they caught the sword man, if he was some sort of thief. He got mad and asked who I had been talking to. He told me to mind my own business."

"Any idea where they might," I gulped, "keep someone that was causing them trouble?" The only place I could think of was the body shop.

She shook her head. "No."

Derrick decided to add his two cents. "We used to have someone watching, but if something went down recently, we wouldn't know about it. Our guys got pulled when Marilyn, when uh, I failed to get additional information. The reports showed some strange activity, but not enough evidence of the place being a drug drop."

Marilyn looked at him and blinked rapidly. "You mean lots of drugs? You weren't just after Ted because he started using drugs?"

He looked uncomfortable. "Of course not. We know a lot of money is being flushed through there. We weren't interested in Ted. I mean, unless he wanted help. We were tracking the money."

Right. Of course the cops would be interested in Ted's welfare. Marilyn and I looked at each other knowingly, and I rolled my eyes.

"The money isn't from a bunch of drugs," Marilyn said. "It only comes in when they get overtime. There's some contract they work that comes in every month or so and Ted gets a lot of overtime then." She sighed. "Ted gets his drugs from one of the drivers, but I don't think anyone else does. Used to be just pot while he was working, but Larry doesn't like them smoking anywhere near the place. He's afraid it will hurt the equipment, so now Ted goes downtown, like the place I agreed to meet you." Her cheeks flushed.

Eileen patted her on the arm, showing her support.

My head was starting to hurt. "I'll just have to follow Ted." I didn't want to cause Marilyn any more pain, but if Ted was involved, he was my ticket to finding Turbo and Huntington. Somehow Turbo had tied Ted to the vans and the stolen computers. Maybe he had seen Ted get into one of the vans after I left and eventually tracked Ted back to where he worked. As for Huntington, he had probably been on the same trail coming from a different direction.

Marilyn stared hard at her feet. "Following Ted is a bad idea."

"Don't worry. Derrick knows where he works." Derrick didn't look like he was going to take me there, but if Turbo could find it, so could I.

She shook her head. "Ted's going hunting. That's why he came by--to have me pack some clothes and a sandwich."

My heart beat so loud, I thought Ted might hear and come back. It wasn't hunting season for any game animals that I knew of; it was July! "Hunting?"

She peeked at Derrick, but kept talking. "He just went hunting Sunday. He doesn't usually go this often, and it's almost always for the whole weekend. While I was making his lunch, he laughed and said this time he bagged a really good one."

"He bagged--" I blinked. "Most hunters brag about their catch after they get back from hunting." I wondered if it was too late to save Turbo and Huntington. "Directions?" I asked.

Marilyn shrugged helplessly. "I don't know. There's some cabin in the forest that he goes to with the guys. I have never been there."

"Who owns it?"

"I don't know. Maybe Larry."

"Where does Larry live?" I asked.

"He lives in the top of the shop."

I looked at Derrick. He didn't look particularly helpful. I turned back to Marilyn. "If Larry does own this hunting place, couldn't we look it up in the county information? Like you found me?"

Her face looked hopeful for a moment and then fell. "I guess I don't know what county it is in either." She thought about it some more. "Ted mentioned the preserve once. It must be near there. I think." She spared Derrick another fleeting glance. "I think maybe once they were on the preserve when they got a deer."

A map would get me the counties near the preserve. If the cabin didn't belong to Larry, I was toast. Worse, Turbo and Huntington might be permanently toast. "Thanks Marilyn. I know you took a chance by letting us in. We won't let you down." I smiled weakly and grabbed Derrick's arm. "Ready?"

He looked like he wanted to ask a few more questions, but he would have had to physically shake me loose. He followed me back to his Dodge and pointed at my missing section of pants. "Lucky that dog didn't get a meatier part."

I was too worried about Huntington and Turbo to care about my pants. "I've got to find that cabin."

He sniffed and looked down his nose at me. "If you know more about what is going on, you really need to tell me. I can help. I can put out an call on Ted's truck, but what's the crime?"

I couldn't prove the kidnapping by any stretch of the imagination. "Can you ask the guys that were watching Larry's place if they know where the cabin is at? I'm going to see if I can find out if Larry owns any property anywhere else besides his shop."

"If Larry ever went to a hunting lodge while we were on watch, we'll know the location. I can check that. Call you at home?"

"And at work and my cell. Leave messages if I don't answer." I wasn't sure where I'd be, but I could pick up messages from either machine.

He dropped me back at my place. It was after two o'clock. I was going to have to hurry to make it back to the condo and to the county offices. If I did find Larry's address, I was going to need four-wheel drive. Since I had spent the last weekend at home, I was driving the Honda. I needed the Mercedes.

I changed into jeans that weren't missing half a leg and grabbed my Colorado map. There were a couple of counties that might have property nearby. I should have asked Marilyn how long it took to drive there or how long he was gone when he went.

I zipped back over to the condo to get the Mercedes. I needed my backpack and maybe some food.

I ran inside, intent on checking with Derrick one final time and maybe Marilyn to see if she had thought of anything else useful.

Michael harrumphed loudly when I pelted around the corner towards the elevator.

"What?" I punched the button, and then had to hold the door opened so he could talk.

He looked pained. "Madam?"

"Madam?" I wasn't sure if I had been elevated or demoted. His face turned red. "Fine, fine, call me whatever, what is it?" I stepped back out of the elevator reluctantly.

He walked towards me and whispered, "You have another visitor."

"Who?"

"A rather large fellow. With a," he looked over my head. "Tattoo."

I grabbed his arm. I think I may have permanently creased his uniform with my grip. "A sword?"

Michael looked at his clothing in dismay and cleared his throat before answering. "He insisted that he was going upstairs. He said he had a key. I was not convinced. However," Michael lifted his head, "It turned out he had a gun."

"What?" Huntington didn't need an escort. Michael knew Huntington. "Wasn't it Huntington?"

"He did bear a resemblance." Michael cleared his throat noisily. "Given the assortment of characters that you have trailed through here, I didn't think it prudent to call in the authorities until I had checked with you." He continued to stare at an invisible point somewhere over my head. I almost checked to see if there was something interesting behind me.

"So…" If it wasn't Huntington, who was it? And what were the chances I was going to mosey on up to my room knowing there was a strange guy there with a gun? Even if it was Huntington with a gun, I would still be worried. The man had originally wanted to shoot me.

"Can I borrow your phone?"

"We aim to serve." His Grand Snobbery couldn't quite contain a smirk. "If you wish me to place the call to the police, I have the number."

I shoved past him and called the condo number. It rang twice before he picked up. "Huntington?"

"Yeah."

It wasn't him. "Who is this?"

"You said it, sweetheart. Huntington."

"Steve?"

"I'm looking for Steve. Where is he?"

I almost missed the touch of panic in his voice since my own was mounting. "You don't know?"

"If I knew would I be chatting your ass up?"

"See now, Huntington--Steve would never have said that."

There was a pause and then the voice came back on, smoother and more cultured. "Under normal circumstances I would be more than pleased to discuss the endless trivia in your tiny little world, but unfortunately at the moment, I am in a bit of a hurry. If you could just help me with some information?" Now he sounded like he had a stick up his ass. Definitely more like Steve.

"That's better. No, I don't know where he is. Well," I hesitated again. "I might. If I come up there are you going to shoot me?" Michael was still staring stoically at the wall, but he was memorizing every word.

I didn't like the fact that whoever was in the condo took a long time to consider his answer. "I guess not." He sounded very disappointed in his decision.

"I'm on my way."

Before I could get the elevator, Michael obliged and pressed the button. One of the two cages was always programmed to wait in the lobby. He held the door for me, still without looking directly at me. Just as it closed, he said, "Some lady was here also. This morning. She asked which condo you were in, but we don't give that information out."

I would have shot the kid if I had had a gun. He had this information and he just let me get on the elevator without telling me?

One problem at a time. And I had a feeling the one upstairs was going to be a big one.

Chapter 38

Steve's brother, and he was surely a brother, was waiting in the condo. I expected him to be draped casually on the couch, cleaning his gun or at least caressing it. Instead, he was leaned against the living room wall, wearing tight jeans and a t-shirt that was small enough it rippled when his muscles did. He had a sword on his arm. I couldn't help but stare at it.

Wow. He was probably a couple of years younger than Steve, but it was hard to tell. "Uh, hi. I'm Sedona."

He knew I was nervous. "Mark." His eyes were creamy coffee brown, not blue. He wore his hair combed back just like Huntington, but his was dark brown, wavier and not black. I wondered if Steve had put a temporary sword on his arm or if it had been Mark in Strandfrost.

I looked at his eyes and knew. "Why was he dressed as you at Strandfrost?"

Mark stared at me. "What makes you think it wasn't me?"

I took in the casual smirk and the challenge on his face. No way. I shrugged. "I…don't know. Why would your brother dress like you?"

Mark glanced away, either annoyed or embarrassed. "Could we just get to the point of this conversation? You said you might know where he is?"

I didn't really want to go there. I only knew if I heard from Derrick in this century. "I have to wait for a phone call. Do you know Larry at the car place?"

His stare was filled with cold assurance. "Lady, I got business to take care of. You just tell me what you know about Steve."

I hated being threatened. It reminded me of bullies in high school. I sniffed. "Larry has or uses a cabin somewhere. I think Steve might be there."

His eyes flickered, just before going expressionless. He knew about the cabin.

"You know where this cabin is at?" I couldn't control the sudden hope in my voice.

He stood away from the wall and came over to me. Gently, he brushed one fist under my chin. "Thanks, babe. I'll take it from here."

He was big, at least as big as Steve. I waited until he turned to walk out and then tackled his knees. Steve would never have turned his back on me, but then he already knew how unreliable I could be. Okay, how stupid.

Mark went down like a big polar bear, but he was even faster than Steve. Before I could crawl up and sit on his back, he flipped over, taking me with him and nearly sending me into the bar halfway across the room.

He sat up. "What the hell did you do that for?" He sounded more incredulous than mad.

I stumbled to my feet, winded. "I want to go with you. They have my friend Turbo too."

"Turbo? Who the hell is Turbo? I thought you were worried about Steve?" His eyes narrowed. "He lets you live in his place and you're worried about some guy named Turbo?"

I was really getting tired of everyone thinking Steve and I were an item. "It isn't Steve's condo. It's mine. He traded me the condo for my house. You can go look it up."

That stumped him even more. He stood up slowly, keeping his eyes on me. "What does that have to do with this Turbo guy?"

"Look, Steve and I are not...anything. He gave me the condo to help with a problem at work. I assume you are involved because he came to Strandfrost the first time dressed like you. He hired me to help him. So you have to take me along."

"He hired you?" Mark didn't sound like he believed me.

"Are you going to take me with you or not? If you're not, I'm going to follow you. If you lose me, I'm going to find you," I promised rashly. "I'll call Derrick!"

"Derrick." He looked amused now. "Just how many boyfriends do you have?"

I glared at him. "None! Derrick is a cop."

That, he didn't find funny. "Who are you? You don't look like a cop."

I thought about lying, but he looked pretty street-smart. "I'm not. Will you just take me with you?"

"I can't. I don't have another helmet for the motorcycle." He waved good-bye and opened the door. This time he kept his body turned sideways so that he could see me coming. I walked forward slowly so that I wouldn't startle him and end up getting thrown out the window.

"The Mercedes has four-wheel drive. We could take the motorcycle if we had a trailer."

He paused, but considered. "Why bother?"

"Was your brother grabbed because he looked like you or because he looked like himself?"

Mark turned to face me fully. "Probably me," he admitted softly, not liking that I had brought it up.

"So we take the Mercedes in. Just tourists. If we can figure out a way to take the motorcycle, we'll have it if you need it."

He watched me for a while without saying anything. "What did my brother hire you for exactly?"

I grinned. "My looks." Technically, he had me to look a certain way. I just hadn't looked it at the time, nor very often after that.

"That," he said, inspecting me up and down appreciatively, "I can believe."

I wasn't sure, but I think I should have said "brains." Frowning, I told him, "I'll get the Mercedes. I'm sure Michael would love to help load the bike." Just thinking about the chore made me happier. I hope the bike leaked oil onto Michael's uniform.

Mark didn't wait. He headed downstairs while I scurried into the bedroom and grabbed a knife and my gun. "Probably shoot myself." I didn't want the gun, but I figured I could leave it in the Mercedes.

Racing downstairs, I handed Michael the keys and cooed, "Could you help us load some things in the Mercedes?"

He was startled, but followed me. Mark's motorcycle was already around front. When Michael saw it, his mouth dropped. I barely kept mine closed, but managed an empty smile and clapped my hands together. "Mark is going to teach me to ride."

Mark looked up in surprise.

"Won't this be fun?" I asked. The bike was beautiful. It was custom painted with a sword that matched the one on Mark's arm. Blue and silver lightning glinted off the magnificent blade, giving the sword the illusion of movement even with the bike sitting still.

Michael looked like he might bolt back inside, but Mark stood there with his muscles bulging, not threatening, but not someone you wanted to piss off.

Mark walked over to the doorman. Eloy, the doorman, seemed to know about whatever Mark was saying because he nodded eagerly three times and headed back into the garage. All I heard was the word seventy-two. Michael had no choice but to follow since I was standing there waiting for the Mercedes.

In short order, Michael drove the SUV around and Eloy returned with a small trailer attached to a golf cart. He happily accepted a tip.

Michael handed me the keys, and I offered to back the Mercedes towards the little trailer. "You guys direct me, okay?"

Michael and Eloy looked rather doubtful. What were they worried about? Did they think I was going to run over Steve's brother?

Mm. Maybe.

Mark didn't even glance my way. He just put his hand out for the keys and waited. I sighed and gave them to him.

We got the bike loaded up and secured. I headed for the driver's side. Mark smiled at me. "I don't think so, sweetheart."

"It's my car."

He gave my shoulder a gentle squeeze. "I know where we're going."

I got in the passenger side reluctantly. "Don't mess up this vehicle. It's the nicest one I've ever had."

"My brother buy it for you?" He asked the question politely, but it was obvious he knew the answer.

I sulked. "It's not what you think."

I caught him grinning and protested again, "It's not."

"Hey, I believe you," he laughed. "My brother never had to buy his women."

He still thought I was Steve's woman. That made me mad enough to leave Steve in the clutches of whoever had caught him. If it hadn't been for Turbo I might have left Steve to rot.

Mark took highway ninety-one out of town. We traveled for almost an hour before he turned off onto a dirt road. We didn't need the four-wheel drive right away, but the sports vehicle was built so that it was available at all times. I hoped the automatic feature worked. I had never tried it.

The forest was full of a mix of deep greens and lingering summer heat. I wished I had had a chance to get snacks. My stomach growled. Thankfully, Mark couldn't hear it over the noise the tires were making.

"How far is it?" I asked.

"Another forty minutes or so."

"How do you know where it is?"

He shifted for an incline. "I followed someone out here once."

"How did you get involved with those people that broke into Strandfrost?" Mark didn't seem like a bad guy, not bad enough to be with the group that had attacked Allen's wife.

Mark didn't answer. A little while later, he pulled the Mercedes into the trees. "Can you walk for a mile or so?"

I nodded. I was feeling less friendly and a lot more nervous. There was little enough traffic on the highway. Out here, there would be an occasional hunter later in the year, but now, there didn't even appear to be vacationers.

"What are we going to do?"

His eyes laughed at me. "You mean you don't have it all figured out?"

I glared at his back while he unloaded the bike and pushed it into the woods. He detached the trailer and hid that also. I wasn't much help, but I scouted around and took a potty break. By the time I got back, he had arranged a gun, knife, flashlight and binoculars on his belt pack. He handed me a jacket from the back of his motorcycle.

"Good heavens." It was a bulletproof vest. I stared at him and wondered if he was a cop. He couldn't be. Could he?

He said, "I'll need it back if I have to ride in there. The jacket will make it obvious that it's me."

That was probably true. It had a blue and silver sword stitched across the back of the black leather. The sleeve had a faded sword painted on it that matched the one on his arm. "Okay." If he was going to be on the bike, where was I?

He headed up the hill. I followed. I could do downhill all day, but my lungs didn't like uphill stretches. I walked quietly enough, but my breathing was loud enough to scare off the wildlife.

Mark stopped frequently to let me rest. Each time, he got more impatient. We were running out of time, and I knew it. Dusk was maybe a half hour away in the heavily treed area even though it was only about six-thirty. It was going to get very dark in these woods.

About halfway up the second hill, I could see a cabin. Whoever had built it hadn't cleared many trees. I might not have noticed it if not for the chimney sticking out around a couple of trees.

"Looks like someone is home," Mark said softly. He used the pair of binoculars that he had taken from his bike. After he handed them to me, I could just see the tail of a white pickup truck. Dying light glinted off something else. It might have been the bumper of another vehicle or maybe a snow shovel that someone had left outside.

"Would they take Turbo and Steve there?"

"Possibly. They got a little too nervous about me trying to deal myself in."

"Oh." His hand was out, so I handed him the binoculars. "Where--"

He cut me off by putting his hand over my mouth. "There are probably at least three of them," he whispered softly in my ear. "Let's not assume they are all sitting there peacefully in the cabin."

Sure, whatever. I swallowed nervously, chills going across my arms and all the way up my back. When he let go of my mouth I murmured, "Do you think Steve and Turbo are inside?"

He continued to scan with the binoculars. "There's a cellar for storing deer. It's off to the right side of the cabin. It's usually covered in pine needles."

Apparently he had scouted the area well. "You think they are in there?"

"Likely. It's far enough from the cabin that if I distract them, you might be able to get the door open and get them out."

I didn't like the sound of that plan. "I don't think that is a very good idea."

He stopped looking through the binoculars and looked at me. "Why not?"

"I assume the door is locked," I hedged. "What if..." What if Turbo and Huntington weren't alive? Was I expected to casually walk up, check and then walk away?

"So?"

"So," I said generously, "I'll distract them. You open the door."

He watched me for a while. "Did you leave your gun in the car?"

I shook my head. I had wanted to really, really badly, but I had this awful feeling that if I got shot and my own gun was sitting in the car, my family would never forgive me. Maybe Huntington would need a gun. I could always give it to him if he was still alive. He acted like he could shoot someone without any guilt.

"We'll try for the door together," he decided.

If Mark hadn't been to the cabin before we wouldn't have found the cellar door unless we tripped over the wood bin that had been put on top of it. Whatever was in the storage cellar wasn't going to come out without help. The whole setup was very worrisome.

It was getting colder now that the sun was gone. What if the people inside the cabin decided to start a fire and needed wood from the bin?

Mark installed me behind a tree and told me to stay put. He circled around towards the cabin.

He came back in a hurry. "There's only two of them."

"You're sure there should be three?"

He made a circling motion with his hand, indicating someone was probably wandering around looking for anyone that might happen along.

"We can't get that wood off without making some noise," I pointed out.

"Do you know how to drive a motorcycle?" he asked.

"No."

"Can you get the wood off?"

I probably could. One or two pieces at a time. "What if they heard us drive up?" My brain was in overdrive worrying about all the possibilities. A shot out here would just be an illegal hunter and probably ignored if anyone heard it. Then they could throw us down into the cellar with Turbo and Huntington.

I thought I heard something. It was still off in the distance, but it sounded like a motor to me. "What is that?"

He cocked his head. "Dunno, but time is running out. Let's get to the door."

We moved logs. Mostly I moved the logs, and he kept watch. Whenever I got too loud, we would stop, and he would check the cabin again. I didn't hear the motor anymore. The bin was almost empty when he came back and dragged me behind the tree. "They are outside. Arguing."

I could hear voices, but not distinguish words. To my surprise, there was a woman's voice in the mix. Maybe someone other than Marilyn had to come clean the place and take care of the men.

I looked back at the bin, but knew I couldn't lift it off that door, even if I wanted to. With a gulp, I pulled my gun out. "I'll watch. If they are arguing, maybe you can slide the bin off."

Before he could disagree, we heard the truck start up. Mark moved quickly, using the noise from the truck as cover. He dragged the bin away from the trap door and then ran back under cover.

No one came rushing from inside the cellar. There was a latch on the door, but I could see from where I was that it wasn't locked.

I swallowed. Mark rested next to me, breathing hard. The sound of the truck died off into the distance. It would be normal for whoever was left behind to come and check the cellar, at least if the occupants didn't already have bullet holes through their foreheads.

"If someone comes through that path, shoot them," Mark instructed.

Ohboy. Would I? Or would I just stand there frozen and let them take shots at Mark?

Mark turned to go back to the cellar door, but as he did I swear I saw it gap up just slightly. I tugged on his sleeve. Maybe it was wishful thinking. If Turbo and Huntington were in there, why hadn't they jumped out already?

Mark ignored my tugging and slithered back towards the door, almost crawling.

I had a nasty little suspicion growing in the back of my mind. What if... they were alive? "Sstt. Mark," I whispered. If Turbo was alive, he had been trapped in a cellar with his own means for several hours. Turbo was first and foremost an engineer, an inventor by trade and a good one.

I had an awful feeling in the pit of my stomach. Mark was almost to the door. I heard a funny creaking just about the time I started out of the trees.

Mark spun towards me, but he didn't move back my way. He must have heard the creaking noise and maybe it did come from my direction. I thought not.

I hit him at a full run.

Chapter 39

Mark grunted and rolled, dragging me under him, using the momentum from my flying leap. The door hit the side of my leg and bounced back. From under Mark, I couldn't see a thing.

There was a kind of silence while I tried to suck air back into my useless lungs. My heart was still trying to escape my body.

If there was anyone left in the cabin, they had to have heard us. I wiggled in anticipation of getting shot.

"She tackle people like this all the time?" Mark asked.

"Sedona? I didn't know it was you!" Turbo sounded shaky.

"Turbo?" I squeaked happily.

"Yeah, she does that all the time."

Huntington! "Mgreh," I protested, wiggling some more.

"I guess this time it was a good thing." Mark pushed himself partway up with his arms and grinned down at me.

"My God, I could have killed you!" Turbo again.

Finally Mark moved enough that I could at least see the other bodies in the shadowy dusk. I could also see the glint of something stuck in the trunk of a tree a few yards behind us. I squinted. "What is that?"

Turbo crouched down. "Meat hook." He still sounded rather shaken. "We weren't expecting you. I jury-rigged the cellar door."

"Mark?" I squeaked.

"Yeah?"

"Will you get off me now?"

He cocked his head to the side, listening.

"Damn," he whispered on a breath of air.

"You pathetic bunch of morons."

I peered around Mark's shoulder. Even in the dim light, I knew the voice and shape. "You?" I gasped. "Dan got you involved?" I wiggled in earnest now, trying to see better.

She grinned, her beautiful white teeth gleaming for a second. "I'm sure you're enjoying yourself there, Huntington, with all her wiggling about, but how about you get off the bimbo, nice and slow."

Mark moved then, and he kept it slow. Before he could stand, she instructed, "No, stay on your knees." He stopped, still facing me. She came up behind him carefully and reached down, picking up his gun. He must have dropped it when I tackled him. Great. It was my fault we were going to die.

"How could you let Dan talk you into something like this? The guy is a leech. He even grabbed my ass!"

"Move over," she instructed Mark. "I like to see the people I'm going to shoot."

Maybe I should have kept my mouth shut.

Autumn said, "Dan doesn't know a thing about it, honey. He was just a convenient access opportunity."

It took a moment for the words to reach my brain. My mouth dropped open. "You mean...you fake the reports? For all the extra equipment?"

"Stand up, next to your buddy over there."

I wasn't sure whom she meant, but when I counted buddies, we were short one. Huntington was missing. I was confused. Hadn't...I was having trouble processing thoughts. I moved slowly, watching Autumn. "Dan fit into this somehow," I insisted.

Autumn smiled again, flashing her perfect teeth. "Oh, he's a big help, believe me. He makes it easy for me to talk to the right people and be where I need to be."

My mind refused to grasp that Dan wasn't guilty. "You're saying Dan doesn't even know? That the scheme is all yours?"

"Of course."

"But...but, how did you get Allen to sign off on the equipment for you?" I took a wild guess. "Favors after hours?"

She snarled. "I am not a slut." She pointed the gun at me.

"Hey," I said, waving my hands innocently. "I just don't get why he didn't tell the Feds what you were up to."

"Because he didn't know! He thinks the whole thing is just a few charity checks." She shrugged. "I made the mistake of letting him in on the deal so that I could get more checks. The loser did fine until he stopped paying my half and worse, he started taking bigger amounts. He ruined a perfect setup."

"He ruined it? You couldn't just keep opening charity accounts forever!"

"Ah, contraire, my dear. As long as I don't leave bogus accounts in existence for too long, and people like you don't get in my way, everything is just fine. He wasn't going to tattle about the equipment because he didn't know anything about it."

"If Allen didn't know about the equipment, how did you get him to sign for it?"

She laughed, delighted. "That's where Dan came in handy. The equipment and expense reports for services were easy to stick in Allen's pile when I was by to see Dan. Allen signs about four million pieces of paper a week."

"He never caught a single item? Not even after he knew you were bilking Strandfrost for the charity checks?"

"Men don't pay too much attention to much else when they're looking down your shirt. Not," she said, "that you would have that problem."

I didn't really appreciate her pointing out that my feminine assets were that much smaller than hers, but she had the gun. "Why did you bother to steal equipment from the shows? Why not just order what you needed whenever you felt like it?"

"Conferences are the best time to add charges. Allen has more paperwork, and he doesn't have time to look at each one. Not to mention it's easier to pick up the equipment when it is already being moved. Show up with a truck and Strandfrost even has people to help load them." She stretched her arms out towards me, taking better aim.

"Game's over now," Mark interrupted. "No point in adding murder to the charges."

She swiveled slightly, just in case there was a threat, but Mark didn't make any sudden moves. "Nice try, buddy. No one is going to tie this place to me. If your bodies are found after the long winter hunting season is over, I'll be gone, just like closing the bank accounts I don't need anymore."

"Your brother owns the body shop. We already figured out that is how you were getting the equipment moved and sold. He's been out to this place more than a few times. I don't think you'll look that clean."

My jaw dropped. It had taken me forever to finally tie Ted and the trucks together. I had no way of knowing that Larry and Autumn were related. Not that I had done any worse than the cops. They had guessed right about the money laundering, but were wrong about where the money was derived.

Beautiful Autumn wasn't swayed by Mark's argument. "You may know about Larry coming out here, but there's nothing that ties either he or I to this property. Even if someone who is still alive after tonight knew he came here, they wouldn't be able to prove he did anything other than stay here now and again."

If Huntington was out there, I wish he would just shoot her and get it over with. She didn't like me so I was obviously going to go first. Before I could take any action, there was a loud crackling in the bushes.

Autumn didn't seem to care whether the noise was a bear or a human. She turned and fired the gun in that general direction. Huntington or not, it was my chance to escape.

I ran forward because to my left was the big gaping cellar.

I don't know what Mark was thinking. He was still on his knees, only partially facing Autumn, so maybe he thought she was firing at me. Whatever the reason, he leaned forward and grabbed my ankle.

One minute I was trying to get past the cellar hole, the next, I was falling into it. With my clumsy momentum and only one foot still on the ground, I toppled right into the blackness with no way to break my fall.

Another shot followed the first, but if it was aimed my way, I couldn't have moved to save my life. There was a lot of noise above me, but I was busy trying to figure out if my head was still attached to my shoulders.

Turbo must have been worried about me because he jumped down into the cellar and landed on my bottom with at least one foot. "Ow," I shouted and then groaned in continued agony. My head felt light and detached.

"Sedona! Sorry! Are you okay?"

Another large body joined us in the cellar. I could tell because the ground shook. Turbo managed to find a candle stub and light it.

I opened one baleful eye and stared at the newcomer. Even with the flickering candle it was too dark to tell which Huntington had joined us. Since I assumed that Steve had come to our rescue, this had to be Mark. "What," I said through gritted teeth, "was that for?"

He leaned down close to my face. I was still flat on my stomach after having belly-flopped into a pool with no water. "You okay? I thought you were going to rush her."

"Are you crazy?" I yelled. It came out a quiet gasp. I tried pushing myself up with my arms, but nothing happened. Turbo grabbed one arm and Mark hoisted on the other. My head spun some more, but I managed to make it to a sitting position. My butt hurt. I glared at Turbo.

"Sorry," he apologized when he noticed the wince.

I turned to my other enemy. "Why in the world would I have rushed her?"

Mark shrugged. "She's okay," he called to his brother. "You have everything under control up there?"

Huntington yelled back, "Trussed like a turkey."

Mark faced me again with a grin. "Why wouldn't you have tackled her? You tackled me twice."

"You weren't pointing a gun at me." Turbo offered a hand to help me out of the hole, but I glared at him and tried to get out without his help.

Mark wasn't as polite. He came and shoved on my sore butt. Huntington met his effort halfway and pulled me out by my arms.

"Sedona, are you okay?" He set me to the side gently. A flashlight was on the ground, throwing funny shadows. We were all strange silhouettes, dancing.

"No." Dirt clung to my hair and bits of it kept falling off the side of my face. I was scratched and bruised. I brushed at the dirt ineffectively.

"You look like you're going to live," Huntington said.

In the dim light, I could see Autumn. She was barely disheveled. Other than the rope that was wrapped around her entire body, she looked like maybe the wind had blown a strand hair out of place.

Life was just not fair.

Chapter 40

Derrick and Sean stopped by on Wednesday. Derrick looked rather sheepish. Sean headed for the refrigerator and instantly discovered the pasta salad I had made. He didn't bother to ask; he just dished some out for himself and for Derrick.

"So," I said to break the ice, "you got them all?"

Derrick nodded and accepted the glass of soda that I handed him. "We were pretty embarrassed that we saw those trucks with computer equipment going in and out of there and never suspected they were the source of the cash flow. We assumed all along it was a drug deal."

"You never guessed? Not at all?"

"My partner, Adrian, followed one of the trucks once," Derrick said, "but it appeared to be delivering the computers from place to place. One of our guys even saw the contract for servicing trucks for some computer company." He shrugged. "The key, as you know, is that half the time the computers weren't being delivered, they were being stolen."

"I take it they weren't selling the stolen merchandise out of the body shop?"

"No, and having a maintenance contract for moving trucks didn't seem that far out of line. The trucks came from multiple companies, because they used guys from various moving places. There was no evidence of certain trucks coming in too often because they used so many different trucks, and even owned a few."

"How long have they been doing this?" I asked.

Derrick shrugged. "At least two years."

"Two years." I tried to do the math in my head. Autumn could have handled several thefts per quarter. Even with only a few thefts and the non-existent vendors at conferences, she had probably been raking in at least a few hundred thousand a year of pure profit.

Derrick continued, "We're still investigating. From the records at the body shop, the large inflow of money from the stolen computers started about two years ago, but keep in mind, we haven't gone through the records for Autumn's printing company. She probably laundered some money through there also, and that may have started earlier."

The doorbell rang. I got up to answer it.

"Do you have any garlic bread?" Sean called as I opened the door.

It was my two Huntington friends. "It's in the fridge," I said over my shoulder. "You better put all of it in the oven. And there are some chicken breasts in there too, ready to be grilled."

"Excellent. I'll start the grill. Derrick, can you throw the bread in the oven?"

"It has to be wrapped in aluminum foil!" I waved Mark and Steve in and hurried back to save the bread. Derrick was tearing off a sheet of aluminum foil large enough to wrap one of the kitchen chairs. I took over.

"Grab something to drink and have a seat," I told the new guests. "The pasta salad should wait until the chicken is ready, unless you're Sean and haven't eaten for a week."

Huntington grinned at me and grabbed the chicken. "I'll take care of these."

Sean looked at him suspiciously. "You know what you're doing? You're not going to burn them, are you?"

I rolled my eyes. "Some people know how to cook and do it often," I informed him. "I bet he can grill without starting them on fire."

Sean didn't appreciate my input. "Who is the one that started that fire at the homeless shelter, Mm?"

It was mean of him to say that.

Within the hour, we were sitting around happily eating our meal. I hadn't really expected all the company, but luckily I always made a huge pasta salad.

"I'm curious," Sean said. "How exactly did you discover the body shop was involved?" Sean directed the question at Huntington, but he glared at me.

"I just work at Strandfrost." I pointed my fork at Steve. "He was doing the investigation."

"You're the one that hired Marilyn," Steve said.

"I wouldn't have met her if it hadn't been for Derrick," I countered.

We quibbled over the details for a while, but Mark had actually been busy infiltrating various computer companies that had done large orders with Strandfrost. "At the time," Mark explained, "we didn't suspect the delivery trucks. We knew someone was submitting orders that were bogus, but we thought the payments were being made without any equipment actually changing hands. I decided to follow a few orders from start to finish to prove it. I got in good with a contract driver. The guy didn't own a truck. He used a van that came from Larry's Body Shop."

"So you caught them delivering the stolen goods there?"

"I might have, had things gone smoothly. When I showed up with the driver, we just picked up the truck from Larry's and the delivery was normal. I expected the delivery to be canceled, the equipment not there, or a reschedule-- and then we'd have proof that the order had never been filled, but had been paid for. Unfortunately for us, part of the order was real so it was all delivered properly. Everything looked legit."

I already knew about the delivery part, but I had other questions. "You never told me what you were doing at Strandfrost with the thugs. How in the world did that happen?"

"That was my fault too," Mark said. "Allen's wife was attacked first--I tracked one of the guys that did it, a two-bit drug dealer name Crane that hired out for muscle. When the second attack was planned, I managed to talk Crane into letting me go along. I thought I could keep things from getting out of hand and figure out who hired him."

"Except that the day the attack was planned," Huntington said, "Mark had already arranged to help with another Strandfrost delivery. He couldn't be in both places at once."

"Steve went to Strandfrost in my place planning on keeping things under control so that no one got seriously hurt. The guys never noticed it wasn't me."

"But you," I pointed my fork rudely at Huntington, "were back near the body shop and met Mark when Derrick and I were talking to Marilyn."

He nodded. "Mark was still watching deliveries, and I was his backup that night. After the delivery, the driver parked the truck at Larry's shop. When that same truck went back out right away that night, Mark followed it. Turns out Ted was borrowing the truck, something he apparently did as a way of using someone else's gas. Mark trailed Ted, but Ted just went to the bar. Even though Ted worked at Larry's Body Shop, there was still no obvious tie-in to the equipment thefts, not at that point. No one delivery guy was used every time; Ted was just one of several. That night, Ted wasn't doing any business that interested us."

"Yeah, he was beating his wife."

"And then you hired Marilyn?" Sean blinked, obviously confused. "For what?"

I looked around my place. It was even cleaner than usual because I hadn't been living in it much.

Huntington grinned. "That reminds me. I brought the paperwork for your house." He went over to the couch to his sports coat. "If you'll just sign my condo back over to me, I'll sign your house back over to you."

Sean's eyes nearly popped out. He actually broke into a sweat. "Do. Not. Tell me. I am a lawyer and you agreed to--" He put his head in his hands and rubbed his eyes. Then he held up a hand. "I do not want to know. If you didn't involve me, then it is none of my business."

"Now there's an idea," I muttered.

"You mean you really don't live with my brother?" Mark eyed me, his brown eyes glinting. One eyebrow rose and a grin spread across his face. He looked at his older brother. "Seriously?"

Huntington ignored Mark, while I protested vehemently, "I told you I wasn't his girlfriend!"

Sean's face reddened dangerously. "It seems to me that you may have tried to take advantage of my sister. You put her in a very dangerous position, solely for your own gain."

"No," Huntington disagreed firmly. "She managed to do that all by herself, just like Turbo managed to get caught all on his own when he tracked down Ted."

"You got caught too!" I said.

Huntington looked annoyed. "Mark had an in with the delivery guys. I showed up at Larry's Body Shop, acting like I was looking for work just as he had on a couple of occasions. Knowing that the last Strandfrost order was stolen, I checked the back of a few trucks. Larry took exception to my nosiness."

"And how is it that you weren't endangering my sister?" Sean demanded. "You couldn't even keep your own cover, let alone protect hers!"

"The part involving Sedona didn't actually work. There was no chance Autumn was going to approach Sedona and ask her to start stealing charity checks or sign for bogus equipment. We assumed all along that whoever was stealing from Strandfrost was working with someone inside, but Autumn's inside man was Dan--he just didn't know he was being used."

"They couldn't even arrest him," I complained. "You can't arrest people for stupidity. That's why Allen got off too. He didn't know enough to be useful."

Huntington nodded. "If we had been smart enough to arrest or fire Allen when we caught him with the charity checks, Autumn might have needed access to someone else with signature power. At the time, we were afraid that whoever was responsible would know the game was completely over if Allen got fired."

"Autumn wouldn't have stopped no matter what," I said. "She is vindictive and mean. That's why she had her brother send in goons when Allen started skimming her share."

Sean tapped his fingers on the table, his lawyer gaze studying each of us. Eventually he threw his hands up. "I'm going home now. The less I know about this situation, the less I'll have to tell Mom and Dad. Derrick?" He hurried into the living room, and then did an about-face and came back to the table. "I told Brenda I'd bring her some food if you had any."

"There aren't any leftovers. You better stop at Albertson's and get some fried chicken or something," I suggested without sympathy.

"You don't have any more of this pasta stuff that you can throw together?"

I pointed to the door. "Out! Go to the store. Get some food for your wife and quit mooching off me!"

He fled with Derrick at his heels. I was left with some papers to sign and two grinning male threats.

Chapter 41

I returned to the condo one last time to get the rest of my things. I didn't know Marilyn was there until I got inside. She was cleaning the place as usual. "Oh," I said. I looked around and wondered how to tell her that I wasn't going to be living there anymore. I couldn't keep paying her.

She smiled. It was a shy smile, but it was a smile. "Don't worry. Mr. Huntington already told me that I've really been working for him all along. He said you were going home."

I was hugely relieved. "He's going to keep you on? That's fabulous!"

She nodded. "I put all your things in a bag. I brought back the sweatpants that you lent me too."

"This is really great news!"

"He said I could keep working here, and he would give me recommendations if I needed them. Ted's in jail," she finished quickly.

I waited, but she didn't continue. "Are you mad?"

"No. It's better this way." She looked down at her hands. "He can't beat me up when I file for divorce. I think the papers can be done and signed and everything before he gets out."

Since Ted was going to be in jail for a few years, it was a good assumption. "Do you have enough work? Can you, I mean, do you think you can keep things going?"

She looked up at me. "I guess if you can act like you belonged here, I could do it. It doesn't seem too hard."

It wasn't all that easy either. "What are you going to do? Pretend to be rich?" I didn't see how that was going to help her situation.

She shook her head. "That isn't what I meant. I mean that I never thought I belonged anywhere. I never believed I was worth anything or that anyone would hire me." She raised her hands and shrugged. "That doesn't appear to have stopped you."

"Oh, well."

"It's like you don't care what other people think. You don't wait for anyone's permission."

"You get like that when you have brothers," I told her. "They're going to make fun of you no matter what. Eventually you stop trying to please the masses, and you certainly don't ask anyone for permission for anything." I thought about it. "And you definitely don't tell them what you're up to."

She smiled. "You don't belong here. Maybe you don't deserve to belong here. But you're here anyway."

"But how are you going to survive?"

"I got three other apartments I'm cleaning. I didn't think anyone would rent me a place, but they did. I showed up with money, and they took it. I listed you as a reference." Her cheeks flushed a bit.

I didn't mind one bit. "So, you have a place to live and three places to clean." I did the math. She had enough to maybe pay the rent.

"There will be more places," she said. "And I'm selling the house. I figure in the divorce, Ted will get half of whatever I get from it, but I'll still have some of it."

"Well, this idea sure beats getting knocked around." I went to my backpack and then had to look in the briefcase because I had finally transferred everything. I found Chuck's name and number. "This guy seems okay. He can probably set you up with other jobs. He's a counselor, but I guess if you tell him you don't want to sit and listen to him lecture, he might help you with the job part. Seems to me you've already done a lot of the other stuff he's supposed to help with." Like finding some self-esteem.

She took the paper. "Mr. Huntington helped with the other jobs. I don't mind asking this guy if he has more. It's not hard and most of the people are nice. I guess if they aren't, I'll just leave." She looked quite defiant at the idea.

I agreed heartily. "That's what I would do." I went to the phone pad and wrote down my home number. "I'm going home again. Could you call me? You know, just in case something happens?"

She knew what I meant. Neither of us really wanted to sit and talk about it. She took the little slip of paper. "Thanks," she said softly.

I got my stuff and let myself out. I felt pretty good about the way we left things.

I got into the Mercedes, knowing it was probably the last time. Huntington could have taken it the other night, but for some reason he hadn't bothered.

Chapter 42

The good news was that when Huntington did show up, he brought Chinese food again.

"Excellent," I said with a smile and ushered him in. "I went to the grocery today since you guys ate me out of house and home, but I haven't cooked yet."

He set it out, and I got some plates. We ate until I thought I was going to have to let my pants out.

When we were done, he started clearing the plates. I went to my trusty backpack and got the keys to the Mercedes. "It's a great car."

He nodded. "You seem to like it."

A thought occurred to me. "If you're driving the Mercedes back with you, how did you get here?"

He grinned. "Mark dropped me off."

I wasn't sure I liked that idea. What was he trying to prove? "Oh?"

He dried his hands from rinsing the plates. "I was wondering if maybe you would like to keep the Mercedes."

Now I was really suspicious. "Oh...really."

He wiped the counter casually with the towel and then leaned back. "I investigate corporate problems. I clean up issues quietly without public scandal. Corporations know they can trust me."

Because he was one of them. He fit in with board members, and it wasn't second nature to him, it was first. It was easy to understand that corporations would prefer to hire someone like him to clean up problems. "What does that have to do with me?"

"I can't always obtain the information at every level, and there's this little job out in California..." his voice trailed off. There was a gleam in his eyes.

There wasn't one in mine. I threw the keys at him.

"Not a chance in hell."

He smiled and moved before I could react. He picked up his sports coat and headed for the door. "I see. That is too bad."

Automatically, I followed him to the front door. He opened it and grabbed my hand. He wrapped my fingers around the keys. "Keep them. Just in case you change your mind." With his other hand, he pushed my chin up to help me close my mouth. Then he leaned forward and brushed my lips with his.

My heart skipped a beat.

He murmured, "You never know when you might change your mind."

Leaving me staring after him, he turned and strolled down my driveway, whistling. I had no idea how he was going to get home.

Executive Retention, the second in the Sedona O'Hala Mysteries, is now available at all fine e-bookstores. The following is an excerpt.

Executive Retention Summary

After solving one case of corporate crime, Sedona expected to get her peaceful life back. Problem: She is still a manager at Strandfrost, and there is still rampant jealousy over her promotion. Is the danger of being railroaded by her not-so-illustrious colleagues worse than taking a new undercover job from Steve Huntington?

Crooks are coming out of the woodwork and family troubles are stewing. Sedona needs to keep her sanity intact, piece together mismatched clues and dodge more than one stray bullet. If she can manage all of that, maybe she'll have time to figure out whether her love life stands a chance.

Executive Retention Excerpt

Chapter 1

As a matter of principle, I don't like working late. The truth is, I don't really like working all that much period. I could sit on a beach somewhere for days on end if I didn't have to worry about how to pay for my next meal.

Burn-out is expected and is almost badge of honor in the computer industry. Then again, perhaps other industries have the same endless meetings where you sit and push around spaghetti. The engineer knows how to make the noodle, but doesn't have any idea why there is a meeting or why he has no say in what kind of noodle they are discussing. Eventually, the engineer realizes that even with his intimate knowledge of noodle creation, no one is listening to him, and he heads for the hills.

I can unequivocally state that despite my recent promotion into Strandfrost management and the Mercedes Huntington left behind as a gift for my investigative help, I am still tempted to drive off into the sunset. If success is so perfect, why am I stuck in the office at eight o'clock long after others have gone home? Why am I not on a beach in a cute little bikini with a cold iced tea and multiple dating prospects to reflect upon?

Steve Huntington, quiet infiltrator for companies with internal problems, finished mopping up the mess at Strandfrost, but he neglected to tidy up *my* life, a mess he helped create. Away he went into the sunset leaving me, Sedona O'Hala, a manager of computer nothingness. Oh sure, I was doing my best, but now that the criminals had been thrown out, I was left trying to help new management understand how business at Strandfrost was done. Out of guilt, I kept trying to piece things together and was therefore stuck at Strandfrost way past closing time.

Whenever I was in this mood, I should take a vacation until things calmed down. I should not stop on my way out in a dark parking lot and talk to strange men in their cars, even if they are driving a brand new Lexus. If the man was Huntington, I should run screaming.

"Sedona, do you want your old job back?"

My heart skipped a beat, and it wasn't his deep baritone that caused it. For a moment I pictured my job in the lab, setting up computers. I could stop attending reams of meetings where everyone used impressive words like "paradigm shift and synergy." I could go back to arguing with my old boss, Turbo, over the best way to prove or disprove a concept and deal only with obedient little machines.

What were the chances? "I want to move to Hawaii. Denton, Colorado will soon be getting very cold, and snow bunny I am not."

"How about the coast of California?"

"Unless the job entails sitting on a beach counting seals, I am not interested," I replied frostily, delivering on my own prediction that Colorado was about to get very chilly.

He was not deterred by the cold front. "Most of the work would be in Denton, but the main office is in San Jose. There's a state park with elephant seals a few miles from there. I am sure we could work in some time for you to go count them."

"Elephant seals?" I had been picturing cute harbor seals, the ones with black button noses and adorable faces. "Don't those have rather large, distorted noses?"

I think he was laughing, but I couldn't recall Huntington actually doing such a normal thing, so I wasn't sure.

"I'll take you there, I promise. I just want you to consider this job at Acetel Services. It should be a breeze for you. The company opened an office in Denton to support computer customers that bought equipment from various providers."

Customers always mixed equipment from different manufacturers. When something inevitably went wrong, if the customer didn't have a tidy service contract, the original manufacturers merely pointed to the competitor product as the problem and refused to look at the mess.

"I'm not interested," I said. Working for a customer that hadn't been able to get support from his original supplier would be nothing short of a nightmare.

Huntington sighed. "How about I take you out to Anthony's Grill, and we can talk about it? You can't stay at Strandfrost forever, you know."

I couldn't? "Why not?"

He purposely misinterpreted my question and assumed I was agreeing to his invitation. Without delay, he hopped out of the pearly white car and went around to the other side to open the door for me.

I wasn't sure what kind of car Huntington really owned and which ones he kept for his various assignments, but this one was certainly nice. The beautiful cream interior beckoned. Huntington didn't look bad either in his black leather jacket and perfectly-pressed khakis. By any stretch, Huntington wore his clothes well on his six-foot frame. His dark hair made his eyes look bluer and the way he used them was...suggestive.

White teeth flashed when he smiled, but only momentarily. "I decided a bit more than Chinese takeout was needed to persuade you to give up your latest position. Anthony's should be a good start."

"The Italian place by Whispering Pines?" Next to Chinese, Italian was my favorite cuisine. Actually, a well-made meal of any kind had a place in my heart, including chocolate chip cookies, chocolate cake and anything else well-prepared. I had never been to Anthony's. It was very upscale.

I looked down at my attire. At least I hadn't yanked my mousy brown hair into a ponytail like I usually did on Fridays. "I probably won't take the job, but it never hurts to eat."

Huntington knew me pretty well. The best way to reach me was through food. Flowers would have been nice too, but we weren't in that kind of relationship. Since he was pretty casual, I wasn't completely out of place in my light jacket, jeans and sweater. Although my last job for Huntington had provided clothes so that I could look the part of an up and coming executive, it had not occurred to me to buy a leather jacket when he was footing the bill. Darn. I was very certain that a sleek black jacket would go nicely with my gray eyes.

Huntington held the door and waved me forward. "Come on. It will be fun."

"I'm still not likely to take the job." I grabbed my wallet from my backpack and tossed the pack into the backseat. I hadn't planned on returning home late and should have brought a heavier coat, but unless Huntington was going to pay me on the side again, the latest job description didn't sound like it would provide a closet full of luxuries.

I expected a hard push for the job, but he was a good deal smoother than that. "How have you been?" He managed to sound genuinely interested--as if he had thought of little else for the past month.

"Oh, just fine. You know how it is, managing a group of people, all the various social engagements and the demands." In my case social engagements equaled "none," which was the primary reason I had never been to Anthony's Grill. The "demands" were work related and felt a lot like being a highly paid short-order cook. When I was lucky enough to grab an order slip, the waitress would immediately change it, leaving me trying to break up a cooked hamburger patty and reassemble it into meatloaf.

"Things are going good for you then." He hid most of his disappointment.

"Couldn't be better. Well, unless I retire early." I hedged because I didn't want to get too caught up in my lies.

"How's Turbo?"

"Fine." Missing the sort of work that he had done to help Huntington, but I wasn't going to encourage Huntington. By this time we were only a couple of blocks from the restaurant. Denton wasn't that big, but it was a Colorado resort town. Anthony's was in the same neighborhood as the Whispering Pines Resort. The restaurant was a quiet little building surrounded by a garden with little outdoor tables nestled under the trees. In the summer it would be romantic enough to sway any woman.

In the winter it was just plain cold, but the setting still had an air of promise as we walked through a wrought-iron arch and along the well-lit sidewalk. I shivered a bit and Huntington did that guy thing, putting his warm hand on the small of my back to guide me.

Where *did* those goose bumps come from anyway?

He leaned in close and whispered in my ear, "The food is great here. You'll love it."

Shivers ran all the way to my toes. I swallowed and tried to ignore my knees. They were probably weak from the wintry air.

Before Huntington was near enough to even think of grasping the door handle, the heavy wooden entrance swung open, and we were ushered inside.

The place wasn't so expensive that I couldn't come here

occasionally; it was the lack of dates that was the problem. Anthony's was not the kind of place you wasted on a lonely meal.

Huntington must have called ahead because the waiter immediately led us across the deep burgundy carpet to an intimate booth with a view. The window looked out onto the faded fall garden; an empty water fountain sat outside, decorated with fallen red and gold leaves. When it snowed, the garden would fill with a magical white carpet and the fountain would drip diamond icicles.

"What?" I asked, having missed the waiter's question, busy with my daydreaming. "Oh, just water for me. No, make it hot tea."

Fleetfoot nodded and soundlessly melted away. He had left the menu by my lifeless hands.

Huntington was bemused by my attitude. "You seem a bit distracted."

"Yeah," I sighed. It had been a long time since I had been treated to dinner and lavished with attention. I narrowed my eyes at the direction of my thoughts. It was necessary to be very careful here. Huntington was way out of my league. If the man thought seduction would get him what he wanted, he wouldn't hesitate, and I really didn't need that type of complication in my life. I didn't enjoy being roadkill, and if my friend Huntington was working a case, I had best be on my toes.

"How can I talk you into taking another job?" he asked.

"Why are you even asking me? The last one didn't go all that smoothly. As I recall, you ended up in a hole in the ground."

He looked solemn and waited with his reply while the waiter presented a boxful of teas. I went with a nice, soothing herbal. We weren't ready to order, so again, Fleetfoot floated away.

"You did come in handy during the rescue."

That might have been stretching things a bit. I was almost positive that Huntington's brother, Mark, could have handled the entire rescue without me. Almost.

"And you did learn some things for me that I couldn't have figured out on my own. That's essentially what I'm after at Acetel Services. There are rampant rumors about mismanagement, but the employees aren't going to tell me what is really going on."

"Are you on the board again?" Huntington had positioned himself on Strandfrost's board during his last investigation. It gave him the power to move players around and become familiar with the politics, but it left him in the cold when it came to the grapevine.

He nodded. "They're usually the entity that hires me."

"Usually?" I wondered who else would bother. And who else could afford to?

He grinned. "Usually."

"Why me? Why not hire your brother Mark to go on the inside?"

"Mark has other skills."

He didn't say whether or not he would be using them in this case. Mark looked a lot like Huntington, enough that they could be twins, especially if one of them wore colored contacts. Mark's eyes were a deep, solid brown, and he spent more time in the sun. Whatever his skills, they resulted in a slightly more muscular build, not that Huntington was hurting in that area. Mark was also a tad shorter and didn't have the kind of suave demeanor that would win him board seats.

"Are you still on the board at Strandfrost?" I asked.

The waiter hovered again. I could have ordered the most expensive thing on the menu, but I wasn't that kind of date. Besides, I loved chicken Marsala, and it was reasonably priced.

"And would you like soup or salad?" the waiter asked.

"Caesar salad please." I handed him the tasseled menu.

Huntington ordered the sirloin Marsala and a salad. When Fleetfoot disappeared, he said, "No, I'm not on the board anymore, why?"

"Wow, that must be nice for them. You get paid to help for as long as they need you, and then they make you disappear. But I guess now you have another board seat."

"I haven't been officially elected to this one," he cautioned. "Strandfrost is privately held so getting on their board didn't require a proxy or stockholder vote. Acetel went public during the dot-com days when stocks flew into the market a few years ago. The board would have to get me on a ballot in order to get me a seat."

The salads arrived, and I dug in. "Why can't you hire someone who is already at Acetel like when you hired me at Strandfrost? Or shoot, just pay an insider to spill the beans on what they think they know."

Huntington glanced up to make sure I was serious. "It's a thought. But not everyone can…blend as well as you do. You actually know the computer job and can do the work. You have a unique way of interacting with management." He frowned. "I don't know what it is, but they don't seem to notice you. Neither do the criminals." It was a thorny sticking point in our relationship. On the last case he had hired me to be noticed. Huntington had pulled out all the stops to advertise my position to the bad guys, to management, to anyone. I had been completely invisible.

"You're thinking I can creep into this company in the dead of night and not get noticed, and maybe I can do some noticing on the side?"

"Something like that. You'll have to blend better than you did the last time."

"I thought you just said I did a great job of blending?"

"You were ignored. But I shouldn't have said you blended. You actually stuck out like a sore thumb and weren't that good at getting people to talk to you. You'll have to spend lunches at this place, date some of the guys, play dominoes, whatever it is they do until they talk to you. It won't be as easy as the last time, hanging out with other managers."

"Hanging out..." I trailed off in disbelief. Apparently Huntington hadn't noticed that the managers, a good ol' boys club, hadn't been the least interested in hanging out with me. And if he thought standing around talking with a bunch of old farts about golf and getting groped was *easy*...what the hell was he asking for this time?

He ignored my sputtering, his attention focused behind my head. He stopped chewing suddenly and put down his fork. "Uh, excuse me."

"What?" I was just getting ready with my scathing reply.

Huntington got up and walked away.

I glanced behind me. To my dismay, two large men followed the direction Huntington had taken. Wearing jackets bulky enough to hide an entire armament, they didn't look much like potential customers. The shorter of the two sported jeans with holes in the knees and the other, a large black guy, wore sweatpants.

The bathrooms were near the front entrance, and that was not where Huntington had gone. Kitchen?

What was going on? I took another bite of my salad. Should I go after him? Riiight. I was prepared to fight off two men three times my size that were probably armed with Uzis. No problem.

The bushes outside the window moved. I looked out, but even with the bright garden lighting I couldn't tell if it was the wind or if Huntington was getting strung up in a tree. I couldn't just sit here and let him get gutted, could I?

Actually...well, no, I couldn't. I sighed, wiped my mouth and got moving. I headed for the door where Huntington and his buddies had disappeared. Fleetfoot was leaning against a counter looking a lot more casual behind the kitchen door than he did when he was serving. I waved at him as I raced by. The cooks were young. They gaped at me. One of them said something in Italian or Spanish.

Luck was with me. I spotted a large cleaver on the counter and picked it up on my way out the back door. Someone, I think it was the head cook, shouted, "Hey! You can't take that. What are you doing?"

"Don't worry," I called back. "My date went out this way." And, it occurred to me, had left me with the check. Another good reason to have the cleaver handy.

...Here ends the excerpt.

About the Author

Maria Schneider has published many other novels and short stories:

Under Witch Moon is the first in an urban fantasy series: When dead bodies start turning up Adriel has no choice but to talk to White Feather, an undercover cop. Unfortunately, Adriel is a witch and White Feather isn't convinced she's innocent of wrongdoing. She's going to have to talk fast—and set spells even faster. *Under Witch Aura* is the second in the series.

The Sedona O'Hala series (*Executive Lunch, Executive Retention, Executive Sick Days*) is a series of contemporary cozy mysteries: Sedona must solve a few crimes while fighting her way up the corporate ladder; mostly she dangles from her fingertips, just trying to survive.

Catch an Honest Thief is an adventurous caper across the New Mexico desert; Alexia is in search of treasure, survival and maybe love.

Dragons of Wendal is a fantasy adventure—can Zoe unwind a dangerous spell before it's too late?

If you're looking for short stories, you might enjoy the anthologies: *Tracking Magic* (Max Killian Investigations), *Sage* (Tales from a Magical Kingdom), *Black-Tie Bingo* or *Year of the Mountain Lion*.

Maria's website: BearMountainBooks.com